OATH OF SACRIFICE: A DARK MAFIA ROMANCE

DEVIANT DOMS

JANE HENRY

Cover art by Popkitty Designs

SYNOPSIS

She may be promised to a stranger...

But we know the truth.

Rosa Rossi is mine.

Mine to have and to hold,

No matter the cost.

If we're discovered,

My life is forfeit,

And she'll be exiled forever.

But I know...

I see through every glance sent my way

I feel every pulse of her heart.

And my heart beats with hers.

Now she's under my protection

No matter the cost,

Even if that means making the ultimate sacrifice.

CHAPTER ONE

Santo

A bead of sweat rolls down my back. I scowl at the landscape that most would find beautiful—rolling green hills that overlook the Rossi family vineyard, almost ethereal with the setting sun. The air's pregnant with the sweet scent of ripe grapes.

Fuck that.

I wasn't bred to harvest *fucking grapes.*

I yank at my T-shirt and pull it off, wipe it across my brow and ball it in my fist. A cool wind skates across my sweat-slicked naked chest. I've grown a beard, gotten more ink, lifted more in Tuscany.

What the hell else am I gonna do?

September's usually the time of year they tell tourists to come to Tuscany, instead of during the hellish, stifling August heat, because the weather's begun to cool. But not this year. This year, September's started off almost as hot as August.

Others might see this as a gorgeous landscape, a little slice of heaven, really.

Not for me.

This vineyard's my fucking prison.

Bare-chested, glaring at the ripe vines that sprawl before me, I want to pound my chest and scream like motherfuckin' Tarzan. I want to claw at the rose tats on my arms, the stark, vivid reminders of who I am.

Who I try to be.

A reminder of the oaths I took.

All of them.

The ones they know about.

And the one… they don't.

I turn my back to the vineyard and stare at the sprawling estate before me, only one of a number of places the Rossi family owns in Tuscany. I once had a place here in Italy, a place of my own, but I sold it when Romeo banished me to the vineyard. It only mocked me with its vacancy and opulence.

Now I have an apartment here at the vineyard, where I oversee operations.

Motherfucking vineyard operations.

A part of me wonders if I'm here because Romeo wants me as far away from his family in America as possible.

Romeo, who's like a brother to me. My Don.

He knows I don't like to sit still and never have. He knows I like to get my hands dirty, whether that's changing the oil in one of my cars or breaking legs as punishment for a crime committed against the family. Romeo knows that the best way to really punish a guy like me is to take him away from anyone who matters and to make him do fucking *menial labor.*

As I head inside, a car pulls up the long drive. It's hard to see with the setting sun, but I cover my eyes to block the sun's rays and try to see. Ah. One of Tavi's, then. He's come to pay a visit. I wait, but he's busy on his phone so I give him space.

Tuscan homes are rustic and sturdy, many built centuries ago. The home set at the vineyard's no exception. Stone columns and benches line the walk to the main house, the most modern part all the recessed lighting and spotlights in the garden. Here, the smell of ripe grapes fades a little.

Laughter comes from inside the kitchen. Maurice, an older guy who's cooked for the Rossi family for decades, makes magic in the kitchen, unless Tavi's wife Elise is here. Elise can cook her ass off. But Elise is pregnant, and hates flying on a good day, so Tavi's got her home with The Family.

I wonder why he's here.

Another burst of laughter floats through the warm evening air. I clench my fists. It's been way too fucking long since I've had a chance to talk with brothers of my own, to feel like I have a tribe that actually welcomes me. I know what'll happen if I go to the kitchen.

I'll find Maurice regaling staff with tales of his many exploits from when he was a young guy in the Italian Army. It's how he met Narciso, the late Don of the Rossi family , and how he got the job here. Kitchen help in the Army.

They'll be sitting around the large, rustic kitchen table with their pints of ale or glasses of wine, probably with a heavy antipasto plate in the center of the table. Maurice is famous for his antipasto boards—handmade cheeses, meats, olives cured from the Rossi's private collection, with jams and dried fruits. They'll drink and eat and talk in perfect amiability.

Until I walk in.

Tavi's still sitting in his car, probably catching up on emails.

I decide to test my theory.

I amble toward the kitchen. Sure enough, the whole crew's sitting around with their drinks and food, and Maurice is speaking animatedly in Italian, waving his hands for dramatic effect. He winks at me and continues his tale. Maurice has known me since I was ten years old, and he isn't afraid of me.

That makes one.

I stand against the doorframe, leaning my hip against it to listen to him.

"And the girl, she says, buddy, you want more than one tonight? I'm a triplet." Snickers and chuckles. Maurice waggles his eyebrows. "And I say to her, I'm glad you told me. Thought I was seeing triple. Still, I only got one dick, sweetheart."

The guys laugh out loud, slapping their knees.

"Ah, Maurice," I say from the back. "Don't sell yourself short, brother. You've got two hands and a tongue, too."

The laughter dies as the guys look back at me, their eyes wide with fear.

And then it begins. First one stands and feigns a yawn and heads off in the other direction toward staff headquarters. Then another, then another, until it's only me and Maurice left. Like I'm a goddamn leper.

Fuck it, maybe I am. Some diseases are invisible.

"Santo," he says warmly. "That hot, you take your shirt off?"

"Yeah, sweatin' like a pig out there." In here, it's much cooler. I head to the laundry room off the kitchen where the house cleaner does our laundry and grab a clean tee. I pull it on, wondering what's taking Tavi so long. I won't invade his privacy, so I'll wait until he comes in.

"They scatter like ants when you come," Maurice says with a laugh. "They don't know the Santo I do. I remember when you were just a boy, ten years old, the first one who ate everything. So thin I could see your bones."

I turn my back to him and close my eyes. I remember, too. The sleepless nights when hunger clawed at my belly until I cried. The way the boys at school made fun of me for my skinny legs and thin, emaciated body.

I remember how I eventually beat the shit out of every one of them in high school, too, and how *no one* made fun of me then, not after Tavi showed me how to lift and Orlando showed me how to fight.

"Yeah, you could say I've filled out," I say with a laugh. I pat my belly. "Maybe even need to lose a few pounds, eh?" I've put on weight in Tuscany, but still work out, so I've bulked up.

"You don't need to lose weight, Santo," Maurice says. "Extra weight looks good on you."

It's extra muscle that looks good on me, I think to myself.

"Santo," he says softly. I turn to look at him. He's laying a hand towel across a ceramic bowl, probably covering the dough so it rises overnight. "Does it make you sad that they leave when you come?"

"Sad?" I laugh. "I don't give a fuck if they like me. I want them to do what they're told."

Maurice waves a wooden spoon at me. "And that's one thing that hasn't changed. You still have the same trashy mouth you did when you were ten."

I laugh. "Only now you don't smack me with that spoon like you did back then."

He rolls his eyes heavenward. "Didn't do any good anyway, did it?"

He'd whack me good for my foul language, and Romeo tried to clean up my mouth a time or two, but it didn't work. The men of my brotherhood swore like sailors, and I always wanted to be just like them.

Always.

It never quite worked.

He takes the spoon, lifts the heavy lid on a pot on the back of the stove, and stirs. "They leave because they're scared of you, Santo."

I know. I know they do.

"Yeah."

"You should try… well, to be a little gentler with them."

"Maurice," I say dryly, turning away from him when I hear the side door swing open. "I don't fucking care."

And I don't. I'd rather they fear me.

I leave the kitchen to greet Tavi in the living room.

"Hey, brother," he says with a grim smile.

Shit.

Something's wrong.

"Hey. You okay?"

Tavi brushes a hand through his short brown hair and heaves a sigh. He's got the Rossi family blue-gray eyes and strong, muscled physique. "Campanelle's calling foul, man."

Shit.

The Campanelles, one of the many rival families that give us shit, have been crying wolf for years. We never listened to them. Romeo assured us that he'd settled outstanding accounts and they had no claim on us anymore, but right after Tavi's wedding and my subsequent exile, the Campanelles provided evidence that the Rossi family owed them several million dollars, thanks to a deal their father made back in the day.

I sit down on one of the heavy sofas and cross one leg over the other. Tavi walks over to the sideboard and pours himself a glass of house Chianti, the very same that's won awards throughout Tuscany.

"What happened?"

He takes a sip of wine and exhales in contentment. "Fuckin' missed this. Haven't touched it at home because Elise can't have it."

Tavi's wife Elise is pregnant and can't have wine for a while.

"How much longer you got? Like six months?"

"Nah, man," he says with a grin. "She's already in the third trimester. Got like a month left."

"Jesus," I mutter to myself. I'm missing goddamn everything being exiled over here. It's been longer than I thought.

I miss Boston. I miss The Family. Romeo knew for a guy like me, no punishment's greater than isolation.

"So what'd Romeo propose?" I ask. We don't want the Campanelles coming after us. We fought them before and won, but not without significant losses to both sides. We don't want to have to fight them again.

Tavi sits heavily beside me, his lips turning downward in a scowl. Before this conversation, I'd have told him that marriage was good for him. Eased his tight-ass ways a little, made him actually fucking smile every once in a while. But now… he looks older. As Underboss, he shoulders heavy responsibilities with Romeo.

He looks up to me with haunted eyes and shakes his head. "He's promised Rosa, Santo."

I don't process the words at first, like he's spoken a foreign language that I don't comprehend.

Promised… Rosa?

I blink. A cold chill skates down my spine.

No.

No.

"Rosa?" I ask, my voice choked. I try to hold my emotions back, so I don't betray feelings I have no business even having.

I knew this could happen. I knew that Rosa, after the death of her husband, was considered eligible to be married. And in our world, the Rossi women are commodities.

They're treated with respect and protected at all costs, but all of us have known from the very beginning that they were never meant to stay here, that they weren't going to stay with us forever. We knew it was only a matter of time before they were given away in marriage to someone else.

I stand and somehow make it to the sideboard. I pour myself a glass of wine, but my hand trembles.

None of them know how I feel about her. If they did, I'd be a dead man walking.

I try to hide the way the wine sloshes on the table, and pour more than I need in my glass. I grab a bar towel and swipe at the dark red liquid. I watch the wine stain the white towel. I've cleaned blood the same way, watching it seep into the terry cloth.

I swallow hard.

Tavi's phone rings, an obnoxious girly ringtone.

I give him a quizzical look. The wine's already dimmed my initial rage at the news, but my knuckles on the stem are still white.

"What the fuck is that?"

He rolls his eyes. "Elise gave me all these damn ringtones," he says and shakes his head. He snorts. "Wait until you hear yours." He hits a button. "Hello?"

Ah, it's not a phone call. FaceTime from Elise.

Her face takes up the whole screen. "Oh, hi, honey!" she croons as she blows him a kiss. "Is that Santo back there?"

She squints, and I wave, then lean back on the arm of the couch and take another sip of wine.

Rosa.

Rosa.

My mind can't help but spin this around, to try to decipher meaning in the black hole of this intel.

I'm not paying attention to the FaceTime call until I hear my name again.

"Santo?"

I look to see Elise isn't home like I assumed, but in her store in Copley, the same one I helped her prepare for retail.

I hate retail. I only helped with the store because Rosa likes pretty things, and I knew because she's friends with Elise she'd end up there as well.

And Rosa is safer in America.

"What's up? How're you feeling?"

All the Rossi women are like sisters to me.

That's a lie. All but *one.*

"I'm good," she says, and she does look like she's glowing. She holds the phone back so I can see her hugely swollen belly. That makes me smile.

"You sure there's only one bambino in there? You can't trust a guy like Tavi…"

Tavi play-punches me, but it still hurts. I duck and laugh, rubbing my arm, when I suddenly freeze.

Elise isn't alone.

I swallow.

Rosa's bent over a display of leather handbags, arranging them artfully. She turns and looks over her shoulder at the phone when she hears my voice.

"Oh, hey, Santo," she says casually. Not a hint of anything more than familial friendship.

I've been a member of this family since I was ten years old, and she greets me like I'm the guy that pumps her fucking gas.

"Hey," I say, an icy tone in my own voice. "How's business?"

Elise speaks up, answering my question.

"Oh, Santo, it's booming. Thank you. I think the marketing guy you found has really helped our exposure. You know how competitive it is in Boston, but he's put us on the map!" She beams. "And Rosa's got the Midas touch, you know."

I swallow hard. "Yeah?" My voice is a little husky. I hope I mask it. I can feel Tavi's razor-sharp gaze on me. "How so?"

"Someone comes in for one little handbag, and the next thing you know, they talk to Rosa, and they walk out with *the entire collection.*"

I smile. "Well done, Rosa. How do you do that?"

Fuck, but I like the feel of her name on my lips. It feels like velvet and chocolate, soft and seductive. I think of her when I see the rose tats on my arms.

She shrugs modestly and looks away from the camera. "I tell them they're worth it. I tell them they work hard, and that it's okay for a woman to indulge herself once in a while." She smiles. "And if it's a guy, I tell him his woman will be very, very thankful and be sure to show her appreciation."

Tavi laughs. "Well done, sis. Looks like you have a calling, eh?"

A calling to be the wife of one of our enemies. Yeah, she's got a fucking calling.

"Guess so," Rosa says. She walks back to her work, and Elise and Tavi chat it up again. She had a visit to the doctor today and fills him in on everything about the size of the baby, how healthy things are, and all the little details that matter. He eats it up like she's feeding him manna from heaven.

Jealousy's a hard pill to swallow.

I turn my back to them and finish my wine, until he hangs up the call.

The room's silent for a minute, until the clock chimes eight. It's two o'clock in Boston, then. They'll be closing in only a few hours.

"Who's watching them?" I ask nonchalantly, as if I'm not holding my breath waiting for his response.

"Amadeo and Tommaso," he says. Amadeo was once reprimanded by Romeo for drinking on the job and jeopardizing his mother's safety, and ever since then, hasn't stepped a toe out of line. Tommaso is new, but trustworthy. I trained him myself.

"You've got two guards on them?"

He nods. "One per person. Not enough?"

He should have a fucking legion stationed out there.

"Need one for your bambino, man." I watch him grin and smile to myself.

I change the subject. "Rosa looks pretty good for someone who just found out she's betrothed to a stranger." I try to keep the edge out of my voice but fail miserably.

I run a hand over my jaw and feel the beard I've grown in Tuscany. I hardly recognize myself these days.

Tavi looks away and doesn't meet my eyes. He twirls his wineglass between his fingers and frowns.

"*Ottavio*." He knows we mean business when we use his full name and not the nickname we gave him as kids.

He still doesn't look at me.

Though technically Tavi's above me in rank, we're brothers. We've taken the same vows to The Family.

Well. Most of them, anyway.

Still, any of us would give our lives for the others.

But I don't push him. I wait.

Finally, he releases a breath and looks to me. "She doesn't know yet, brother."

CHAPTER TWO

Rosa

"Rosa! No cheating!" Marialena's sitting cross-legged on the carpeted floor of her room in The Castle. She's got her Tarot decks lined up, one deck in hand that she's fanning like she's a poker dealer.

It's the full moon, and Marialena's been begging us all to read our cards. I finally caved. None of us are as into it as she is, but we all love her, so we occasionally indulge her. She grabbed them from me when I kept trying to peek through them.

"I'm not cheating," I tell her, rolling my eyes. "I was just trying to see what they looked like."

Marialena frowns at me.

"Here, Rosa, you can come cheat with me," Elise says, patting the tufted ottoman beside her. She's nestled snugly into the armrest of the chair she's in, her swollen ankles propped on a little stool.

I've known Elise longer than my brother Romeo's wife Vittoria, and Orlando's wife Angelina. Angelina and Elise are best friends, but I only met Angelina after she'd married Orlando. I met Elise long ago in Tuscany. We didn't know until after we met we were each in rival mob families.

"I am happy to sit by the pregnant lady," I say with a laugh. "She's the one with all the good stuff."

Typically fit as hell, Elise has grown a bit plumper with pregnancy. She grins at me and hands me a bowl of dip with sprinkles in it. "Pretzel dip?"

I shake my head and reach for the bowl of popcorn.

"Ah, right, you and the sugar." She rolls her eyes. "You've got the willpower of a saint. Did you gain even a pound with Natalia?"

Natalia, my daughter, is six years old and sleeping under the watch of Mama, since it's her nanny's night off.

I laugh. "Uh, I gained like forty pounds during that pregnancy!"

Elise's eyes go wide. "Well now *that* makes me feel better," she says, dipping a pretzel into the bowl and taking a ridiculous amount of dip with it.

"What *is* that?" Vittoria asks Elise. "It looks like jarred frosting."

Elise only shrugs. “Maybe it is, maybe it isn’t.”

“Oooh,” Marialena, who eats literally everything, says to her. She abandons her cards and scoots over closer. “I *love* jarred frosting.” I watch her take six pretzels and dip them into the bowl, lift them, then shove them all into her mouth at once.

“Rosa,” Elise says around a mouthful of food. “Are you exaggerating? How does someone gain forty pounds and not eat any sugar?”

I sigh. “Homemade bread, homemade pasta, buttered popcorn. It was a lot easier than you’d think.”

“Oh,” Elise says with a grimace. “I believe it. Yet somehow Angelina defied all the odds and managed to stay fit as a fiddle. How’d you do that, girl?”

Angelina grabs a plate of nachos from the buffet table and sits cross-legged on the floor. She digs in with gusto.

“Stress,” she says. “Anxiety. I don’t recommend it.”

Elise grimaces. “Oh, right.”

Angelina was incarcerated right here in our family home during the beginning of her pregnancy, because she and Elise had concocted a plan to fool my brothers. They’d switched places and fooled all of them into thinking Angelina was Elise. When the real Elise turned herself in, Angelina was forced to watch *her* be punished for the same crimes.

My brothers can be seriously ruthless. Maybe, if I'm honest, they're not the only ones.

"Those boys are incorrigible," Marialena says, but in a low enough voice that if any of "those boys" were in the hall outside her room, she wouldn't be overheard. Romeo once threatened to send her to Tuscany for openly defying him, and she hasn't forgotten it.

Vittoria smiles from where she sits, sipping a cup of tea. "I don't disagree," she says, shaking her head. "Now, Marialena, I'm dying to hear what my cards say."

Marialena reaches for Vittoria's cup instead. "I think I'd like to start by reading your tea leaves, Vittoria. May I?"

Vittoria nods, her mass of wild amber hair swirling around her face. She's got pretty, vivid eyes and lips that are almost always tipped up in a smile. I like her. "Ah, a smorgasbord tonight."

Marialena swirls the remaining tea, then pours the tea leaves onto a paper napkin. She frowns at the little design they make. She turns the napkin around, as if trying to see a way into the knowledge they hold, then her eyes light up.

"Oh, wow, Vittoria. I'm seeing nothing but good fortune."

I tune it out as Marialena goes on and on. I have no use for things like this.

Finally, she pulls out the cards again. "And here we go," she says happily. "I am so glad I finally got all of you together to work on this. I've been dying to, you know."

I laugh. "It only takes someone's birthday for us all to finally find the time to do it, huh?"

"Well, yes, if the birthday girl wants to corral us all into her mystical woo-woo ways," Elise says with a wink at me. She and I share similar views on all mystical, spiritual things, and love to pull Marialena's leg.

"Watch it, girls," she says. "I *do* have voodoo dolls in my chest."

Vittoria pokes a pinky finger at Marialena's free-swinging breasts. "Oh, do you? All I see is a pair of free birds."

Angelina snorts with laughter. We all know Marialena's talking about the chest that sits at the foot of her bed, where she carefully packs away her Tarot cards and crystals and books, and I suspect a good supply of candy, as well, which she knows would be gobbled up in seconds by our gluttonous brothers.

"Oooh, Voodoo," Elise says, waving her hands over her belly. "Don't curse the baby, Lena!" She gasps, her eyes go wide, and she sits with her legs spread wide apart. "Oh my *God,* did you see that?"

We all crowd around her huge belly and croon our little praises to the tiny baby, whose feet are kicking up a storm like they're doing a little jig in there. Elise and Tavi haven't found out the sex of their baby yet. I'm kinda hoping for a niece so my Natalia isn't the only girl, but I'll love any little baby that comes our way.

I stare out Marialena's window at the garden below and stroke my hand absentmindedly over my own flat abdomen.

I don't want a baby. Not now. God, it would complicate things so much, the very thought pains me. But that doesn't mean I don't allow myself a little space to dream of a baby with light brown hair and pale blue eyes, as soft and pretty as a rain cloud...

"Now, listen," Marialena says, turning to face the girls. "Tarot can't predict the future. It doesn't *work* like that, okay? But it can help you, like, make decisions and know what the right thing to do is."

"So can logic and reason," I say under my breath. Elise snickers, but Marialena is unperturbed. It's Marialena's birthday. I can give my little sister a little grace for today.

"It's a good way to stay *grounded,*" she says, gesturing without a trace of humor on her face. Always one to crack a joke, she takes *this* very seriously. "When things are overwhelming or I'm struck with indecision."

"Red dress? Or white? Loves me, loves me not?" Vittoria teases. Marialena tosses a throw pillow at her. She goes on and on about the standard deck of seventy-eight cards, how each set has a different name and artwork. I tune it out. I'll be here for the company and to wish Marialena a happy birthday, but I have no interest in Tarot.

My mind's still focused on the call earlier today.

It seems Elise calls her husband every hour, and while I think that's adorable, if not a *little* clingy, and I love that the two of them are so close, I never know when... when Tavi will be with *him.*

I didn't expect that he'd be in the same room with Santo earlier today.

I didn't know he'd be sitting there, in all his badass, tough-as-nails, tattooed, bearded, angry glory. How anyone could look like the centerfold of a men's weight training magazine wearing nothing but gray sweats and a white tee is beyond my comprehension.

Ah, Santo.

I still remember him as a gangly, ten-year-old boy who was wise beyond his years. Some might say jaded, even cruel, and I won't lie and say he isn't both of those as well. But there's a difference between someone who's scarred and someone who's ruthless.

I know the difference with him.

Marialena screams with laughter at something Vittoria says, and I quickly turn back to the girls.

Elise is wiping tears away, and Angelina's got her face planted in a pillow, her shoulders shaking with laughter. I missed the joke, so I only smile and laugh along with them.

I've gotten used to just going along with everyone. Pretending to laugh, when I have to. Pretending I care.

I don't really understand why Santo's in Tuscany now, but we're an ocean apart, and we both know that's for the better.

"Now, Rosa," Marialena says, turning to me. "Your turn."

I shake my head, "I'm good, thanks. You girls go on without me."

Marialena looks sternly at me. "If you squint, the card on the right looks a little like Matt Damon, you know."

The girls laugh so hard, I wonder if Marialena's snuck them all edibles. She doesn't know that I know she's got a stash right along with her crystals in that chest of hers.

"Ha, I'm good. Go ahead, I'm enjoying watching you girls read," I lie.

I wonder what he's doing tonight. I glance out at the full moon as my phone buzzes with a text.

My heart races.

Santo: Hey. You okay?

I swallow hard. We don't text anything serious to each other on our private phones because both are under surveillance by Romeo. He says it's for everyone's own protection, but I know he keeps an eye on anyone and anything that could threaten the family.

And a relationship beyond brother and sister...

Me: I'm good. Reading Tarot cards with Lena on her bday haha

Santo: Read a good one?

I look out at the moon and smile to myself.

Me: I read one with a moon on it. It said I'd fall in love with a handsome, dashing Italian man. Shows how silly those things are, huh?

My finger hovers over the text as I think about sending it. My cheeks flush hot. No, I can't go there. I don't want even the faintest trace of flirtation on a text one of my brothers could read. I delete the text.

Me: It says I'm going to be a millionaire heiress and move to Italy. So insightful, eh?

The little dots start, then stop. Start, then stop again. Finally another text pops up.

Santo: Wow, impressive. Hey, it's past my bedtime. Tell everyone I said hi. Night.

My heart sinks. I don't let myself think long about why. I swallow hard.

Me: Good night. Thank you for checking in.

I blink, then go for broke and send him a red heart emoji. I hope he feels the sentiment in that little, tiny image sent across an ocean.

I put the phone down, deflated, and quickly close my eyes at the surprising well of emotion that rises in my chest. The girls laugh, oblivious to the inner turmoil I battle with. Oblivious to the inner torment that eats me. The grief that tears at me from the inside out.

I look out the window and stare at the stone wall that overlooks the sea. Here, right here, was where I sat, but further down so no one could see us from a castle window, just before his exile to Italy. It was the only time I've ever seen Santo cry.

"Horoscope, Rosa? C'mon, they even have horoscopes in Cosmo," Marialena chides. "Just this once?"

I smile and decide the hell with it. I turn to her. "Let's hear it."

I love the way she squeals and pulls out rolls of paper where she apparently gets the horoscopes? Weird.

"It is high time for Aries to start moving and shaking," she begins.

"Oooh. Aries. How'd I know Rosa was the stubborn ram?" Elise teases. I flip her the bird, which only makes her laugh.

Marialena continues, unperturbed.

"September is a *busy* month for them. Due to the appearance of a full moon at the start of September followed by a new moon like September bookends, a doorway to improving work and life balance opens. Be aware of the hint of love coming your way, Aries."

Marialena grows still and worries her lip. She looks up at me, then back down, and rolls the paper up.

Okay, what's that about?

"Hey. You didn't finish reading it," I tell her. Not that I care, but I don't want her to hide things from me. None of this matters anyway.

"Oh, the rest is just... you know, nothing."

The other girls grow quiet. Elise speaks softly to her. "Hey. Babe, what does it say? You can't only read half of a horoscope. Isn't that, like, bad luck?"

She laughs, but it's a nervous laugh. She looks to me and I only shrug. I do want to hear the rest, but I don't much care.

"C'mon, let's hear it," Angelina says, dipping another pretzel in frosting. "Then we'll read the rest."

Marialena sighs and goes back to it. "Okay, but just keep in mind that, like, this isn't gospel."

What the hell? She never gives us warnings about these things. If anything, we're the ones warning *her*.

"Read it." My voice is harsher than I intend.

She wets her lips with the tip of her tongue and finishes reading.

"Beware wolves in sheep's clothing, Aries. Love that was once lost may be found, but all isn't what it seems. Guard your heart against tricks of the eye and sweet talk. You may experience deep, abiding pain in the coming months, but terrible pain can be avoided if you guard against it."

The room is silent. Marialena scowls and balls the scroll up. She stands and walks to her wastebasket and tosses it in.

"What bullshit," she says, but none of us believe her. "I mean, what sort of horoscope is *that?* It sounds so doomsday." She rolls her eyes. "Deep, abiding pain my *ass*. Whatever."

I look out at the stone wall and remember how it hurt so badly. I remember how Santo caught me and nestled me against him and held me.

I stare at the ocean and stand up straighter.

I don't need anyone to hold me up. I can stand on my own.

"It's just bullshit," I tell her, but the truth is, it's the first damn horoscope I've ever actually believed.

CHAPTER THREE

Santo

The driver pulls around the bend that takes me back to The Castle and whistles a happy tune. The sun's lower in the sky than it is in Tuscany. It's cooler, too, thank fuck.

It's been months since I've been here, and *Jesus,* I missed it. I missed it so much.

Mama loves the fall months, and it shows. Ripe orange pumpkins decorate the front steps to the Castle. The elevated portcullis, the heavy closing gate with a wooden and metal latticed grill which is lowered when we lock up for the night, is decorated with orange and gold-tinged ivy. Mama lives for the cooler days of a New England autumn, and when we were younger, would pile us all into the Great Hall to carve pumpkins, drag us into the heart of

Gloucester to go on hayrides, and even sewed our costumes with Nonna for us to go trick-or-treating. She did everything she could to keep things normal for us.

I liked the costumes. Those were fun.

Behind the mask, no one knew who I was. I blended in with everyone else.

My stomach rolls with hunger as we pull up the drive. I haven't eaten anything all day in preparation for the feast we'll have tonight, to celebrate the induction of our newest member into The Family.

It's the only reason I'm here, the only reason I've been granted a temporary reprieve from my punishment. No one can be inducted without the express consent of the ruling members of The Family. Even now, that includes me.

I look up when the two large Rottweilers Romeo trained stand at attention. Heavy chains keep them locked in place with ample room to move but far enough away to not hurt anyone but intruders. Romeo has a remote control he can activate on his phone to release them if necessary, but we keep them locked up so they don't attack anyone mistakenly.

When they hear my voice, they wag their tails so hard their whole bodies shake. They whine and cry until I kneel in front of them and let them lap my face.

I hear laughter behind me. "You're the only one they kiss." I turn toward The Castle to see Mama waiting for me. "Cain Master was here recently. And his wife Violet, too. Those dogs are as docile as lambs around her, but they don't kiss her. Only you, Santo."

Even though Tosca Rossi isn't my birth mother, she's always treated me like a son. I wonder at times if she knew Narciso took me under his wing in a way he never did with the other boys.

"I love these mutts," I say with a laugh. "Good to be home, Mama. How've you been?"

She waves her hands in the air. "Better now that you're home, too, Santo. Get up here and give *me* a kiss."

I trot up the stairs two at a time, but she doesn't give me a chance to give her a kiss. She grabs me by the shoulders, stands up on her tiptoes, and kisses each of my cheeks, one at a time, then repeats the gesture.

"Now, Santo, you know I've been cooking," she says, waving for me to follow her. The heavy, ornate door swings open, and Romeo stands in the doorway to greet me.

A myriad of emotions swarms me at once—my first thought to deck him, to lay him out right here on the front lawn of The Castle for subjecting Rosa to the marriage he's arranged. How fucking *dare* he?

I can't do that, and we both know it. I'd be dead before he hit the ground.

I'm not even sure he knows Tavi spoke to me yet.

He's more detached since he exiled me to Italy but can't help the warm smile that spreads across his face at seeing me.

I bow my head to greet my Don, but he pulls me to him and kisses each cheek, just like Mama did. My throat feels weird, and my eyes burn. He may have exiled me to Tuscany and spared my life, but Romeo's a brother to me as well. I try to repay him but can't help but keep aloof and cold. That's nothing new for me, though, so if he notices my reticence, he doesn't let on.

"Welcome home, asshole," he says affectionately in my ear, before he ruffles my hair like I'm ten. My stony heart melts a little.

"Thanks, asshole," I say back, and quickly duck his playful jab. It's been months since I've been home.

Home.

The Castle, the Rossi family home, has been the place I've called home since I was ten years old.

God, how I've missed it, even as a part of me screams inside at the injustice of it all. Of everything.

I've never been one to sit on my ass while the world burned around me.

I've always been the one to hold the fucking torch.

But now... Jesus, *now...* there are a world of secrets in me I've held for years, and a part of me wants to tell everything. But I can't. Not yet.

They know that I had gone to Tuscany when Tavi and Elise were honeymooning there, that I had gone without permission from Romeo or a word to any of them. Everything I did smacked of betrayal, until I saved Tavi's and Elise's lives in a shootout with some of the Regazza family.

It was the only move that saved my life, and why I'm not buried six feet under in one of the Rossi family graveyards, or worse, an unmarked grave somewhere in Boston.

So, meeting with Romeo... seeing my Don in the flesh... feels bittersweet.

It damn near killed me to stay in Tuscany for the past few months.

"Santo's home!" Romeo shouts, and I feel like the prodigal son as hurried footsteps sound throughout The Castle. "He's home!"

I stand in the entrance, home but detached. My gaze travels to the huge window that overlooks the sea, giving us a full view of The Castle wall. From here, I can see the well-worn path I've walked thousands of times. It's the only place on the whole damn property not covered with video surveillance. Tucked against The Castle wall, overlooking the sea, Mario—our resident techie—says video footage will be damn near impossible because of a combination of crossed interception and darkness. The only way to fix that would be to run wiring or a spotlight out there, and Mama would lose her ever-loving mind over defacing her family castle.

So it's the one spot that's untouched. The one black hole in the Rossi family cosmos.

And I've used that to my full fucking advantage.

"Santo!" Marialena trots down the stairs with a grin. The youngest of the Rossi family, Marialena's always been like a sister to me.

"Hey," I say warmly. I brace myself for her tackling hug, and I'm not disappointed. She throws herself at me like she's five years old again, squeezing me so tightly I can hardly breathe.

"Not the same here without you," she says in my ear, and her voice sounds a bit wobbly. That's not the Marialena I know. I pull back and hold her at arm's length, but before I can ask her any questions, Romeo's bringing me into the Great Hall.

The Castle, as always, is teeming with people. Back in the day, when we were all kids, the Rossi family would occasionally show the public this house. It was featured in magazines and news articles, but Narciso, the late Rossi family Papa, put an end to that. He felt it was an invasion of privacy. It's still talked about, though, and every once in a while we see tourists casually driving by and taking pictures. The dogs usually scare them away before we do.

With fourteen bedrooms, eight bathrooms, and ten fireplaces, this place was a childhood fantasy come to life. So many places to explore. So many places to hide, with turrets and towers, and main living areas such as the dining room, library, and even an inner courtyard with a swimming pool. And while the place is under heavy surveillance, the cameras are trained on areas we're most likely to be compromised or attacked. And I know every damn one of them.

There was a reason I became the expert on surveillance when I was younger. Now, we all know how to use the equipment to our advantage, and Romeo oversees the vast array of cameras in his office, but I know how to manipulate them well.

Uniformed staff walks about, dusting furniture and straightening area rugs, wiping down windows, while others take my coat to the coat room. Mama's gone ahead to the kitchen to oversee the food prep and cooking, because in full Rossi family tradition, we'll be feasting tonight because I'm home.

My heart warms. *I'm home.*

"Hey, there he is." I don't even know who says it, because when we enter the Great Hall, they're all there. I don't have much reason to smile and don't much care for shit like emotions, but I can't help but smile when I see my brothers.

Suave, wily Mario, with his charming looks and forked tongue that melts the panties off any girl he meets.

Big, burly Orlando, the group heavy, his eyes twinkling at me. He's bigger than ever, between lifting and eating good food since he got married.

Stern, aloof, detached Tavi, the one I probably relate to the most.

One that's noticeably absent is Leo. But his memory isn't even worth the mental energy of conjuring it up. I mentally spit on his traitorous name and my gaze sweeps the room.

"Ah, Santo!" Nonna, portly and friendly with her ever-present black dress and apron, round face and twinkling eyes, waddles over to me to give me the biggest hug she can muster. I hold her, enjoying this little minute of comfort. The feeling of belonging that's been absent since I was exiled to Tuscany.

"I make your favorite. Tosca can make you those little panazarotti, but I know *my* boy likes calzone." She holds me tight, and my heart swells. "*Tutto bene?*"

I whisper back in her ear, "You know me well, Nonna. Thank you. And I'm good, thank you. How are you?"

She pulls back, but only enough so she can look me in the eye. Her aged, wrinkled face is lined with worry as her brows knit together. "Only okay," she says with a sigh. Her gaze swings to Romeo, but she reserves judgment. For now. Though she and Tosca are likely the only ones who can ever speak their minds without repercussion, they rarely intervene in our affairs.

"*Mangia*," she says, her voice a little softer and sadder than usual. She pats my belly. "You get skinny."

I've been working my ass off in Tuscany and lifting. She thinks everyone looks skinny if they haven't eaten vast quantities of her ravioli. I lift heavy in Tuscany, though. What the hell else am I gonna do? Harvest *grapes?*

I grin at her. "Maurice ain't Nonna," I tell her. He's a damn good cook, but the truth is, food tastes better in good company.

I look around the room casually, hiding my eagerness to see the one face I need to see above all others.

There's Vittoria, with her crazy auburn hair and petite features. She smiles shyly at me and gives me a tight wave before turning back to chat with Elise. Vittoria's Romeo's wife, and as loyal as they come. She upholds her husband's leadership at all times, as she should.

Orlando's Elise smiles at me and waves, then goes back to chatting with Vittoria. She's always friendly to me, even if she did shoot me months back. Of course, she thought I was a traitor back then. I saved her husband's life, and she's thankful for that, though.

I told her not to think anything of it. It's my duty.

They might not believe it, but I'd lay down my life for any motherfucker in The Family. Any of them—man, woman, or child.

Some days, I wish I'd get the goddamn opportunity. To prove myself.

"Uncle Santo!" I turn just in time to catch the whirl of pink taffeta, ribbons, and curly brown hair that buries herself in my arms. I close my eyes as uncharacteristic emotion wells in my throat. For years, I've learned how to deal when emotions surprise me that I don't expect. Most of the time, I only feel anger, or a detached sort of cold apathy. That's what's familiar.

I remember the school psychologist stamping a label on me to my foster parents, before Narciso and Tosca adopted me.

Sociopath.

Sometimes synonymous with psychopath.

When he repeated it after I was adopted, I told him to fuck off, broke his nose, and got expelled. Mama cried, but Papa rewarded me with my first hunting knife. I still have it.

I shove the memory out of my mind and kneel on one knee in front of Natalia.

"Natalia," I say warmly. I take in her mother's vivacious blue eyes, as pretty and precocious as ever. Thankfully she doesn't look a thing like her cheating asshole of a father. "How are you, baby?"

Her hair's gotten darker and wilder, curly and unruly, and her affinity for pretty pink things hasn't changed. She's enrobed in miles of pale pink with a matching hair bow attached precariously to her curly hair. Usually, Natalia's accompanied by her nanny, but when I'm around, the girl stands well in the background unless I call her.

"I am *so good,* Uncle Santo," she says solemnly. "I have missed you so much. I bring Fluffy to bed every night, and do what you told me to."

Fluffy, a stuffed golden retriever, is a special little toy with a hidden video camera. I gave it to Natalia as a parting gift, and told her to put it on her nightstand every night before bed.

I want to know they're safe. And I like to sit at home in Tuscany watching Rosa, her hair down and makeup off, dressed in her pajamas, sitting on the edge of the bed and reading her a bedtime story. I imagine I'm there.

Maybe it's fucked up. Fucked up's my middle name.

"Shhh, baby," I say, bringing my finger to her lips to keep her quiet. "Remember, that's our little secret."

Her blue eyes go wide and she nods solemnly. "Right," she whispers, loud enough to wake the dead.

The night before I left for my exile, I took Natalia out for a walk. I'd miss her almost as much as I'd miss Rosa. "Look out for your mama," I told Natalia. "When I'm not here to do it myself."

Simple words. Fairly innocuous. But it's best if I keep my instructions between the two of us.

"And where is your mama?" I ask as nonchalantly as I can. My eyes are on my brothers when I ask, but they're all preoccupied. But before Natalia responds, I *feel* Rosa—*my* Rosa—enter the room. My heart begins to beat a little faster, my skin prickling with awareness. It's as if the very pieces of my heart are knit back together when she's near.

With expert skill, I close that door and assume my usual detached mask.

"There she is," Natalia says with a grin. She grabs my hand. "C'mon! Go say hi!" Her smile fades a little. "She misses you when you're gone. So much."

A pang hits my heart.

How does she know Rosa misses me?

I brush Romeo's arm as we walk past. He nods coolly. I wonder if he heard Natalia.

I look around until I spot her, like a radiant beam of light, at the entrance to the Great Hall.

Rosa's scanning the room. She hasn't seen me yet.

Rosa.

My entire fucking world stands on stilettos at the entrance to the Great Hall, cast in a soft yellow glow from a lamp in the hallway behind her, giving her an almost ethereal glow.

She ain't no angel, though. This woman's not even mine. Still, I swallow the lump in my throat at the sight of her.

I've seen models that were less stunning than Rosa. The only word that comes to mind when I see her is… *regal.* On the taller side for a Rossi woman, she stands on death-defying heels that make her legs look fucking *stunning.* She has a taste for fine clothes, and it shows. She wears a slim-fitting pair of designer jeans that fit her like a glove, and a vibrant, slouchy red top that's gauzy and transparent, over a thin white cotton tank.

Rosa may be older than me by a few years, but she's been smaller since we met, and age never meant a damn thing to us. The angelic scent of her perfume wafts through the air when I get only a few feet away.

I almost don't want her to see me. There's only so much familiarity I can show.

Her gaze comes to me, but her eyes are as cool as the last time we met. Hardly any recognition.

It's for our own good, I know it, but it doesn't mean I don't feel the coolness like a stab of ice. Her lips glimmer with the trace of a smile that doesn't reach her eyes. "Santo," she says softly. "How are you?"

I'm tempted to shake her fucking hand like she's a distant relative, but Natalia will have none of it.

"Mama, he's been gone so long, *hug him,* Mama."

She yanks me forward.

Rosa lifts her arms to me and hugs me. I'm engulfed in her scent, the warmth of her, the way she fits as if she were carved right here into my arms.

I'm glad my back's to the whole damn lot of them, so I can close my eyes and revel in this moment. I swallow the lump in my throat and hold her, a stolen moment of perfection right here among the men that would dig my grave if they knew the truth.

"I missed you," I whisper in her ear. "I fucking missed you."

I expect her to go rigid, to keep her distance from me. To play the role she was meant to play and has since before she came of age. Since before she ever married the motherfucking traitor Mercadio.

But she doesn't. I feel her sigh, and she gives herself one second to rest her head on my shoulder. "I missed you, too," she whispers in my ear.

A crash of glass comes behind us, and we release each other on instinct. When she wobbles a bit on her heels, I grab her elbow to steady her. But it's only another Rossi brother fight over goddamn food.

"Boys, boys," Nonna scolds. "Santo home for one day, you no fight over food! Ottavio!" She calls over the crowd. Tavi looks over. "Focaccia?"

"Always, Nonna." He mutters under his breath, "Dumbasses." Then, louder, "I brought a catering tray for a party of a hundred."

Orlando releases Mario's collar, and Mario glares. "Son of a bitch," Mario says, straightening himself. "I *told* you I didn't eat the last piece. Jesus. You should eat once in a while instead of just drinking those goddamn protein shakes."

"Oh yeah?" Orlando says, taking another step toward him. "Just like you said you didn't eat the last fucking manicotti the other night?" Mario stands his ground and cracks his knuckles.

Shit, I've missed these assholes.

"Guys." Romeo's deep voice cracks like a whip, and we all look to him. "Enough. We only have a short visit with Santo."

A strange feeling settles in my chest, a feeling I can't put my finger on. I swallow at the sudden rise of emotion.

We only have a short visit with Santo. As if he doesn't want to waste the few minutes they have with me on bullshit. As if I matter.

They settle down, but Orlando points to his eyeballs then swivels his wrist to Mario and glares to warn him he's watching him.

Romeo nods to me. "Let's hear about the vineyards."

Fucking great. Can't wait to talk about the goddamn vineyards.

We take our seats at the huge table in the Great Hall. We eat our formal meals in the dining room, an ornate affair with hung tapestries and fine Persian rugs, a gleaming table custom-made to accommodate the large Rossi family and their guests, wineglasses made of crystal. We eat on fine china, and drink wine procured from Tuscany. I personally oversee the first shipments home.

One entire wall of the dining room is comprised entirely of bottles of the Rossi family wine, which we drink liberally and replenish every weekend. On Sundays we have our family meal in the formal dining room as well, but every other meal takes place in the Great Hall. And today, we have business.

I settle back in the chair Romeo gestures for me to sit in, take the glass of wine offered to me by staff, and prepare to fill them in. Before I do, I make a casual sweep of the place to see where Rosa sits.

But Rosa's gone.

CHAPTER FOUR

Rosa

Natalia's with her nanny, which is all I should care about.

No, it's all I *do* care about.

Natalia's safe, and she'll be feasting on all the food with the rest of the family. Nonna's ravioli is her favorite, which Nonna made especially for her today. Her other great-grandchildren are still too young to eat everything we do, so Natalia gets the special treatment.

From here, I can sit with my back against the fence that surrounds the pool, and hear Santo's deep, confident voice in the Great Hall. The courtyard's only a small staircase away, but busily decorated with pillars and columns and greenery galore. Enough to hide me.

I was surprised Santo didn't notice me slip away, but I waited until he was fixated on Romeo. Romeo holds the keys to Santo's entire world in his hand, so it only makes sense Santo focuses on him. It's easy to get swept away in the crowd with my brothers and their ridiculous obsession with food.

I have no appetite anyway. How could I?

I close my eyes and will myself to breathe more slowly. In and out, in and out, as slowly and as purposefully as I learned to breathe through labor pains when I was pregnant with Natalia.

It's a different sort of pain, but it's every bit as consuming now as it's ever been.

A gentle hum comes from the pool, either the heater or filter or both, but it's only white noise against Santo's deep, melodic voice. I don't catch all the words, but I hear him say *vendemmia,* the Italian word for the harvest of the grapes, one of the most special times of the year in all of Tuscany. In late August or early September, the grapes of the vineyards are harvested. Some people make it a holiday in Tuscany.

"Success," I hear him say, telling them we harvested a greater abundance of perfectly ripe grapes than ever. I hear Romeo respond and hope he's praising Santo for once. Romeo's sparing with his praise, but I know the guys need it sometimes.

I lean back and let Santo's voice wash over me, the rich intonation of it rising and falling, as steady and as calming as a magician's incantation. I love Santo's voice. I could fall asleep to the sound of the inflections painted with calm authority and confidence.

He looks different, these days. He's let his beard grow in thick, as if it's a vineyard keeper's job to look like a biker. A part of me wonders if he just doesn't care anymore.

It suits him, though. It suits him *fine.*

I tune in to his voice, trying to piece things together.

But even though his voice is every bit as resonant as it ever was, there's something missing. He speaks coldly, as if reciting something he memorized for school. There's no... no *passion.*

And Jesus if that isn't all I ever had with him.

I can still feel his hands in my hair, still feel his lips on mine. When he held me in the hall, I felt our hearts beat together in that stolen moment of time.

I ball my hands into fists and shove them in my eye sockets.

I will not cry, I will not cry, I will not cry.

I've been through so much that never made me cry, from my father's cruel backhand to marriage to a man I married for the sake of the family.

They all thought I loved him. It was a narrative I told for the self-sacrifice I knew was inevitable.

The only love Anthony Mercadio ever gave me's sitting in the Great Hall surrounded by her family, feasting on Nonna's homemade pasta and Mama's handmade bread. To Papa, I was a commodity, nothing more than a Rossi jewel on his tilted crown.

Anthony's and my marriage deteriorated quicker than I would have anticipated. I thought I could hold things together like everyone else had.

But I won't think of that now. Not now.

"We expect next year's harvest to outdo even this one," Santo finishes. This time, his voice rings loud and clear.

"Excellent," Romeo says, before he orders another round of drinks. Someone will say my name in a minute and my private moment of solitude will evaporate. But I'll enjoy this while I can.

I close my eyes and remember, the words of my brothers and Santo fading into the background like music. I remember sitting right here the night Santo was brought into our family.

"Rosa! Rosa?" My mother's voice carried through The Castle as she called for me, and I knew I only had a small window of time before I'd get into trouble. Five-thirty on a Sunday meant Sunday dinner was in half an hour, and if I didn't show up promptly, I'd be grounded for eternity by Mama, if Papa didn't find me first.

I swallowed hard and fingered the little note in my pocket, crumpled and hidden away. A new classmate, a boy from out of town, who'd joined us late in the school year. While every other boy in St. Anthony's eighth-grade class knew enough to leave any Rossi family member well enough alone, the new boy hadn't learned yet and the other boys didn't trust him enough to warn him.

I was on the cusp of womanhood, prepared to go to high school the next year, so eager for attention from the male of the species it pained me how they treated me like a pariah.

But not the new boy. He was a young guy from the West Coast, with short red hair and a friendly smile.

"Hey," a guy from class whispered to the new kid when he saw me talking to him. I didn't hear the rest of the words he said except "Rossi" and "brothers." My brothers were younger than my classmates, but it didn't matter. They'd already earned their reputations.

I got the note after gym class, folded in a triangle sitting on my desk.

"I can't talk to you anymore."

No reason. No explanation. Nothing at all.

I didn't ask questions. I didn't have to. But the pains of continuous rejection still stung when I was so young. It wasn't until much, much later that I learned to mute them.

Most of the time, anyway.

"Rosa!" Mama called, her voice taking on a more concerned edge. With a labored sigh, I pushed myself to my feet and went to go see her.

"Here, Mama." I waved to her from the courtyard. The water in the pool behind me lapped quietly, as if sighing that I had been found.

"Ah, where've you been?" She walked rapidly to me in her signature high-heeled shoes, grabbed me by the elbow, and pulled me along. While Mama was a lot gentler than Papa, she grew rougher when she feared his wrath would focus on one of us. "Please, Rosa," she pled. "Don't make him angry. He has news he's excited to share with all of us."

Ah. "News." It typically bored us all to tears, but we all listened attentively, giving my father the god-like attention he demanded. We'd acquired new property, he'd bought a new car, we were going on a trip, blah blah blah.

And then I saw him. Standing in the doorway of the dining room. I stifled a gasp.

He was the most beautiful boy I had ever seen.

Younger than me maybe, yes, but taller, bigger, with the air of someone who hadn't grown into his own yet. And those eyes... eyes that were much older than his years. A stark, vivid blue that pierced my soul.

Eyes that had borne pain and survived.

Yes. Survived. The stranger in the doorway was a survivor.

Just like me.

He faced me fearlessly, his jaw clenched tight and his stance welcoming anyone to try to knock him down. This boy was a born fighter. He was as tough as my brothers, but there was something... different about him. A brilliance in those eyes unmatched by his peers, as if he held the knowledge of some long-hidden secret.

Time would reveal him to be a brilliant strategist, an expert chess player, and the most skilled hit man my father ever trained.

He also became my father's favorite, the one child unrelated by blood, the only one my mother couldn't control. The only one my father would truly take under his wing.

Some say the only one of us unencumbered with a conscience.

And yet, I knew a kinship with this beautiful, haunted boy with the world-worn eyes within seconds of meeting him.

"Rosa," Mama said, beaming, but even I didn't miss the hesitation in her voice before she continued. "Meet Santo." She cleared her throat. "He's your new brother."

"Rosa?" Mama stands in the doorway just like she did so many years ago. Her brow's knit in concern. "Are you okay?"

I stand and brush imaginary dust off my dress. I give her a forced smile. "Oh, fine. It was a little hot in there, so I needed to get some fresh air."

She smiles sadly at me. I walk to her, the sound of my own heels clicking on the floor of the courtyard. I like the sound the fabulous Jimmy Choos make when I walk. It's… empowering.

I reach for her when I'm by her side.

She clucks her tongue when she looks at my feet. "My God, they're incredible." She shakes her head. "I did pass down good taste in shoes, didn't I?"

I give her a wan smile, and she tucks me against her shoulder. She hugs me tighter than I expect. "Warm, is it?" she whispers in my ear. "Right." She doesn't buy my excuse. "Ah, my love, you carry so many things in your heart, don't you?"

Why is it that a mother knows so much more than anyone else?

I've never talked to her about Santo. To her, I'm a daughter. To her, he's her son.

But he's never been like a brother to me, not since the very first day I saw him.

I can't reveal what's in my heart to her. It would be strange, and unexpected, not to mention put her in a dangerous position of having to choose sides.

I can't do that to her, not after everything she's been through.

I can't cause any more ripples in the peace of my family ever, ever again. *I won't.* And I won't make anything more difficult for Santo.

I wish he would tell me why he went to Tuscany that fatal day.

I wish he would talk to me. Romeo thought I knew, and he pried as hard as he could without crossing a line. Orlando tried as well, but I told him I didn't know. I didn't.

And Santo won't breathe a word to me.

"Rosa," Mama says in my ear. "My love. Do you think at some point it might help to put down what you hold that's so heavy?"

I release her and step away. "I don't know what you're talking about. It's warm in here, and I needed to get away from everyone."

I shiver as I say this and brush my hands over my arms.

"Right," Mama says, her tone hardening. "I understand. Come, love, let's have dessert before the boys begin their initiation process."

When they do, just as always, the Rossi family tradition will trump all. The women will take their leave, and the men will perform their initiation.

It's just as well. I know initiation involves a sort of hazing I'd rather not see the men I love perform.

I walk in as discreetly as possible beside Mama. Santo's in deep conversation with Tavi and doesn't even look up. I can feel him tense, though, as if his radar's been flicked on by my presence.

I wonder sometimes if I've imagined his attraction to me, if I'm only someone who helped him pass the time until he could bed another woman.

And we all know he's had no fucking *shortage* of them.

I turn away from him and for the thousandth time, let him go.

I know it's for the best. I know it's even necessary.

Then why does it make my heart feel so heavy to be invisible to him?

"Mama, Nonna made ravioli," Natalia, swinging her legs at the table, says around a mouthful of pasta.

I smile at her. "Mmm, your favorite, isn't it? Don't speak with your mouth full, though, sweetheart." I hand her a napkin and show her how to lay it on her lap, just before I take my seat beside her.

Her nanny's taken the rest of the day off, which is just as well. The girl acts like a scared little rabbit around me, but I don't know why, since I've never done anything to her that should frighten her.

Santo's four chairs down from me, beside Orlando and across from Romeo, but sitting on Orlando's other side is a dark figure of a man I've never seen before. Ruggedly handsome with classically masculine features, dark eyes frame his square face. The set of his chin hints at a stubborn streak, a feature that will serve him well here. But even though he's hot—like all men of The Family, strong and muscled, with an athlete's physique and a general air of authority that knows no compunction—he might as well be wallpaper to me.

There are no men I'll ever be attracted to again except the one who knows every curve and secret of my body. The only one I'll never have.

Romeo clears his throat, and the room grows silent. I put my finger to my lips for Natalia and she rolls her eyes. Naughty little thing. If Santo were beside her, she'd be a little angel. All he'd have to do is raise that stern eyebrow of his and she'd eat out of the palm of his hand.

"As we all know, we're here today for a special reason," Romeo begins. His deep, authoritative voice resounds in the Great Hall, no need for a megaphone. This hall was designed for meetings just like this.

What he doesn't say is that we're initiating another man into the brotherhood because Uncle Leo betrayed us.

Bastard.

"The rules state that the inner sanctum of The Family be fortified within a year of a core member's loss," Romeo continues discreetly. "And Orlando suggested we recruit outside The Family. To be clear, later this year we'll initiate cousins on the Montavio side as well, but we'll wait until their jobs in Italy are complete." It's odd to hear Romeo, the king of using "motherfucker" in any grammatical way possible, speak so formally. But right now, he isn't my brother but The Don.

Romeo turns to the man sitting beside Orlando. "Welcome, Dario."

Dario stands, and I can tell before he speaks that Orlando's chosen wisely. He's as big and intimidating as the other guys and fills out his suit well. And while he carries himself with an air of respect and intelligence, there's a cunning edge to his eyes that I note a mile away.

They all have it. You have to, to do their jobs, or you'd fold like a house of cards.

Dario clears his throat. "Thank you for the warm welcome, Mr. Rossi."

"Romeo," my brother corrects with a bit of a grimace. He will never allow the men of the inner sanctum to call him *Mr. Rossi.*

Dario smiles, revealing straight white teeth. "Thank you, Romeo, and thank you Orlando for suggesting me. It's an absolute honor to be included among the ranks of men such as you, and I will do my best to make you proud."

Amidst the clinking of glasses and cheers, the smacks on the back and fist bumps, Dario meets my eyes. I give him a small, aloof smile, my go-to. As a Rossi family widow, I'm prime real estate, and it would pain me to mislead any man, even with the hint of a smile that's too warm.

But Dario doesn't look away. He holds my gaze for another heartbeat before he looks over at Orlando and sits back down.

I won't look at Santo. I won't. I know without confirming that Santo's giving Dario the death stare that would incinerate a lesser man, and I can't… I can't bear that. Not now.

Feasting commences.

Natalia got an early sampling, likely to keep her occupied while the adults conversed and drank their wine. Now, staff bring out large trays of crostini, bacon-wrapped scallops, and Santo's favorite panzarotti, the decadent little mini calzones Mama fries up just for him. She gets up at the crack of dawn to make the dough, then hand-cuts each piece before she stuffs and fries them.

I watch as one of the staff brings an entire tray and places it right in front of Santo.

I purse my lips. Of all the goddamn things...

First to exile him. For what? We don't know, because he won't tell us. Then to treat him like a king when he returns? It's cruel. Too fucking cruel.

"Earth to Rosssaaaa," Marialena singsongs beside me. "Yoohoo…"

I swivel my gaze to meet hers. "Yes?"

"You okay?" she whispers in a stage whisper.

Natalia grins. "She's just hungry. I think she wants Uncle Santo's panzarotti."

My cheeks flush, but I quickly calm my pounding pulse.

I sniff. "Not me. I'm here for the scallops and steak." I ran an extra mile this morning just so I could feast with the rest of them. I fill my plate with the savory dishes and a few crostini but leave room for Nonna's delicious insalata.

I listen to the conversations around me but feel an odd sort of detachment from it all, as if I'm a fly on the wall observing, and not one of the Rossi own.

"Dario is well-known in Southie, brothers," Orlando's explaining to them all in a low voice. He'll wait until they're alone to give details, but I listen to him attentively. I'm intrigued.

"Where'd you two meet, Lando?" Marialena asks innocently. She leans back in her chair as staff clear our plates.

Orlando grins at her. Her pet name for him always makes him go soft as a marshmallow. "Dario was my right-hand man in The Big House. Saved me from more than one a—" his gaze travels to Natalia, and he quickly amends— "butt kicking, had my back. You need a guy like that at your side." He nods, and I watch as a shadow flickers over his face. Orlando may be the one whose fist falls heavier and faster than any other brother, but he's got a gentle heart that ironically dislikes violence.

It's been a while since any of them have served time. His reference to "The Big House" goes right over Natalia's head. I'm thankful my brothers keep their language and references in check. If I have my way, it'll be a long, long time before she knows who our family is.

My mother clears her throat. "Dario, we've welcomed the men of the brotherhood into the Rossi family, a select few outside of our bloodline."

I feel Santo's eyes burning a hole in me. I want to look away. I need to stay detached. But as if he has a magnetic pull on my heart, my gaze swings back to his, and I swallow hard.

I forget when we're apart how piercing his eyes are.

I forget how stern and cold he can be, his profile rigid and strong, but how light glimmers over his hauntingly handsome face with icy radiance, how his straight white teeth contrast with the olive tone of his skin.

Mama continues. I hold Santo's gaze for a risky length of time, until I fear someone will think it inappropriate, but I don't want to be the one that looks away first. A beat passes. Two.

Natalia pulls at my dress, and I turn to her. I release a breath I didn't know I held.

"When's dessert?" she whispers. "Uncle Tavi brought me a surprise."

I put my finger to my lips to admonish her to be quiet, but whisper back, "They're taking it out now, and I'm sure you'll be the first one we serve, baby."

She silently claps her hands and dances in her seat. Santo's watching her, a rare ghost of a smile on his lips.

Mama continues. "Dario, we trust Orlando's judgment, and as you know, after the passing of my brother-in-law, our family could stand to fortify ourselves."

Dario nods. "Thank you."

We've taken blow after blow over the past few years. Romeo ascended into his position as Don after my father died. For us, it was a welcome death, one my brothers oversaw and allowed. My father ruled with an iron fist, and every one of us bears the scars as a result.

I still remember when it was Romeo's turn to lead. How I took him aside and begged him not to be the man our father was.

"Do better, Romeo," I said. "Do better."

But now my future… my everything rests in the hands of my brother who sits at the head of this table.

My brother, who holds the fate of us all in his hands.

CHAPTER FIVE

Santo

The unmistakable sound of someone crying stopped me in my tracks. Eight years after joining the Rossi family, I knew every possible hiding place on the sprawling grounds of The Castle. I'd been to each place time and time again, whichever locale served the purpose I needed, to hide a smoke, to hide contraband, or to hide forbidden tears when I was younger.

I was way too old to cry now. Narciso taught me that the hard way.

I looked down at the papers he sent me to retrieve, a scroll from the chapel bound in burgundy ribbon, and glanced at my wrist. He expected me in five minutes. I knew he'd beat the shit out of me if I was late.

Eh, whatever. He might beat the shit out of me if I was on time, too. Said I needed to learn to deal with pain without crying.

And I was almost there.

I sighed, made the choice to take whatever hand he dealt me, and went down to The Castle wall. Every beating I took was another plate in my armor.

I expected to see Marialena nursing a wound over something. Papa yelled at her, Nonna kicked her out of the kitchen, Mama told her she couldn't have biscotti before dinner or buy another dress.

I stopped short when I saw Rosa.

She was so beautiful she made my heart beat faster and my palms grow sweaty. No other girl ever had that effect on me.

Over the years, her cheeks hollowed, and her body filled out, though she was always slender and fit. Only now, her hips were wider and her breasts fuller.

For a while, I dragged my sorry ass once a month to the confessional at St. Anthony's, but I didn't know why. I did wicked shit for Papa, damn near every day. I swore like a sailor. But it ate at my conscience to jerk off in the shower to someone who was supposed to be my sister. I felt like some sick, twisted deviant.

But Rosa wasn't my sister and never had been.

I walked slowly, so she didn't hear me, but I didn't want to startle her. My heart broke to see her like this, balled into a fetal position with her fists in her eye sockets.

So when I was only a few feet away, I cleared my throat.

She sat up straighter, her eyes coming straight to me. She glared at me like I didn't belong. And hell, maybe I didn't.

"Why are you here?" she snapped. "Leave me alone."

She eyed the papers tucked under my arm. I ignored her and sat down beside her. Her barbed comments didn't touch my armor.

"Dunno, thought it might be fun to intentionally piss Papa off today."

"Santo," she said, her eyes softening. "Don't. Don't do it. I hate it when he hits you."

I cut my eyes to her, anger flaring in my chest like the light of a match. "And one day I'll fucking kill him for hitting you."

She turned her face away from me, as if she didn't want to acknowledge she'd been on the receiving end of Narciso Rossi's rage. It was nothing to be ashamed about, though. He didn't play favorites.

"You shouldn't say that," she whispered. "Don't say that, Santo."

"Only a fuckin' devil hits a woman," I snapped, but I kept my voice low. I was already in trouble for being late, I didn't need to add confinement to the dungeon, or worse, on top of my inevitable punishment.

She sighed. For long minutes, we stared at the angry sea, and a rough wind kicked up over the water. She shivered in the cold. Wordlessly, I shrugged out of my hoodie and draped it over her shoulders. It was what I was taught to do by Mama. Still, looking down in surprise, Rosa gave me a rare, heart-melting smile.

"You're a gentleman now?"

Only for her.

I shrugged. "I was gettin' hot is all. I gotta get this shit to your Papa. So spit it out. Tell me why you were crying."

She stuck out her chin and gave me a decided shake of her head. "Ah ah. No way. Nope. I'm here alone for a reason and you won't take that from me."

But the way she didn't meet my eyes said she wanted to tell me. She wanted to reveal everything.

And why not?

Everyone needed a confidant.

Everyone.

"Rosa," I warned.

"Don't you Rosa *me," she responded. "You're younger than I am. I've got enough people to boss me around."*

"Well add me to that fuckin' list," I snapped.

I've been taller and bigger than her with more power and experience since I fucking came here. We both knew age was no excuse.

Furthermore, as a sworn-in member of the Rossi brotherhood, we both knew I was in authority over her and would be until she was married.

"Since when has that meant a damn thing?"

She shook her head and didn't respond.

Her elbow touched mine. An electric buzz skated across my skin as if she bewitched me with her magic. I covered up the hitch in my breath and swallowed, already hard just at the scent of her perfume.

"Since never," she finally said. Her lip wobbled, and I knew on instinct that if I just gave her time, she'd tell me why she came. Didn't mean I could make it better, but I'd try.

"You know I'll be married someday, Santo, don't you?"

I knew it. She knew it. We all fucking knew it.

I nodded.

"Likely to someone I've never met. Likely to someone who'll never love me." Her voice shook. "And sometimes, it makes me want to just... to just throw myself off this cliff and end it all."

I grabbed her arm and held her.

"Don't you fucking say that, Rosa. Jesus. If you ever say anything like that again—"

"Oh, now you're *threatening me?" She yanked her arm out from mine, but I only reached for her again. Her skin felt like silk to my touch, but it didn't pacify the raging*

anger I felt at her mentioning suicide. I wanted to yank her over my lap and spank the shit out of her for saying such a stupid thing.

"You're goddamn right I'm threatening you. You're talking like a spoiled brat."

"Santo!" she hissed. "How dare you? I'm old enough to—"

"We covered that. I don't fucking care how old you are. You want to talk about bullshit like ending it?"

I pulled her to me. My chest heaved from the effort of controlling myself. The thought of a woman as brilliant, as beautiful, as perfect as Rosa, throwing it all away because life got hard made me want to shake some sense into her.

"You think you should even say that shit out loud, even give it any power at all?"

We were too close. Closer than we'd ever been. She was on the taller side for a Rossi woman, but not as tall as me. She was slender and willowy. I could overpower her so easily it was laughable.

"I can't believe after everything we've been through you'd want to threaten me."

I shook my head. "I can't believe after everything we've been through you'd be so stupid. As if—as if none of us cares about you."

And I thought she was the coward?

She blinked, and her lip trembled. We'd crossed a line and we both knew it, a line that couldn't ever be uncrossed.

I touched a Rossi woman unbidden.

They'd kill me for this.

But I'd always liked the adrenaline rush of breaking the rules, and I wouldn't stop now. When she blinked again, a tear rolled down her cheek.

"You're the only one who ever gets it, Santo," she whispered.

I'd wear that honor like a badge.

And just like that, I wanted to hold her to me. I'd never wanted to do that to another human in my life.

I reached my thumb to her cheek and brushed a tear away. While she watched me, I placed my thumb in my mouth. I drank her salty tear.

I pulled her closer to me. My dick was so hard it was painful, but I ignored it. I'd rather cut off my own balls than violate her. And if we did anything consensually, her brothers would happily do the deed for me.

"Don't be gentle, Santo," she said, shaking her head. "Please."

"Why not?" I whispered back.

"I'm afraid I'll fall in love with you."

"Motherfucker." Mario scowls at the cards in my hand as he tosses his on the table and folds. Orlando eyes me warily and pushes more bills onto the growing pile. Romeo watches with his arms crossed on his chest. He folded his hand first.

I bring myself back to the present and stop thinking about the past.

I don't think he cares. I think he wanted to watch more than anything.

But Tavi gives me a look and tosses more money into the pot.

"You're a fuckin' cheat." Mario glowers at me, but I give him a cool look.

"You wanna talk about that outside, brother?" I haven't lost at poker in ten years, and haven't cheated a day in my life.

Mario scowls. "Nah, man, I'm racing tomorrow."

Dario grins. His arm's still bandaged from the intentional knife wound inflicted by Romeo that made him bleed. All of ours had bled, but Dario's was the deepest cut.

We sealed the blood oath between us last night. Tomorrow I go back to Tuscany. My flight leaves first thing in the morning, but I wanted one more night with my brothers.

It was my suggestion we play cards, and I totally fucking manipulated them into playing in the back room of Elise's shop downtown.

A risk, maybe, but a risk I was willing to take.

I want one more night with Rosa, too, even if she's on the showroom floor. I know she's here. I can feel her. I can hear her voice as she talks to customers and Elise.

She doesn't know I'm here yet.

The back stockroom for Elise's store connects to a warehouse where we conduct business. Romeo secured this place for the sake of all of us. Located in Copley Square in Boston, it's a perfect place to do the clean work, while the dirty work often takes place in Orlando and Tavi's North End locations.

Here, we conduct business, place orders, and have necessary meetings in Boston without having to travel to The Castle on the North Shore .

I hear her. Rosa's voice sounds right outside the door. My heart smacks against my ribcage, but I keep my poker face.

I wanna see her one more time before I go, and this is the safest damn way.

I toss my hand down.

They curse me out and shove money at me. I take my time picking it up.

"When's the last fucking time Santo didn't beat us?" Orlando asks, scratching his beard. He leans back in his seat and scowls.

"I think Mario was still in fuckin' diapers," Romeo says. Even Mario laughs at that. "Y'all should've known better than to agree to a farewell card game with a motherfucker who's got nothin' to lose."

I shrug.

"You agreed, Rome?"

"I knew you'd win," he says with a flash of white teeth as he grins at me. "Thought I'd give you a parting gift, just make you fuckin' earn it first."

"Aw, thanks," I say, as the door to the back room swings open.

"Oh my *God.*" I don't look up from gathering my earnings at the sound of her voice. I've learned to use my poker face more often than at the card table. "Tavi, Elise is gonna *kill* you."

"She'll do no such thing," Tavi says, shaking his head. "She doesn't mind when I play cards. And I fuckin' own this place." He leans back in his chair to match Orlando and gives her a look that dares her to push back.

Every Rossi man is the head of his respective house, and every Rossi woman, whether married into or born in the family, knows this. Still, it's a dick move.

"Not for the goddamn *cards,*" she hisses. "For *smoking in her stockroom.*"

Tavi eyes the joint in his hand as if he'd forgotten it was there, then passes it around. "Elise loves to smoke, though, Rosa."

"Not since you knocked her up, and she does not want her fucking handbags imported this very day to smell like an ashtray or a joint!"

"Wow," I mutter, as Mario shuffles then stacks the cards and starts dealing them out again. "You kiss your mother with that mouth?"

Rosa turns to me, aghast. Her jaw falls open. "If I had to censor your conversations with a beeper, Santo, every other word out of your mouth would be a *bleeping bleep bleepity bleep.*"

I shrug. "I'm not a lady."

"Ooohhhhh," the guys say in unison, because they know I just threw the gauntlet down.

Rosa's gaze grows frigid. Fuck it, I love when she gives me that look. Still, I don't react, even when she snaps at me. "A man named *The Saint* who swears more than a bookie thinks he has the right to tell me what to do?"

Romeo's phone rings before I open my mouth and regret the next damn thing I say.

"Shit," he mutters. Everyone's eyes go straight to him.

"What is it?" Tavi asks, always cool and collected when shit goes down.

"Got a cryptic message here. Gotta run footage in the warehouse, guys." He blows out a breath and jerks his chin to Mario. "Show us the new surveillance equipment, will you, while Santo tallies his goddamn earnings?"

He knows I'm no damn use looking over surveillance this time. I'm back in Tuscany tomorrow with my *fucking grapes.*

Chairs scrape as they're pushed back from the table. Mario grabs the cards, and the doors swing closed behind them as they walk away from the stockroom and off to the connected warehouse.

We're alone. I wanted this. I hoped for this.

What she doesn't know is that I laid surveillance in this room before they opened the business, and I know every angle the camera captures.

And every angle it doesn't.

My mouth goes dry, but I keep my face impassive as I pocket my winnings.

"Think you can still boss me around, do you?" she asks tersely, her arms crossed on her chest. I bet she thinks she sounds cold. Aloof. But I hear the thread of want in her voice, and my dick hears it, too.

I pierce her with a look and have half a mind to throw caution to the wind, just like I did that day on the cliffs by The Castle. The day I not only didn't bring the scrolls to Narciso but dropped them. We watched them flutter like birds with broken wings, before they were swallowed whole into the sea. I didn't care. I'd sacrifice myself for Rosa any goddamn time I could.

Still, I spent three days out of school after *that* beating, though.

And now I've got the *entire* fucking Rossi brotherhood here. They would tie me up and take turns beatin' the shit out of me before they cut out my heart and disposed of my body.

If they were feeling generous. I'm already on goddamn probation.

"Ah, Rosa," I say quietly. The only sound in the stockroom is the ticking of a clock on the wall. "I don't *think* I can still boss you around." A true enough sentence, even if we're overheard.

What I'd fucking give to *really* boss her around. Tie her up and punish her and see how wet it made her before I made her come for me. I'd revel in every moan and spasm I'd draw from her. Revel in the way she'd fight me. Relish that sweet moment of submission.

Her eyes go half lidded, and her breathing hitches. Rosa might be smaller than I am, and in some ways, more powerful. One shout to her brothers, and I'm a dead man walking. But she knows who I am. She knows what I'm capable of.

We've spent decades skirting this dance.

We've taken other partners. I've had no compunction about sleeping around after her marriage to Anthony Mercadio. And now...

I put everything down on the table and crook a finger at her and go for broke.

"Get over here."

My pulse quickens when she takes a step closer to me.

I swallow as she nears, her high heels clicking on the concrete. Her rounded, beautiful eyes meet mine with a little curiosity and a *lot* of lust. Thick lashes frame her eyes, making them stark and vivid against the soft creaminess of her porcelain skin. Her eyebrows arch dramatically, and her lips part in a wondrous sigh.

"You gotta move, baby," I whisper in a heated whisper. "Faster than that."

We have minutes, maybe seconds, before heavy footsteps tell us they're coming back.

"The cameras," she whispers.

"I disabled them before we played the game," I whisper back. "And right here we're out of the line of vision."

Her eyes go even wider. "Wh-what?"

"You heard me, beautiful." When she reaches me, I brush my hand across her cheek and capture a lock of hair. I give it a little tug before I gently place it behind her ear.

"Why'd you do that?" she asks.

"Because I didn't want any evidence of what I'm about to do, if I had the chance."

Tomorrow I go back to Tuscany. I won't miss my chance.

I shouldn't do this. I'm playing with such fucking fire, I'm damn near scorched already, and it isn't just me. If they see what I'm doing, her marriage to that fucking Campanelle could happen tomorrow. We're on such thin ice I can feel it cracking.

I reach for her and tug her onto my knee. "You think I can't tell you what to do?" Footsteps come nearer and we both freeze, but they retreat just as quickly. I go for broke. Without giving myself a chance to overthink it, I reach my hand to her face and trace it gently. I lower my mouth to hers and give her a tender kiss while I brush my finger over the fullness of her breast. I slide my hand down the front of her dress and gently stroke her nipple. I drink in the delectable moan she gives me.

I don't care what happens to me.

I don't care what they do.

She feels so good like this, smells so good, I need to taste her.

"Santo," she whispers, but instead of getting off my lap, she only snuggles in further. "Santo," she says, no longer a protest but a plea. "Soon, they'll marry me off. I know they will. And it's not fair you're being punished." Her voice hitches. "Santo, I—"

We hear the footsteps right outside the stockroom door too late. She flies off my lap and runs to a box, frantically grabbing things out of it. I dive behind a pallet of boxes and press my belly to the floor.

"Hey, Rosa."

I let out a breath. Elise. Elise might not tell Tavi if she saw us together.

"Oh, those aren't the ones I needed to look at. Sorry, it's the smaller boxes we got earlier today that I think they messed up. I asked for the XL and I'm pretty sure—"

A flash of light flickers in warning on the stockroom wall. I stare in disbelief. Our hidden security system. Someone just pulled the alarm.

Elise and Rosa go still.

Fuck.

That light means *get the fuck out of here.*

But it's too late.

Half a second later, sirens sound outside the warehouse.

"Oh my God. Oh my God!" Elise runs toward the warehouse and Rosa follows behind her.

She never saw me. I leap to my feet and follow them, just as a swarming team of armed State Troopers break down the back entrance to the warehouse.

Fuckkkkk.

"Oh God!" Rosa cries openly, her hand over her mouth. She knows as well as I do what it would mean if Orlando got taken back to jail. She knows that can't happen. "What is it?" she asks. "Who is it?"

I join my brothers with my hands in the air, but it isn't me they're after.

"Romeo Rossi, you're under arrest."

No.

No.

Romeo looks mildly surprised, but he's always calm under duress. Slowly, he raises his hands in the air.

"Now what the fuck—" Mario begins, but Romeo shakes his head sharply at him.

"Not now, brother. Call Flynt," he says. Family lawyer, hired after a will fiasco before Narciso died.

Rosa's crying softly as they drag Romeo's hands behind his back and cuff him.

They don't even look at any of us.

I don't hear what they say for the ringing in my ears.

Why Romeo? Why now?

"Santo," Romeo says, as they march him away. "Stay, brother. I lift your exile. They'll need you here."

I watch him be taken out in stunned silence.

We all do.

Then it hits me.

I'm staying home.

CHAPTER SIX

Rosa

We stand in silence as the fading sounds of sirens disappear. I wipe my tears and quickly get myself together. I can't fall apart, not now.

"Of course they had to make a fucking show of it," Mario mutters, shaking his head. "They couldn't just arrest him." He swivels his gaze to Santo. "Why'd they take him?"

"How the fuck do I know?" Santo snaps, but his eyes are bright, and my mind still hasn't caught up to what Romeo said before he left.

Santo's staying right here.

He isn't leaving for Tuscany.

"Because you're the one who's the brains behind everything," Mario says, running his fingers through his hair. "You're the one who knows what's happening before we do."

I don't know if it's my imagination, but it sounds like there's accusation in his tone. Does he suspect Santo knows something he isn't letting on? I bite my tongue to avoid snapping at him. I won't let my family descend into chaos and bickering because we're stressed.

Most of them have been arrested at one point or another, and most of the time with good reason, but none of us has ever seen the Don taken since Romeo's assumed the throne as Boss.

I choose willful ignorance when it comes to what my brothers do, what all made men do. But I have a basic understanding. I know Mario's skilled at all things techie, Orlando's the group heavy and enforcer, and Tavi, as Underboss, consults with Romeo on all internal operations, but his keen mind is also behind everything. He's often the group strategist, similar to Santo.

Santo, however, is skilled intellectually, and often sees one move ahead of everyone else. He's also the one that may not have a conscience, which gives him a decided advantage.

I know this is why he was in Tuscany. Even though he hasn't told anybody the details, I know that he saw something nobody else did, a threat to the family that hadn't come to fruition, maybe. I'd bet he even suspected Leo was a traitor long before we knew he actually was.

I wish I knew why he was in Tuscany. I have a niggling suspicion that...

No. No, I won't go there.

It's none of my business.

There was a time when I wanted to learn everything, to know every decision made, penny paid, and deal signed with whatever stakes they chose. But I regretted that choice. Since I couldn't control damn near any of it, I was only left frustrated and often angry.

So I've written myself out of my brothers' work. And even though I love my family with all my heart, I don't follow where they lead.

But now... now we're reeling from a devastating blow.

Santo paces and Tavi takes a call, likely from the lawyer. He turns his back to us and talks in a low voice.

"I know this," Santo says, his deep, gravelly voice commanding the attention of the whole room. "Romeo is innocent. I know he ain't perfect, but I know he's kept his hands fuckin' clean."

"How do you know that?" Orlando asks.

Santo scowls. "Because he wants to have a baby with Vittoria. He doesn't want to risk anything that will take him away from home, not now."

Vittoria was once pregnant with a child, soon after their marriage and before Orlando's, but she lost the baby early on. And they haven't been able to conceive a child since. It's something we rarely speak of. Santo understands this.

"So I'm thinking, then... that Romeo was set up," Santo says. His words fall like a gavel. "Someone wants him out of the picture, don't they?"

Mario's jaw tightens, and his normally jovial expression hardens. The brother that stands before me isn't a boy anymore, but a man, and has been for some time. It only took me a while to see it.

"Yeah," Mario says, and I can see him piecing things together, though not at the same rate as Santo. Santo, always one step ahead.

Finally, Dario speaks up. He clears his throat as if to get everyone's attention, but he doesn't need to. With a simple syllable, his voice commands the room. I don't know his role yet here, but as a newly made man, I'd guess he begins as one of Romeo's Capos.

"I know I'm new here, but I feel the same. Someone wanted Romeo out of the way. Someone wanted us ruffled. Maybe someone who knows I've been inducted, and that Elise is having a baby, someone who knows we're solidifying the power of the

Rossi family." He frowns, and his gaze swings to Orlando.

"Right," Orlando says.

The pulse in the room is heated and angry, as if we're sitting on a ticking time bomb. Santo looks to Tavi. "Tavi, thinkin' we should convene at The Castle. Lock everyone down. Cancel the flight tonight, re-assign every motherfucker here. Yeah?"

A shiver skates down my spine at the low command of authority in Santo's voice. He isn't the one that technically holds the most authority, but it seems when shit goes down, he takes the natural lead. And damn if that isn't hot.

Tavi blinks as if just realizing with Romeo being locked away, he's the one in charge. A natural-born leader himself, he'll rule fairly and intelligently. He and Orlando will share responsibility, as will most of the made men, but Tavi's like the Vice President. He'll get the final call when Romeo's unable to lead. Still, he'll lean hard on all made men of the Rossi family.

"Glad he told you to stay, brother," he says in a low voice to Santo. I wonder if anyone else heard him.

Elise walks up to him and laces her fingers through his. She rests a hand on his belly as Tavi's eyes come to hers, heated and intense, and a part of me longs for someone to look at me like that. My brothers love me, but there's a different kind of intensity between lovers. "You do not leave my side. You don't fucking use the toilet without me next to you, you get me?"

She pales. Elise is one of the few women married into The Family that was raised in the mob. She gets it. "I do," she whispers. She knows the danger she's in. I've seen my brother personally vet every bodyguard that watches her.

"Everyone back to The Castle," Tavi says. "We'll close the store down for the night, Elise. Keep it closed over the weekend. We'll have more intel and security in place so you can hopefully reopen on Monday."

Tavi turns to Santo. "You take Rosa back to The Castle. I want my sisters safe, do you understand me?"

Santo's jaw tightens and I watch as his hand goes to the harness on his hip by instinct. I can almost hear him whisper a silent command to make his fucking day. I swallow as surprising emotion rises in me.

I'd give anything for the simplest reassurance from him. Finger touch to mine. Knowing look. Soft whisper in my ear. But this is Santo, and he's keeping this clean as fuck.

I remind myself, I'm Rosa Rossi. And I don't need a man to make me feel safe.

I check my own gun in my purse, and finger it lovingly. We keep it on the down-low, but Marialena and I are skilled with gun use and take refresher self-defense classes twice a year.

Tavi accompanies Elise to the front, where she tells her staff they're closing and helps customers finish packing. I go to help her when I feel a firm hand on my elbow. The Rossi made men may pride themselves on keeping us safe, but we pride ourselves on not needing them.

"No," Santo says, holding me in place. "Let Elise and Tavi go. You come with me. I'm taking you back to The Castle now."

Who knows how long it's gonna last with Santo being my temporary bodyguard, but I have mixed feelings about this.

I hated the thought of him going to Tuscany, and a part of me's relieved he's here. But at the same time… it's a lot easier not to think about him when he isn't *right in my space* all day long.

And if I know him, he'll command my every breath.

Gah-reat.

I clench my jaw and whisper a heated, sarcastic, "Yes, *sir.*"

A muscle twitches in his jaw while he looks straight ahead. "Watch it, woman," he whispers back. I ignore the little zing his threat gives me.

We march together to the waiting cars.

Though we have security here, The Castle's a veritable fortress, nearly impenetrable. We've been under attack before, but the few times that happened, retribution was so harsh and immediate, no one's dared to attack on Castle grounds again.

"We should put better security in place everywhere," I mutter, my hand trembling as I reach for my leather bag.

Santo nods. "We've been adding additional security measures for the past year, Rosa."

Well. Shows what I know when I willfully try to ignore everything.

"Did you drive here tonight?"

"Of course." Again, the twitching jaw. He looks like he wishes he had one good reason to deck someone, or, preferably, slice a throat and watch their blood run, or perhaps shoot someone between the eyes and watch them sink to the floor.

While the other guys often go places with drivers, Santo's one of the few that doesn't. He's a car guy and has been since he got his license. And he's *shit* at letting go of control.

"Which one?"

Before he left for Tuscany, he sold two of his six cars, but before then, he was known for trading out once a quarter or so.

He doesn't have to ask what I mean but knows immediately.

I watch as he sweeps his eyes across the room as if to confirm everyone's occupied, before he whispers in a low voice that makes my nipples furl, "Red Maserati, baby." He knows that's my *favorite.* My absolute favorite.

"Oooh."

Why does every vibration of his voice feel like foreplay? *Why?*

Did he somehow hope he'd be the one to drive me home tonight? Or did it just remind him of me?

Is that wishful thinking?

The door to the back opens again and Tavi comes in with Elise. "Store's closed, everyone's gone but us. I want everyone to stay together, make sure—"

An explosion sounds so loudly, I hit the floor before I know what's happening. I don't even have time to scream. Santo's heavy, muscled body's atop me, pinning me in place. "Don't move," he barks. "Stay there." Then louder. "What the fuck?"

There's nothing in here, no sign of an explosion. It was outside, then.

I hear rapid footsteps. Mario's run to see what it was, the explosion right outside this door. I can't see anything with Santo on top of me.

"Let me up," I manage to get out even though my lungs are constricted from being squashed. My heart's beating like mad. I want to know what happened. I don't want to be pinned beneath his weight as we wait to hear the news.

"Stay right fucking there," he snaps.

I try to roll him off me, but he is, not surprisingly, completely immovable.

"Santo," I growl, gritting my teeth together. "Let me fucking up."

"*No,*" Tavi says, overruling everyone because *of course.* "You stay there."

Fucking ganging up on me.

Mario returns. "Jesus," he swears under his breath. "Who parked a red car in the back lot?"

"Mother*fucker,*" Santo mutters. "Jesus, mother-fuckin' *douchebags.*"

No. *No.* My heart aches at the knowledge that someone destroyed Santo's pride and joy. Tears, actual tears, prick my eyes.

I better get a good swing in myself at whoever did this to him. They don't usually let the women in our family get their hands dirty, but this one… this is personal.

Mario curses. "Hope you had good insurance." He curses under his breath in a stream of rapid Italian. "You guys get the fuck out of here. No one wants me and Dario, we don't mean shit to anyone."

Dario chuckles coldly, as if this is something to be proud of. The sound makes a shiver of fear slide down my spine. "Yeah, agreed," Dario says. "We'll hold things down, the rest of you go back to The Castle. We've got things covered here. We'll run footage, make sure we're clean."

They make a plan while, I should note, *I'm still under Santo,* my cheek pressed unceremoniously against the cold concrete floor.

"Santo," I begin again with a sigh. "Let. Me. *Up!*"

"I. Said. No." He leans down and whispers in my ear, "And if we were alone, I'd whip your pretty ass raw for not doing what you're told. *Shut it.*"

Oh, how *romantic.* Maybe I *don't* care his pretty car's blown to smithereens.

I buck at his huge body fruitlessly.

"Tryin' to get me hard?" he whispers in my ear, a low rumble of warning I crave with every fiber of my being. I'd die before I'd admit that. "Go ahead," he whispers in my ear, while chaos still reigns around us and no one notices. "Fight me. You know how I like it when you fight me." I tremble in frustration. I try to draw in another breath, when finally Tavi speaks up.

"Caravan of armored cars outside this door will take us home. Lawyer will meet us in the Great Hall in an hour. Every one of you, weapons drawn as we exit."

Finally, *finally,* Santo's heft moves off me and I can lift my cheek off the disgusting concrete floor. I make a face and smooth my fingers over my face. I'll have to use the cleansing charcoal face mask after *that* disgustingness.

Santo takes me roughly by the elbow and brushes me off. I'm sure he wants this to look fastidious and unsexy as fuck, but every touch of his fingers on me makes my skin prickle with awareness.

And then I remember. And I can't be angry with him anymore.

"Santo, your car," I say, my legs still tingling when the blood flows through them freely again. My voice cracks. "Your beautiful car."

Scowling, his face unreadable, he shrugs and glances at the door. "Only a damn car. I've got others."

If I close my eyes, I can still see him, the angry young boy with a chip on his shoulder to beat all chips. He melded into our family life like he belonged here… because he did.

Because he *does.*

But nothing was his own. He shared parents with us, he shared a home with us, and he knew from the minute my parents adopted him that everything he had was given to him.

Not his cars, though. Never his cars.

The first one he bought after years of scraping money together, even though my father would've gifted him one off a lot. But no. He had to pay for it himself.

He hadn't even legally gotten his license yet when he bought it. It sat in the garage at The Castle while he learned how to fix it, how to make it the car of his dreams. And when he finally did, when he finally made it his own, he babied that thing as if he'd given birth to it himself.

Romeo took him driving himself instead of my father, for fairly obvious reasons. No one wants to learn how to parallel park under the threat of a backhand. Romeo was rough on all of us, but I learned later that it was mostly for the same reason my mom was—to spare us from the boiling wrath of my father.

No emotion shows in Santo's eyes, after decades of schooling sentiment and feeling.

Santo might be playing this off, but he knows this was personal. He knows it. We both do.

He wraps his fingers roughly around my elbow. Calloused, rough fingers touch bare skin. Gentle words and soft touches would repulse a woman like me, but his hard grip... I ignore the flare of warmth where he touches me and internally scold myself, while he escorts me to the waiting caravan of cars outside the warehouse door.

He opens the door to one of The Family's large, armored black SUVs, missing nothing, his eyes like a hawk's, zeroing in on anything that breathes within a twenty-foot radius of us. If there was an invisible ghost tracking me, he'd see it.

Several of the Capos march out first to his car while sirens blare in the distance, probably firefighters coming to put out the damn fire. Santo doesn't even look at the rising flames. My throat aches.

We're out of here.

Santo shoves me in the back of the car roughly, as if proving to my brothers that I mean nothing to him. I bang my knee on the door and shoot him an angry look, but he only narrows his eyes to slits and buckles me in.

"Push me, Rosa. Fuckin' dare you," he says under his breath. And nothing's ever tempted me so much in my life. Maybe it's his perfect control, the perfect picture of *calm, cool, and collected.* Maybe it's because I want to know what he thinks, what he *feels* inside.

For too long, I've wondered if my attraction to him was one-sided. I've seen him take so many women to bed over the years, I've muted the zing of pain I felt wishing I was the one he paid attention to.

But I didn't imagine what happened in the warehouse before Romeo was taken. I didn't imagine any of it.

Orlando and Mario enter the car after us; Tavi, Elise, and the others are in the third car.

"Gun it," Orlando orders the driver. My belly drops when the huge car peels out of the parking lot, just as a second *boom* explodes around us.

I gasp and cover my mouth, my eyes scanning all around us, but Santo only shakes his head. "Same car. Ignited fuel line."

Flames light the sky as the sirens of firefighters grow nearer. Flashes of red and blue light the sky.

Santo grabs his phone and makes a call.

"Lock them down. Tavi will give you direct orders, but I'm calling a soft lockdown now. Yeah. Explosion at Copley, Romeo's been arrested." Cursing at the other end of the line. He barks out more orders, then shuts his phone off.

Orlando nods. "Amadeo?"

Santo nods.

I throw my hands up in the air. "Is *someone* gonna fill me in here or what?"

"We're expecting another ambush," Santo says. "We need to call in reinforcements. Tavi's in command, but any of the made men of the inner sanctum can call a soft lockdown at any time and Tavi's got his hands full."

Orlando gives one short nod. "Good call, brother. Good fuckin' call. Tavi's on the phone with Flynt and he can only work so fast."

I want to hold his hand. I want to reach for him, to sit closer to him so I can feel the steady, confident warmth of him beside me. But Orlando and Mario will notice if we do anything more than we're doing now.

Goddamn it.

"What's a soft lockdown?" I ask.

Santo looks to me, his piercing blue eyes holding mine. I ignore the way my heart beats faster, and I swallow hard.

"Hard lockdown means there's an active perpetrator and we're in imminent danger. Might hit a safe house or barricade in the dungeon until the coast is clear. Soft lockdown means doors are locked and barricaded, and no one goes in or out. Hard lockdown is a defensive move, soft lockdown offensive."

Santo always prefers taking the offense.

"Why soft lockdown?"

Santo blows out a breath and looks at Orlando and Mario. They both nod.

"Because everyone knows better than to directly attack a made man of The Rossi family," he says.

"Why?" I ask again.

Santo's jaw clenches. "You never ask anything, Rosa. You've chosen to stay out of it. Why the twenty questions now?"

I look out the window. "Because this feels... different."

Because if it were Papa taken to jail, I'd rejoice.

But it isn't Papa.

I love Romeo. And I have a daughter who could be in danger.

Oh my God.

Natalia.

I sit up straight and feel panic hit my chest. "Natalia," I say in a choked voice, shaking my head. "Her nanny's useless. I don't trust her to follow protocol, to make sure that anything's safe for her."

"Natalia's fine, Rosa," Santo says calmly. He places a brotherly arm around my shoulders. "I promise."

"How do you know?"

He doesn't answer.

Orlando has his wife Angelina and his son Nicolo to worry about, Tavi has Elise and the baby they're expecting, and Mario will watch over Mama and Marialena. They'll make sure Romeo's Vittoria has guards on her 24/7 as well.

Someone's got to watch over Natalia. And me.

A little thrill ripples through me at the thought. Santo, at my door, standing guard. Being so close to him without being able to do what I long to…

Not touching him, staying apart and aloof, keeping my distance, is the only thing that will save me. It also may very well kill me.

CHAPTER SEVEN

Santo

I go over everything in my mind that I know to date.

The Regazza betrayal and their conniving ways. Elise's family had an ax to grind after the death of her father, but her mother wanted the inheritance for herself. She actively plotted against Elise's marriage and had a firsthand role in pushing Elise to run from her arranged marriage to The Family.

Who knows how many of the Regazzas she hired to turn. At least two lie dead.

We later discovered that Leo conspired with Anna Regazza, for reasons we may never know. Money is only part of a rationalization for betrayal. But Leo was Narciso's younger brother, and I suspect he had underhanded motives.

Everyone else trusted him. I never did. But then again, I never could trust a man with mistresses and a spoiled wife. It smacks of nothing but selfish motives.

In Tuscany, however, my dealings with the Regazzas only scratched the surface of why I was there.

I piece everything I know, everything I've seen, together. The attack tonight that destroyed my car, no accident, I'm sure. And Romeo being taken to prison…

Did they know he'd lift my banishment to Tuscany and make me stay? Was that part of the plan?

Or did they remove the most dangerous man in New England to prepare for a worse attack?

Only time will tell. Time, interrogations, and a shit ton of money.

We reach The Castle in record time, and the soft lockdown's in full effect. Rosa looks out the window, the tips of her fingers grazing her collarbone. She absentmindedly traces a path from her neck to her shoulder, then back again.

I can feel her presence like the rising of the sun, warm tendrils of awareness kissing my skin. I imagine my pulse beats in time to hers.

Rosa. I told myself that distance was the only way to keep her out of my mind, but it was a lie. Every soft breath of warm air over the vineyards, the scent of ripe roses, the way the sun set over Tuscany's rolling hills… everything reminded me of her.

I want to hold her to me. I want to remind her that she's safe with me. But I know that actions speak louder than words. Probably now more than ever.

I can feel her concern over Natalia, but she doesn't know I've got the hidden camera. Natalia's safe.

The first thing I did after the car explosion was check on Natalia with the hidden camera I had installed and thank fuck she was playing with her dolls in bed. Her useless nanny was, as always, on her phone while Natalia chirped away at imaginary friends.

It's uncanny how much the kid reminds me of me. Likes to be alone. Doesn't really fit in here. Has no peers that really know who she is or why she's here. And I get that.

Wheels crunch on gravel as all the SUVs pull up the winding drive that takes us to The Castle entrance, just as my phone rings with a call from Tavi.

"Yeah?"

"Take the dogs, Santo," Tavi orders. "Bring 'em in with you." He knows I'm the only one they'll obey in Romeo's absence, and they're two of the most powerful weapons we own.

I nod. "On it."

Rosa's eyes come to me, and she can't quite hide the fear. I draw in a deep breath and let it out again. I don't believe in luck, and I don't believe in chance. But tonight, Rosa will spend the night with me, under my watch, and even though we'll walk a razor's edge so no one knows how I feel about her, we won't have an ocean separating us.

I'd rather watch over her a hundred times than watch the fucking grapes grow.

"Tavi wants me to get the dogs," I tell them. "I'll meet you up at the house."

Orlando's gaze registers mild surprise, but he only nods. He defers to Tavi like all of us do in these circumstances.

"The dogs?" Rosa asks in surprise. She knows how volatile and fierce they are. "Why?"

I shrug. "We'll see. Get behind me."

I ignore the way she purses her lips at me. She's never been one to like being told what to do but is experienced enough to know when to pick her battles.

We march to The Castle gates with guns drawn. Guards flank every entrance to The Castle—the main entrance that leads to reception, a second entrance at the pavilion outside the courtyard, the entrance to the chapel which leads to the secret wine cellar, and the last that I can't see from here, another entrance by the central sun room. With a touch of a button, Tavi's called our security to full strength.

We march in unison to the front entrance, Rosa behind me and only inches away. Elise is tucked under Tavi's arm. I pass Rosa off to security at the main door, and head to the chain-link fence where the dogs stand at attention.

"Time for action, boys," I say under my breath. They wag their stumpy tails in greeting, the most friendly gesture either of them ever display. I give them a quick scratch behind the ears, then survey their surroundings for any sign of foul play. Something in bubblegum pink catches my eye. Frowning, I kneel in the dry grass to look closer, shove the blades of grass away, and extract a miniature doll-sized shoe.

My *God.* Natalia. If she came here...

I shove it in my pocket. We'll deal with that later.

The chains are so heavy they take effort to lift and move so I can unlock them. The powerful, muscled dogs vibrate with excitement at the possibility of action.

"Don't get so excited," I mutter under my breath. "Could be nothing."

I've seen these dogs tear the throat out of a man that tried to attack Narciso, and tear through the flesh of an attacker who once tried to hurt Marialena.

I gave them extra meat from my plate that night.

I snap their solid leather leashes on and hold them taut. "Heel," I command. The dogs instantly fall into line.

When we reach the entrance to The Castle, I tether them on a short lead secured to a sturdy column behind the portcullis. They whine, but when I snap my fingers, they sit quietly.

"Good," I tell them. "Stay there. Watch." Their eyes are keen as hawks. They'll miss nothing and immediately alert us if anything's amiss.

Mama stands in the entryway, her lips pressed tight, but she's otherwise composed. Marialena paces by the window.

"Where's Rosa?"

"Went to fetch Natalia from the Great Hall," Mama offers. "Guards are with her. What's going on, Santo?"

I shake my head and lift my finger. "We'll tell you soon. Have to secure everyone first."

"Is everyone okay?"

Okay's a relative term. We're all alive.

I nod, as a car pulls in the drive. I look out the window and sigh.

Vittoria.

She must've been out when she was called to come back here. I wonder if anyone's told her what's going on yet.

"And everyone else?"

"Tavi's in the war room," Mama says. "Orlando's securing Angelina with Elise in the Great Hall, where everyone else is heading. Tavi wants a family meeting." She swallows and draws in a breath. "I'm told he called the Montavios, Santo?"

Montavio is Tosca's maiden name. Before Narciso took over this castle, it was owned by the Montavio family. We're on friendly terms with them, though the Montavios run a mob separate from us. We haven't called them in here since I was kid.

"Good call," I mutter. I run my fingers through my hair and watch as the dogs wag their tails for Vittoria. She bends and kisses them both, earning her wagging tails, before she enters. They're gentle with Romeo's bride.

"Why?" Mama asks. I'm not holding anything back. The plan of attack and who might be implicated will come into play shortly, and I'll give Tavi the space he needs to lead, but Tosca and Vittoria deserve to know.

The door opens and Vittoria steps foot inside. "I know," she says to me. Her eyes look red-rimmed but are now dry, and her voice is as strong as ever. Every Rossi woman, those wed into our family and those born into it, has a spine of steel. "Tavi's already talked to me."

Mama makes an impatient sound as Nonna enters the room behind her. "Well no one told *me.*"

I sigh. The sooner they all know, the better.

"Romeo's been arrested. We have reason to believe he was set up. He has nothing he should be convicted for, and as soon as he was taken into custody, someone blew up my car."

Mama gasps and covers her mouth. "What do you mean?" she whispers.

"The red Maserati," I say with a sigh.

"Oh, Santo," she says as tears spring to her eyes. Goddamn, if I don't love her for feeling for me. She was the first one who ever did.

"It's alright, Mama," I say, shaking my head and swallowing the lump in my throat. "Cars are expendable. People aren't."

"I know, son," she whispers. She reaches for my hand and gives it a little squeeze. "But that one was special."

I look away. That car signified my move from childhood to adulthood. It meant almost as much to me as the vows I took and the ink on my arm.

I'll enjoy beating the fuck out of the motherfucker who pulled that trigger.

Natalia flies in front of the doorway and sees me. She waves excitedly, clearly thrilled to see us all here for once. And then she sees the dogs secured by the portcullis and makes a beeline, running toward them.

"Natalia!" I yell her name, but it's too late. She's already thrown herself at the dogs. They strain at their chains, growling, pawing at the ground. One snaps at the air inches from her face. Mama screams. I launch myself at them and bark out a sharp command. I can't reach them, but I do reach the chain, wrap my hands around it and yank so hard they whimper and fall to the ground.

"Down!" They obey.

I heave a sigh of relief before I grab Natalia and yank her away from them. I fall to one knee and wrap my arms around her. She's trembling and crying.

I want to shake her. I want to punish her for doing something so stupid and reckless, to drive home the edict that she's never to come anywhere near them.

"What were you thinking?" I snap. "You know better than to go anywhere near them. You know better!"

I want to shake her so that her teeth rattle but restrain myself.

I'm not Narciso.

I am not Narciso.

I will not strike a child.

"I'm sorry," she sobs. I close my eyes and hold her to my chest, rocking her. Composing myself. Reminding myself that she's okay.

She's okay.

"They'd kill you, baby," I whisper. "Kill you."

"They won't, Uncle Santo, they won't—"

I hold her at arm's length. Tears stream down her cheeks. I'm still shaking from the effort to restrain myself when I hear Rosa.

She yanks Natalia up, hugging her and scolding, "Natalia, if I ever catch you anywhere near those dogs again, you will be in the biggest trouble of your little life. Do you understand me?"

Her cheeks are flaming red, her eyes bright. She stands only inches from me, the look on her face reminding me so much of Tosca scolding us when she caught us smoking that it's uncanny.

I release a trembling breath.

"I second that," I say sternly. "Don't you let me catch you anywhere near those dogs." I hold her gaze and purse my lips. "Is that clear?"

She nods, and another tear falls down her cheek. I take the little pink shoe out of my pocket and hold it in my palm.

"That yours?"

Natalia's wearing a soft pink dress with taffeta and glitter, and a crooked tiara sits on her curls. She looks so cute I want to pinch her cheeks and buy her an ice cream. I hate scolding her. I'd hate worse knowing she was hurt by the dogs we keep as goddamn weapons.

She squirms uncomfortably, and I almost soften. But I can't. She needs to know how dangerous it is for her to be anywhere near the dogs.

I clear my throat. Rosa watches both of us keenly.

"Maybe," Natalia whispers as Vittoria comes outside with Angelina. Nicolo's over her shoulder, asleep.

"Is it, or is it not? I could watch security footage to get the truth, but I want you to tell me."

"What's… a security foot?" she whispers.

I school my lips that want to twitch. "The cameras we have that record everything that happens outside."

"Ohhh," she whispers. "Okay, it's mine," she says in a rush of words. "I get so bored, Uncle Santo. I'm always alone, and my nanny's always on her phone, and my tutor doesn't even *smile.*" She frowns and twists a lock of her curly hair. "I brought my dolls down to see them and… I just played. I didn't touch them."

I give her a steady look, and she winces.

"Okay, I snuggled them a little, but they're sweet and they licked my cheek."

I close my eyes against the heat of anger that flares through my chest and release a breath. I look to Rosa.

"I'll fire her," she whispers.

"Immediately," I agree. "And let me talk to her before you let her go."

Natalia watches us. I'm not sure she understands we're talking about her nanny.

"She'll be with me and Vittoria until you get a replacement," Tosca says gently. "You can guarantee she won't go anywhere near the dogs with us."

I know it. Tosca never liked us having the dogs but knows they're for our own protection.

I reach for Natalia. "Come here, baby." She buries herself in my arms, and I give her a tight squeeze. "You have to stay safe," I whisper to her. "Don't scare Uncle Santo."

A bell rings, a signal we haven't used in years. I hand Natalia back to Rosa and rise.

Mama used to ring the dinner bell to call us down from homework or the yard or the workout room, but now the few family meals we have are scheduled.

Tavi wants us in the Great Hall.

"You two sit with me," I tell them. "And Natalia?"

She looks at me, those pretty eyes just like her Mama's. "Yes?"

"If you want a dog, I'll get you the softest, prettiest little puppy so little you could put her in your pocket, okay?"

Her eyes light up.

"Santo," Rosa groans. "You could ask me first."

I shrug. "I know how to train dogs. It's a cakewalk."

Rosa shakes her head as we enter the Great Hall and whispers so no one else hears, "Don't let anyone ever tell you you're heartless, Uncle Santo. No one. You may have a Grinch-sized heart, but it still beats."

CHAPTER EIGHT

Rosa

I yawn in exhaustion, still sitting on one of the hardback chairs in the Great Hall.

Tavi filled everyone in on what happened today, told us he was in touch with the lawyer, Flynt, and that we'd have a meeting of the inner sanctum the very next day, after the arrival of the Montavio reinforcements.

"We expect another attack, and any minute," Tavi says as we all look to him. "So we stay on soft lock-down until we're clear, or have to move to hard lockdown."

"You hear from Romeo yet?" Vittoria asks.

"No, but it takes some time to get everything sorted. I promise you, Vittoria, you're the first person we'll notify if anything comes up."

"Is he guilty, Tavi?"

These are questions she's allowed to ask, questions all made men and women of The Family are allowed to know.

"I'll fill you in later, Vittoria, but no. He's kept himself squeaky clean."

Staff and the goddamn nanny I'll fire as soon as we're finished have not been allowed in.

I can't believe she let my daughter near those vicious dogs. I've seen them attack.

"Tavi?" Mama asks. We all look to her. Only my mother and grandmother interrupt Romeo or Tavi when they're addressing the group.

"Yes, Mama?" Tavi asks. His jaw tightens but he's being patient with her.

"Why are the dogs in the house?" We all know how she feels about them. "They tried to attack my granddaughter."

"Your granddaughter knows better than to get anywhere near those dogs," I interrupt. I will not let Natalia think for a minute she got away with that. Santo's eyes are cold, but he nods in agreement with me.

"Rosa!" Mama says. "They could've hurt her.'

I keep my own voice tight. "Which is why she will never, ever get within ten feet of them again. Will you, Natalia?"

She shakes her head and looks properly abashed. I heard that dressing down Santo gave her and fully support him.

"The dogs are outside by the front entrance as added security. They are well trained. And yes, they're dangerous, but the children will be kept away. This is only temporary, until the Montavio family arrives, which should be within the hour."

Mario snorts. "I love that the Montavios are replacements for our guard dogs."

Laughter erupts in the room, and I breathe a sigh of relief. We all needed that.

"Fitting," Orlando says, running a hand through his hair, referencing the pit bull-like ferocity of our cousins. "We done here, Tavi?"

Tavi nods. "We'll reconvene when the Montavios join us." He looks to Mama. "Mama—"

But Mama is already on her feet, joined by Nonna.

The Montavios are my mother's family. She'll be eager to feed them. Nonna married into the Montavio family, and though she didn't care for her husband, she likes the Montavios.

It's getting late, but they'll have a welcome spread. I'd join them, but tonight I want to be with Natalia.

While most families of our caliber have hired chefs and the like, Mama and Nonna prefer to make every scrap of food we eat by hand. I dabble a bit but don't cook as much. Tavi's Elise, however, loves it.

I always thought when I was younger Mama and Nonna did our cooking because they liked feeding us. Now I know it's also because they know no one can poison the food they prepare.

Yeah, my family's something else.

"Before we adjourn," Tavi says. "I want to go over where everyone will be at all times. *No one* goes outside The Castle until I lift the lockdown. We'll remain on the first and second floors of The Castle only." So no one will be allowed to go to the chapel or wine cellar. "Orlando will be with Angelina and Nicolo. Their nanny's been sent home for the night. Their guards will be with them as well. Elise is, obviously, with me and our guards. Mario will take main guard over Mama and Marialena. Nonna has her own guard, and Vittoria hers as well." He looks to Santo. "You'll take Natalia and Rosa to their rooms. You'll take the nanny's quarters."

My heartbeat spikes, but I keep my face placid.

Santo nods and stands. We'll have an attached room, then. He'll be right on the other side of the door.

"Santo, before they go upstairs, I want you to be the one that dismisses her nanny. Give her six months' severance and an escorted armored car to accommodations. She leaves tonight. I'll call everyone down after the Montavios arrive."

I clench my jaw. I wanted to be the one that did it, but I know it's probably wise that it's Santo. She won't cry or beg for her job if Santo does it.

"Mama?" Natalia holds onto my dress and looks up to me. I look at her large, luminous eyes and hold her to me.

"Yes?"

"Can I stay with Aunt Vittoria tonight?" She looks to Vittoria, who sits alone at the table, nursing a glass of sparkling water. "She's lonely. Uncle Romeo isn't home." We kept the part about him being taken into custody away from her.

Vittoria looks up at us and smiles sadly. She has a pullout sofa in the little sitting room upstairs where Natalia often spends the night. I can't ask her to take Natalia for the night. I can't imagine what she's thinking. Feeling. There were many times when I was a child my father was taken into custody, but my parents weren't as close as Romeo and Vittoria are. I think when my father was arrested, all of us actually were relieved.

"Hey, girls," she says, as Nonna and Mama clang in the kitchen and everyone packs it up for the night. "I was thinking. I really don't want to be alone tonight. Do you think Natalia could spend the night?"

Natalia's eyes light up and she pulls my arm to her excitedly. "Please, Mama?"

"If it's not too much trouble, Vittoria," I begin, but Vittoria only shakes her head and smiles softly.

"We'll watch that new Disney movie," she says. "And pop popcorn."

It's nearing Natalia's bedtime, but I know she'll want to stay up late for their sleepover. And maybe a night with popcorn and a children's movie will keep Vittoria's mind off things for a little while.

"Oooh," Marialena says, joining them. "I'll join you. Pretty please? Nat, we can wear those new pjs we bought."

"Of course," I tell them. I mean, they'll only be right down the hall from me.

From… us.

I look over at Santo, all six foot whatever of tall, muscled, tatted, brooding male.

There will be nothing but a thin wall between us, hardly anything at all.

The rooms we occupy don't have cameras in them like every other inch of this house. When Romeo first came into the throne, it was only his room that went dark, but he soon granted us all the privilege as well. Said he didn't need to know what his siblings did behind closed doors, and any threat to our safety would be captured on camera outside the doors and windows.

No footage.

No cameras.

Nobody watching.

My brother's been arrested, and my family's in lock-down. Santo's car was blown up. We expect another attack at any moment.

And all I can think about is that I get to spend the next—however many—days and nights in close proximity to him.

Off the radar.

Tavi never would've assigned him to watch over me if he didn't *completely* trust him. He did, of course, position us in such a way that we'll have two rooms with separate entrances.

Like that matters.

I close my eyes and breathe in through my nose and out through my mouth.

I shiver.

"Cold, Rosa?"

I jump. Santo's so close to me his breath ruffles my hair.

"Yeah," I say on a sigh. "It's been a long day."

"It has." He shoves his hands in his pockets, and for one moment I imagine it's to stop himself from touching me. Placing his hand right there, on the small of my back to give me comfort. Sweeping my hair out of my eyes and tucking it behind my ear.

But no one can ever see how we feel about each other.

No one.

Even Mama would lose her mind. They all would. And I can't imagine the punishment he'd earn for betrayal that deep.

I let my eyes rove over the strong forearms covered in ink, the way his shirt stretches over his biceps. He's gotten new ink, and lots of it.

I like.

"Where's Natalia?" He looks around the room.

"She's, uh… she's having a sleepover with Vittoria and Lena. They're watching a Disney movie or something." I feign a yawn. "We should go upstairs. Damn, I'm tired."

I look away from him so I don't see the flare of heat in his eyes when he realizes we'll be alone tonight.

"I'm checking all the locks first."

"Tavi ask you to?"

One quick shake of his head. "No, but Tavi's got a lot on his mind."

My heart does a little twirl. I have this strange, inexplicable attraction to competence. Competence porn. *Sigh.*

"I'll go with you."

He jerks his head at me wordlessly to follow. I swallow hard.

"You staying up for the Montavios?" I ask, as he heads to the back door by the kitchen. "I'll see them in the morning." Tavi will want to get right down to business, and I wasn't lying when I said I was tired.

"Yeah, I'll be back down to see them. After I get you settled."

My heart beats faster.

After I get you settled, like he has to tuck me in bed and pull up the covers first.

Oh, Santo.

Santo.

I've missed him so much. I've missed what we had.

I've missed who I was when I was with him.

We've never had any kind of relationship anyone else could know about. We were discreet, and we were cautious.

Most of the time.

But even if we'd never touched each other… even if we'd never gone to the places where we did… we shared a bond I imagine no one else has. Something just between the two of us.

We walk in silence up the carpeted steps and land on the second floor, where my room and Natalia's are. We live sometimes here and sometimes in Tuscany, though I spend more time here since Santo's exile.

Not of my own choice, though. I need to keep him safe.

As our footsteps reach the landing, I talk out loud, in case anyone's listening. I know the cameras are trained on every doorway, I know that guards are in the shadows.

"I'll have your sheets changed and make sure you have everything you need."

He nods. "Thank you. I'll get what I need from my room."

He steps aside when we reach the doorway and lets me open the door.

My heart beats faster.

A part of me's on edge, as if holding my breath, like Tavi or Orlando or someone will come around the corner and point their fingers at us. "Traitors! Liars!"

As if.

And yet…

And yet I'm nervous about what might happen next. Maybe a small part of me hopes someone will stop us. Fate's thrown us in close proximity… and I fear what will happen without an ocean between us. With nothing but principles and rules between us.

Santo and I have no future together, and we both know that. At any moment, Romeo could arrange for me to be married to someone and eventually will. Though I'm not as exclusive a commodity as Marialena, in her untouched virginity—*God*—I am a Rossi, and that means something. Marriage to me would strengthen any family we joined forces with.

I open the door to my room and enter, and he follows behind me. Even if I didn't know he was there, I could… *feel* him.

I can't look at him. I can't even make eye contact.

My heart races as I turn the lock, my fingers trembling on the cold metal. Downstairs, I hear cars approaching the house. Santo immediately stalks to the window and opens the shade.

"Montavios have arrived early, looks like."

I join him. Our elbows brush each other. "Ah, just a few. They're not all here yet. Some come from further away than others. They're party animals, you know."

"Oh, I know," he says with a laugh. I give him a sharp look. Is there a reason for that comment?

"Don't get your panties all in a wad, baby," he says, drawing the shade back down. "Jesus, I didn't bang your cousins."

Yet. Hmph.

Maybe he doesn't remember how lovely they are. Mama comes from strong stock.

Our rooms here are large and expansive, Natalia's and the nanny's all attached to mine. The nanny's door's shut tight.

"Let me have a word with her," Santo says, his heavy brows drawing together over piercing eyes. I almost feel bad for the girl, until I remember in my negligence that she allowed my daughter into danger.

And I don't feel so badly anymore.

"Go," I say with a nod. "Should I join you?"

"Better if you don't."

"Alright, then. Good. I'm going to take a shower."

His eyes drag lazily from my face to my bare chest. Across my cleavage. To my slim waist and curvy hips, before dragging back up to my eyes.

"Go, baby," he whispers. "Go shower."

I hitch in a breath when he reaches a finger to my cheek, the mere ghost of a touch, before he turns away, straightens his shoulders, and heads to the other room.

I don't release my breath until the door shuts.

I look around the rooms. Impeccably tidy, thanks to twice-daily housekeeping. I love having my space clean. There's a window in the large sitting room that overlooks the stone wall, the ocean churning and crashing behind it. We had this wing outfitted with comfortable Italian leather furniture and a plush, vibrant carpet. Simple but bold art adorns the walls, chosen by Mama and Marialena when we remodeled this wing.

I have a small but functional kitchenette, where I make our tea and small meals when we're not eating with the rest of the family. A short distance from the kitchenette is the door that leads to my room and the bathroom.

I have a white desk in the corner of my room with a matching white leather chair. I've always liked white. Maybe because it's a sign of purity, something I've always craved but never could quite have. Not when you have a family like mine.

My notebooks and laptop, pens and paperwork sit in neat piles and bins, beside a small bookshelf with my favorite books.

It's a simple, well-furnished place, but I much prefer Tuscany. It feels... stifling here. Too stifling.

I kick off my heels, pick them up, and carry them to the walk-in closet. I wipe them clean and neatly place them on a rack before I head to the bathroom. I step out of my clothes and put them into the laundry hamper before I reach for a soft, sky-blue satin robe. I breathe a sigh of relief. It feels so good to relax.

If I didn't want to see Santo before he has his late-night meeting, I'd treat myself to a bath. But now there's no time.

I head to the bathroom and start the water, grab a handful of shower salts, and toss them on the floor in the line of water. A gentle, relaxing scent of lavender and vanilla fills the air, and the steam in the room comforts me. I hang my robe up and step into the hot, steaming shower.

All the while, I'm listening for him. I'm wondering how things went with the nanny.

I'm wondering how things will go with *us*.

I spin under the steady stream of warm water but pull a shower cap on to keep my hair dry while I lather up my legs and begin to shave.

The sound of a turning doorknob makes me freeze with my hand outstretched to a bar of soap.

He wouldn't.

Would he?

The bathroom door opens. I can see his shadow silhouetted on the frosted glass.

"Hey!"

"Hey."

"That was not a *hey* in greeting. That was a *hey, what the hell do you think you're doing?* hey."

He grunts in response, shuts the door behind him, and sits on the closed toilet lid.

"Ah, hello?"

He doesn't respond.

"Santo," I whisper.

"Rosa," he whispers back.

I crack open the shower door and peek out. "How'd it go with the nanny?"

He shrugs. "She's gone."

"She take it okay?"

"Kind of."

I don't push any further. Closing the shower door, I rinse the soap off my body and change the subject.

"What are you doing in here?" My words are swallowed up by steam.

"Watching you," he retorts.

"I don't think this is the type of watching Tavi had in mind."

"He didn't specify."

Oh God. *Oh God.*

"Pretty sure I'm safe in here."

"You are now."

Why does that make tears well up in my eyes?

With trembling hands, I finish shaving my legs and washing until I'm squeaky clean. I'm nervous about leaving. What will he do?

"Will I still be safe when I get out of this shower?" I ask.

"That depends," he says in that deep, melodic, yet almost sinister voice.

"On what?" I whisper.

"If you behave yourself."

"Santo, we can't—you shouldn't."

"Go ahead," he says in an angry whisper. "Tell me what I can and cannot do, Rosa. Tell me what I should and shouldn't do. Try me. I'm dying for a chance to remind you who I am."

His pet peeve, being told what to do.

Why does the sound of his voice make me deliciously squirmy inside? The threat of being reminded of *exactly who he is.*

The most fearless man I know. The most ruthless.

The most passionate.

I yank the handle to the water to "off" and stand in front of him, the steam still rising like mist around me. "Go ahead, then," I say, unable to mask the feeling in my voice, the challenge. "Watch me."

I put one long leg on the edge of the tub and reach for my towel, giving him a full view of my ass. I don't know why I'm doing this. I don't know why I'm teasing him. I don't know why I'm pushing anger aside before it chokes me, but he makes me so angry I want to scream.

"Come here." His voice snaps in the warm room.

"Oh?" I say coyly. I give him a curious look with my head tipped to the side. "Why?" My voice is a whisper, laced with curiosity and lust.

No man has ever made me crave his touch.

Until Santo.

No man has ever broken me in all the best ways.

Until Santo.

No man has ever made me forget every other man I've touched before or ever will.

Until…

"Because I told you so. And I think you remember what happens when you push your boundaries with me, Rosa."

"Oh, Santo," I say, shaking my head. "We don't have boundaries. We don't have… there is no… there is no *we*, and you know it."

My words ignite a flame in him. He's on his feet, his eyes flashing, before I can respond.

"Don't lie to me, Rosa." He stalks over to me. "Don't tell me that every time that fucking traitor Mercadio ever touched you, you didn't pretend it was *me.* Don't lie to me." He stops himself inches away from me. I grab the towel and wrap it around myself, but he only grasps the front of it in his fist and yanks me closer. He can't mask the pain and fury in his voice. "Don't tell me that every time you lay beneath him, you didn't wish it was *me.*"

And just like that, like a long-lost wound, he splits me open again until I bleed.

Just like that, I'm laid bare.

Every word he said is true, *every word.*

How does he delve so deep into my mind he knows my thoughts?

"Why, Santo?" I whisper.

He doesn't ask me what I mean. He knows.

I hold my breath as he draws nearer. He leans in so closely, I fear I'll faint before I can breathe again. He has to bend to kiss my cheek. His hair's damp, falling on his forehead like he's a carefree boy. But he isn't.

He never was.

His lips brush my cheek.

"You know why, baby. You know."

I close my eyes. He's so close. I want him so badly I can't think beyond the blood thrumming in my ears. So close. Every raw, vicious inch of him.

"But I want to hear you say it," I whisper.

He utters the words as if they're torn from him, as if it physically pains him to say it. "Because you're my addiction, and I don't want a fucking cure."

I don't realize I'm crying until he wipes a tear from my cheek. Cupping the back of my head, he pulls me to his chest. He's still fully clothed, probably boiling in here, but he doesn't let on that it bothers him. He just… holds me. I'm half-naked, wrapped in a towel, and he holds me to him like it's the only chance we'll ever have to be this close.

"There are no cameras in these rooms, Rosa. We'll have visitors, you know that. We'll have places to go, and we can't make anyone suspicious. But while I'm here and you're here, we'll have the privacy we need."

"To do what?"

As if I'm innocent, as if I don't know exactly what he wants or what he has planned. As if it isn't exactly what I want, too.

Tomorrow, Romeo could be home. Tomorrow, Romeo could announce my engagement to be married or Santo's return to Tuscany. Tomorrow, Tavi could tell us he's found a woman for Santo to marry, someone to form an alliance with. It's doubtful any of those will happen that soon, but they could happen the day after... or the day after... or any day after.

All we have is the present. The past is gone, and we may never have a future.

Santo and I definitely don't have one.

His low, dark chuckle is his only response.

CHAPTER NINE

Santo

The sun set an hour ago, but I was not going to leave the job until I was done. Inside The Castle awaited central air, good food, and even better company, but I had a job to do, and I was not gonna quit until I finished.

The chrome gleamed in the overhead light. Papa was overseeing a business deal in Tuscany and wouldn't be home for another week, and damn, it was nice to work without fear of his wrath or the call to do his fucking dirty work.

I almost whistled to myself as I checked the oil and wiped my hand on a dirty rag. The heat was oppressive, but I only needed another hour—

The soft, soulful sound of crying caught my attention. I lay still under the car, thankful I hadn't put the radio on like I'd planned to. The click of a door closing meant someone had come out from the house.

Not Romeo. Romeo didn't cry, not at his age. Not Orlando or Tavi, either, for the same reasons. Maybe Mario, but even he was too old for shit like tears now. And it couldn't be Marialena, because everyone *knew when she cried.*

That left only one person.

I waited until the tears began to subside before I wheeled out from underneath the car.

Rosa, beautiful, stunning Rosa, with her large eyes and thick, long hair, sat hunched in the corner staring at me. Crying. Again.

"I didn't know you were here," she whispered, pushing to her feet.

"Sit."

She blinked, staring at me as if processing my command to sit. I hadn't thought about our age difference in years. I always felt older than she was, and I found it easier to take command. It was in my nature.

She sat. Her hair fell over her face and covered her from me.

"Stay right there."

I stood, wiping my hands on a rag. I went to the sink we had in the corner and washed up while she sat. Staring. I looked down at myself, curious as to what she saw.

I'd taken off my T-shirt in the heat. Fresh ink across my back and shoulders, though my arms were still mostly a blank canvas. I was not one of the preppy boys from college, but I worked out, had finally gotten the body of a man, and it had finally started to show.

I cleaned thoroughly in case I had to touch her.

Hidden in the shadows as I was, her guard didn't hear me when he opened the door from the house to the garage.

"Miss Rossi?"

"She's with me," I said, dismissing him.

"You sure?" he asked.

"Yeah. The lady needs some privacy, man. Watch the door for us, and you can take over when she comes back inside."

Without another word... he did.

They all knew better than to piss me off.

The door shut, and I turned back to face her. There were cameras in here, I knew, that would catch our every move, but that was okay. I wouldn't touch her, even though it was the epicenter of every fantasy I ever had.

I grabbed my tee from the hood of the car and yanked it on. She stared at me, unabashed, and swallowed.

"You've... filled out, Santo," she said in wonder.

I looked down at where the tee stretched across my arms but lay flat against my abs.

"Helps a guy get laid," I said, and I wasn't joking.

She gave me a sad smile. "Of course it does," she whispered. "I wouldn't know."

I sat across from her, only feet away, and thought about that. It was the first time I actually had. God, but I could be a selfish son of a bitch sometimes.

I'd forgotten their father's expectation of virginity until marriage. The women of the Rossi family were expected to marry to benefit the family, and no one would accept a woman who was blemished.

Widow was the one exception, I found out later, but we didn't know that then. Kids didn't need to think of shit like that. It was like thinking of taxes, or mortgages, or death.

I couldn't imagine being in college, as stunningly gorgeous as her, and not be able to do... well, damn near anything.

"You can't... you ever even been kissed?" I asked her. I felt the rising response of my dick at the thought of kissing those full lips of hers. The way her back would feel pressed against my palm, the scent of her hair when I brushed it away...

She flushed pink. "Maybe," she said, then looked away. "But it was nothing memorable."

Goddamn, I'd give her a kiss she'd never forget.

I cleared my throat and changed the subject. I didn't need to do a damn thing that would encourage my dick or my thoughts to get any of us killed.

"That why you're crying?" I asked, giving her a half smile. "Shitty first kiss?"

She gave me a wan smile and rolled her eyes. "Not because of the guy that kissed me. Like I said, it was... forgettable." She actually cringed.

"Who?" I asked, unable to mask my sudden anger at this revelation. I watched as her eyes went from slightly amused to guarded, as if she just remembered I was a sworn-in member of the Rossi family.

"As if I'd tell you," she said, shaking her head. "No way."

She knew I'd kick their ass. No one was supposed to touch a Rossi girl.

I'd find out.

It would take me a few weeks, but I'd find out and still give the thorough ass-kicking they'd earned for breaking the rules, for touching her.

Her brothers would kill me if I were the one...

"Then why are you crying?"

She looked away and bit her lip. It wasn't uncommon for Rosa to be upset about something, but it wasn't often she cried. Like all of us, she learned to mask her emotions and follow the rules.

Life was simpler that way.

"Papa found out I had a friend, and he—"

Goddamn Narciso. Always the fucking dictator.

I held up my finger to her, and she paused.

I tried to remember if the cameras in here had audio. Just to be safe, I stood and turned on the fan, pretended to check something under the hood. The deafening noise would hide the audio.

She frowned at me. I leaned in close. "It's too fuckin' loud," I told her. "Will drown out our words if there's audio in here."

"Oh." She nodded. "Good thinking."

Damn, that made me beam. I schooled my face and shrugged it off. I felt the flicker of warmth that only came from Rosa's praise.

"So your Papa found out you had a friend..."

"Yeah. And she's Irish, like Irish-American, and really poor."

Dammit. Narciso hated non-Italians and poor people. Douchebag.

I winced.

She laughed mirthlessly. "You know then."

"Yeah. What'd he do?"

"All the way from Italy, he told my guards not to let me see her anymore or talk to her anymore. Forbade it. Told me if he caught me near her again, he'd put me in

boarding school."

Always the Rossi family threat but damn if we didn't all think they'd actually do it one day.

"He called her scum," she whispered. "And she's the sweetest girl I know. She's wholesome."

I knew what that felt like, craving the company of someone who was better than you.

I nodded. "Jesus, I'm sorry. God, that's unfair."

The only friends I had were right here. I hated people at school. They probably hated me back, but at least they feared me, and that was good enough for me.

If they feared me, they'd keep their distance.

"Thanks," she said softly. "I... I don't have any other friends anymore." She looked down at her hands and shook her head. "They shun you when they know you're a Rossi, you know."

Yeah. I knew. Only I kinda liked it. Figures she didn't, though.

"Mama says I don't need friends. Says I have all that I need right here at The Castle."

I shook my head. "Nah," I said, agreeing with her. "Not sure I agree with that."

My life was a vast canyon of emptiness before I had the Rossis. I scrapped my way to money, then scrimped and saved every penny I could. Learned how to con my way into places, make myself good money. The night I pulled a fast one on Narciso, he could've killed me, but instead he brought me home. Knew I'd be an asset to them and by God, I was.

She nods. "People say you're—" She clamped her mouth shut as if she'd said too much.

"People say what?" I asked, my voice harsh.

She shook her head.

"Rosa." My voice took on a warning edge. "Tell me."

She shook her head again. "It's nothing."

"It isn't nothing. Say it."

"They say you don't have emotions," she said. "They say —you have no feelings." She shakes her head and looks away, her eyes over my shoulder as if looking at something far, far away. "But I don't think that's true, Santo. I think sometimes you have the strongest feelings of all."

Her words filled my chest with a sort of buzz, a keen knowing, as if she'd stumbled on a truth I hadn't realized myself yet. As if she spoke a truth that somehow set me free. I mulled these words over, holding them for a little while.

"Rosa," I finally said, holding her gaze. I watched her eyes flicker over the tat on my bicep and the tee before she looked back up at me and blushed. The girl was checking me out, and shit at hiding it.

Well if that didn't make my fucking year.

"What?" she whispered.

I reached a fingertip to touch hers, too low for the cameras to catch, and gently touched her. "I'll be your friend."

I could lie to myself, make myself believe that I've got nothing to lose. Tell myself that she's gonna be married soon anyway, and if I don't take this one chance I have now, I'll never have one.

But it would be a lie.

I could lose damn near everything.

Nah, not *damn near* everything.

Literally *everything.*

I don't care if they hurt me. I don't care if they beat me or punish me in whatever sick, twisted way Romeo or Tavi could concoct.

But I'd have to give up the only family I've ever known.

A small part of me wonders if Tavi knows how I feel about Rosa. Why would he station me here, to watch over her? But he was the one that told me about her arranged marriage. And we've been nothing but careful. He sent me here, with a room between the two of us, and I'm sure his primary concern is his immediate family.

He can't know anything. He can't fucking know.

But goddamn, I'm here now. And the next time I'm home, she could be a married woman.

Not that that means anything, only that she'll be completely out of reach forever.

I want to tell her what I know, that her life's about to drastically change. But I can't complicate things any more than they already are, and I haven't even heard confirmation from Romeo yet. We'll wait to see what happens after he's released from prison.

If he's released from prison.

So I hold her to me. I caress her soft, damp skin. I relish the way her breath hitches, the way she moves closer with the gentlest suggestion of my palm on her back. I kiss her bare cheek and close my eyes. Her skin's soft and warm, and I want to taste every inch of her.

I want to do more than *that.*

I take her hand and lead her out of the bathroom, shut the light off, and bring her over to her bed. Here, in her room, we're furthest away from the door than any other place in here. If anyone walks by the hall, they won't hear a thing.

This room and the next, as well as Natalia's, are connected by doors, so we have at least the illusion of privacy. If we get too close to a window or door, we risk shadows or even images caught on camera. But here, in the privacy of her room, we're off the map.

"Lay back on the pillows," I tell her. I barely recognize my own voice, deep and husky, affected by the nearness of her.

"Why?" she asks in a whisper, but she can't hide the need in her eyes, the way she swallows and squirms. "Santo, we can't—you know we…"

"You let me worry about what we can and cannot do."

A flash of those beautiful eyes like beacons in a storm. "I'm not a brainless female, Santo, who caves to you. I don't give my submission away to *anyone,* and you know that. Sure, we played, and it was fun, but…"

My heart thumps, my pulse races, and I can barely hear over the pounding of blood in my ears. I love it when she fights me. I grasp both wrists in my fingers and pull her arms by her side, then march her backward to the bed until her ass hits the edge.

We played, Rosa and I.

Like it was a childish game we outgrew.

"Don't you lie to me. You know you like it when I boss you around. Damn near fuckin' came the first time I spanked your ass and pulled your hair."

"That was years ago," she whispers, but she can't hide the way her pupils dilate, and she shifts on the bed. "Santo—"

"This a game to you?" I whisper against the shell of her ear. "You think I'm fuckin' playing, Rosa?"

"We can't—you know we can't. You can't touch me. We can't… touch each other." She shakes her head, her voice trembling.

"Romeo's in jail," I whisper, laying her on the bed. "Your father's dead. And any goddamn minute, I'll get shipped off to Tuscany and you'll get sent wherever the fuck." I can't tell her the truth.

She presses against me when I try to lay her on the pillows, but I overpower her.

She lets me.

Her thick, damp hair splays on the pillow, and her face, free of makeup, looks almost innocent.

Almost.

"Santo," she whispers.

Slowly, like I'm peeling back a layer of a Christmas gift, I remove her towel and feast my eyes on her perfect body. The trim waist with its little dimpled belly button, her shapely legs, the full breasts that heave with excitement.

"Yeah, baby?" I whisper back.

She reaches for me slowly, as if asking permission. She knows I don't like to be touched unaware. I give her an almost imperceptible nod. I watch her as her fingers trace my forehead, down the side of my face, then over my lips. She runs her hands over my beard and groans.

"I missed you," she whispers. "God, I missed you so bad."

I nod. I do know. She wasn't happy in Tuscany with Marcadio, any more than I'm happy in Tuscany watching grapes grow. The two of us aren't like the rest. Fierce almost to the point of being uncivilized, we never pretended that any of what The Family does is normal, or acceptable. We didn't make the best of the cards dealt to us.

We embraced the life of corruption.

I like to think I understand her better.

I like to think the feeling's mutual.

"Then don't try to stop me," I whisper back.

I don't think of the past, what lays behind us. We were only kids then, with a lifetime ahead of us and rules that bound us tightly.

Before we knew who we really were.

I don't respond at first. Gently, I glide my finger over her shoulder, relishing the soft, silken skin beneath my touch. I trace a path from her shoulder across her collarbone and circle the hollow in her neck. Feeling her breathe. Watching the way her breath hitches, her pulse racing. I trace my way to her right shoulder, over the curve, then down the slope to her elbow. She watches me, mesmerized, as I gently trace the length of her body.

Down to her fingertips. Up the inside of her arm. Down past her breast, but I don't stop to linger, before I go lower, down her side to where her hip swells. Down the top of her leg to her knee, then down her calf to her foot. She giggles when I trace the soft, delicate arch of her foot.

"That tickles," she whispers. I bend my bearded face to her thighs and gently tease.

"Does that tickle?"

"Santo," she whispers, squirming. "Oh my God."

I sit up straighter and go back to touching every inch of her like I'm memorizing each cell, every membrane.

When I trace my way back up her side again, this time I graze the tops of her breasts, but I don't touch her nipples. Still, her breasts get fuller, and her nipples harden. She closes her eyes and squirms. I bend and kiss the fullest part of her breast. First one. Then the other.

My dick's aching, hard as fuck, but I don't care. I don't want to fuck her, not tonight. I want to remember her.

"Why are you doing this?" she whispers, her voice thick with arousal.

"Because a woman like you deserves to be worshipped."

I kneel over her, and her eyes come to where my jeans are tight. She doesn't miss my raging hard-on.

After I've traced her, I decide to kiss my way down her.

Collarbone. Shoulder. Elbow, and fingertips. Hip, thigh, and her pretty little kneecap. When I get to her foot, I lift it and kiss the arch until she squirms and giggles. I place her foot back down and kiss my way back up the other side.

By now, I can smell the sweet, seductive scent of her arousal. I can feel her trembling when I get closer to the most sensitive parts of her—the damp skin between her legs, her breast, her collarbone.

But I don't touch her pussy. I don't kiss her nipples. I touch nothing but her perfect, creamy, olive-toned flesh.

"Santo, I—"

My phone buzzes. Tavi.

"That'll be Tavi, baby," I whisper. "I gotta go."

I look at the screen.

Tavi: Montavios here. All report to the Great Hall.

Her eyelids flutter closed, but when she opens them, she only nods.

"I'll be back. I'll tell them I'm tired. I'll tell them you're asleep and I want to stand guard."

She nods, trembling. I bend and brush my lips across hers, relishing the way her back arches into me, then whisper in her ear, "When I come back, I'll do more than kiss you, baby. I promise. But keep your hands to yourself until I do, and don't fucking push me, Rosa."

I give her a warning look.

I love the way she captures her lip like a coy little girl. "Or what?" she whispers.

I cup her pussy suddenly, and her back arches. She gasps and squirms, pressing against me for pressure, but I don't give it to her. Not yet.

"This pussy's mine," I whisper in her ear. "While I'm with you, all of you belongs to me. That means your orgasms, too. If you touch yourself before I come back, I'll know. And the punishment will be severe."

My dick throbs at the thought of her earning a punishment.

"Severe," she whispers, squirming. As if she's thinking it over.

"Severe," I promise.

I stand and adjust myself to fix my hard-on and groan when a knock sounds at the door.

Rosa gasps and reaches for her towel.

"Relax," I whisper. "Don't look so fucking guilty."

"Can't help it," she whispers.

"Santo?" Mario.

"On my way," I shout to him. In her doorway, I wave a warning finger in her direction, which only earns me a wicked grin. I shake my head and shut the door gently before I meet Mario.

CHAPTER TEN

Rosa

While I'm here.

You're mine.

While I'm with you.

I can't worry about tomorrow. Tomorrow, we could be gone. It's true that all we have is today.

But that's a shitty reason to do anything that could jeopardize any of our safety.

Especially Santo.

I hate the thought of him getting in trouble with Romeo. I hate the thought of my own exile, which would almost certainly be in the form of a swift marriage I have no control over.

My brothers love me, and I don't doubt that. But they're loyal to The Family and always have been.

Likely always will be.

My mind comes to a stuttering halt when he touches me. When he gives me that dark look that promises even darker actions, when I imagine he's thinking about every wicked thing he could do to me.

The first touch of his finger on my skin felt like fire, and my pulse skittered harder and faster. When he didn't stop, my pulse ratcheted so quickly I got dizzy. Flames licked my core, and heat pooled in my belly. I wanted him to touch me, and not the chaste, explorative touches of before.

I wanted him to bite me, to lick me, to suckle and tease. I wanted him to pull my hair and spank me. I wanted him to overpower and dominate me, like only Santo could.

He wasn't wrong when he remembered how I responded once. And a woman's craving for the taste of dominance doesn't fade like some thinks it does. Maybe it can become muted when she's with the wrong guy or worse, an asshole, that's true… but my body knows Santo means business, and there's no logical explanation for telling me to get my shit together.

Beyond my doorway, I hear the door to the hall click. Voices rise, then fall.

No one will be looking for me this late. They'll know I'm asleep, especially as Natalia's having a sleepover with Marialena and Vittoria.

And God, I hope no one would suspect that Santo was… doing what he did just now. I shudder at the thought of what anyone would do. Even happy-go-lucky Marialena would *lose her mind* if she knew I fucked around with the iron-clad family rules.

I don't want Santo to be punished.

But he seemed so certain we won't be caught.

I've been turned on since he walked in on me in the shower.

Santo's a twisted man. His taste for the dark side infiltrates every part of who he is.

And yet… I'm drawn to him, irrevocably, like he's got a string tied around me I can't pull away from. One little tug, and I follow.

I know he'll be my undoing. Because he's right.

There will be no man after him.

Hell, there never was.

People think sex is what binds you, that somehow spreading your legs for someone joins you together at the hip. And I guess that might help, if there were anything else there to begin with. But a real connection, the type that binds you to someone's *soul*… it's so much more than physical. So much more.

Santo and I played with each other, and maybe that's what we're doing now… playing. But we never went all the way. It was a line we couldn't cross, though we defied every other boundary.

But it's more than a physical connection. I feel I know him, and he knows me, like he—and then it hits me with such powerful honesty, tears spring to my eyes.

Santo's the only one who's ever loved me unconditionally.

Unconditionally.

And those are the ties that bind.

I close my eyes and will myself to think of something, anything, but putting my fingers where I throb and relieving the pressure that builds with every passing second. He could be gone for minutes or hours, depending on how much Tavi wants to cover tonight. My guess would be closer to a shorter visit this evening, after everything that's happened, and they'll reconvene tomorrow and start taking action.

I squeeze my legs together and recite the alphabet.

Lame.

It doesn't work. I roll over and grab my phone from the bedside table, but nothing, no amount of scrolling or reading or playing mindless games distracts me from the pulsing need he ignited.

Oh, fuck it.

What's he gonna do? *Punish me*? Oooh, I'm so scared.

I roll my eyes at no one.

Fuck it. He can punish me. He can give me that bullshit about my body belonging to him and all that, but he's got a lot of work to do before I'll just hand it over to him.

This body is *still mine.*

So I do what I've been doing for years, since Anthony was a dick and only cared about his own needs. I part my legs and gingerly touch myself.

I'm not breathing. I'm waiting for him to barge in that door any minute and catch me red-handed. Or maybe he's got goddamn cameras set up in here or a spy. There's nothing I wouldn't put past Santo.

But I don't care.

If I take care of my own needs, I won't need to depend on anyone else.

That philosophy's gotten me pretty far, anyway.

I close my eyes and conjure up a fantasy.

One stroke.

I whimper at the first touch. I'm so swollen and slick it should be illegal. My mouth is dry at the second swipe of my fingers. My hips convulse at the third, I'm that aroused. I casually conjure my favorite fantasy.

Santo walks in the room and catches me touching myself. His dark eyes go broody and angry, his lips pressed thin. Leaning against the doorway, he shakes his head from side to side.

"Bad, bad girl. What'd I tell you about touching yourself?"

I can almost hear him standing right there, lecturing me. I have no idea why someone like me, who hates being in trouble and hates even worse being scolded, gets so excited at that deep, dangerous tone of his. I can imagine him shaking his head and clucking his tongue as he reaches for his belt and touches the buckle.

"I told you I'd punish you if you touched yourself, didn't I? Bad, bad girl. What's a bad girl like you deserve?"

"Punishment," imaginary me whispers.

I stroke harder, faster. One hand travels to my breasts and I graze a finger over first one nipple, then the other. My hips jerk with the intensity of my arousal.

"Get on your knees," he barks, snapping the belt in his hand. I can hear the snap, leather on leather, as I scramble to my knees and give him my bare ass. He's never spanked me with his belt before, but damn if I haven't fantasized about it over, and over, and over again.

The first spasm of pleasure ripples through me, and I'm whimpering in earnest now. My fingers grasp my nipples, first one, then the other. I stroke and circle and stroke until I'm on the very edge, on the very cusp.

Crack! The leather snaps against my ass in my fantasy as another wave of bliss washes through me.

Whack! The deep, burning pain aches so deep I scream against the onslaught of lashes, as ripples of pleasure consume me.

Over and over, I stroke my pussy, so consumed by my orgasm I can't think straight.

And then I'm sinking. Sinking. Falling back into bed. I open my eyes.

I'm alone. Alone, in the dark room, still floating on the throes of aftershocks. I keep stroking, my hips jerking from the too-sensitive feel of my body underneath my fingers, but I'm greedy. I'm so damn greedy, and it's been so long since I've felt anything like this, so good, that I can't stop. I close my eyes and stroke again, on the cusp of a second orgasm.

Again, I'm being punished, but this time I'm over his knee. Just like the first time he punished me. The first time he yanked me over his lap and spanked me to tears.

And then after he punished me, he held me. I was so turned on I begged him to touch me.

"Please, Santo. Touch me. Oh, God, I need you to touch me. If you'd kept going, I would've come."

He turned me back over his lap without a second thought. We were down by the wall and could've been caught at any minute, except one knew we were here; no one could find us.

I don't remember why he spanked me, but he'd been looking for a reason. He'd threatened it so many times it'd become the focal point of my fantasies, imagining him punishing me over his lap. And then he did it.

Over his knee, my ass in the air, he spanked me again.

"Go on, then," he said, stroking between my legs before he spanked me again. "You said you could come by being spanked."

My clit throbs, my core contracts. He yanks my hair and growls, "Come, then. Come while I redden your ass. Show me. Come, or I'll punish you harder."

I come a second time. This orgasm way more powerful on the heels of the first. I cry out, unable to stop myself, and dimly hope no one in the hall heard that. But the door's shut tight and I'm alone in here, still stroking myself to the aftershocks of a second climax.

Oh, God, *oh God,* I can't believe I made myself double climax to memories of Santo.

Yeah, this is not gonna end well.

Still riding the post-release wave and comforting warmth, I pull the covers up over me and close my eyes.

Oh, Santo.

How I've missed you.

God, it feels so right having him home again.

Santo.

My Santo.

I hid myself from everyone at The Castle. Even though I was a young adult now, I was still under the thumb of my father, and I hated it. I didn't go to prom in high school. I never went to any of the sorority dances or social events in college. And now, as most of my family's in Tuscany, I was alone. And so lonely I wanted to cry.

"Rosa?" I looked over to see Santo in the darkened corner of the room.

"Yeah?"

"You okay?" he asked.

How did I not realize he was still here?

"You didn't go to Tuscany."

He shook his head. "Nah."

"Why not? They all went."

"Not all," he said with a frown. "Mario stayed home, and I said I'd keep an eye on him."

I narrowed my eyes on him. "Right. You said you'd keep an eye on both of us, didn't you?"

He flashed me a wicked grin.

"The boy whose name means saint who couldn't be more of a little devil, could he?"

He shrugged with a pleased smile, as if I'd just paid him a compliment.

"Take a walk with me," he said. "It's been a long day and you seem under the weather."

"I'm okay," I lied, while I grabbed my hoodie and shoes.

We walked out in the cold, a light rain misting from the heavens. I shivered, but he didn't touch me. Cameras were trained on every inch of the grounds of The Castle. It wasn't until we got to the wall that the surveillance disappeared. Still, for the sake of safety, we never went directly together to the blind spot by The Castle wall. Nor did we go when everyone was home.

But tonight, with mostly everyone in Tuscany, it couldn't hurt to escape down to The Castle wall. Where no one would ever know where we were.

When we were younger there was no tracking capability on cell phones. But we were careful. We'd leave no evidence for anyone.

Santo and I had parted ways when tracking was more fine-tuned.

Good, I suppose.

My heart beat faster as we walked down. We took our separate paths, him to the left and me on a circular path that went right, circled back to the front of The Castle, then back down again until we got there together.

Finally, when we made it, we faced each other and grinned.

Grinned.

Neither of us ever had a reason to grin.

"Come here," he said softly. He sat with his back up against the wall and pulled me to him. I fit between his arms, my back to his chest. I leaned back and closed my eyes. It felt so nice to be held by him. I fantasized about this before I went to bed at night.

Here, away from the prying eye of the camera, with most of my family overseas, Santo and I entered our mysterious world, as if we'd stepped through a portal to another time and dimension.

It felt right laying here with him.

"Now will you tell me what's bothering you?" he asked.

"Ah, Santo," I whispered. "What's ever bothering me?"

He shrugged. "Could be anything. Your Papa pulled another asshole move, someone was a jerk to you at school, Romeo got heavy-handed and domineering, Mama yelled at you for not getting good enough grades." He shrugged. "Or, I guess it could be something like you gained two pounds or the bag you wanted to buy on clearance was all sold out."

"You make me sound so shallow."

I felt him shaking his head behind me. "No, Rosa. You aren't shallow. Jesus, girl, you're the least shallow person I know."

I looked up at him over my shoulder. "You're just saying that to get laid."

A glimmer of a smile crossed his lips before he shook his head. "Nah, babe. I'm smarter than that. Remember what Orlando did to the douche who assaulted Marialena at that party?"

I winced. "Beat him thoroughly, then castrated him and left him to bleed out on the bridge."

But he wouldn't assault me. That was a bird of another color. Not my Santo.

He grimaced. "Yeah, so there will be no gettin' laid here, thankyouverymuch."

I released a sigh. "Bummer."

"Bummer?" When he tickled me I giggled and squirmed but kept it quiet. I still didn't trust anyone. "The boy whose name means saint couldn't be more of a devil, could he?" I asked with a smile.

I felt him shake his head again.

"No, Rosa. And don't you forget that."

I looked up over my shoulder at him again.

The moment froze in my memory like a vignette, a little glimpse into the past that made me the woman I am today.

I knew he'd kiss me before he did.

I knew it would be a kiss I'd never forget...

I fall asleep, darkness pulling me under the warmth of the blanket.

I wake to the sound of a key turning in the lock. It could be minutes or hours later, I have no idea.

I open one eye, still groggy, as I hear Santo locking every door and fastening the deadbolts.

He opens the door to my room.

"Are you asleep because you're asleep, or are you pretending to be asleep because you touched yourself and you don't want to go over my lap? Hmmmm," he finishes thoughtfully before he makes it to me.

I murmur and roll over and open both eyes.

"Sleepy. You know I love going over your lap."

He gives me a grim smile. "Not for punishment you don't."

I close my eyes. Lie. *Especially* for punishment. But I'm tired. So damn tired.

I feel his weight on the bed next to me as he sits, his heft making the bed sag.

"Sleep, Rosa," he says softly. He bends his mouth to my ear. "And tell me the truth before I find it out for myself."

"Mmm. Got it."

"Rosa," he warns.

I yawn and fall closer to sleep. I'm so damn tired.

I hear him strip and climb into bed next to me. He settles his hand up to his flank and throws an arm around me.

Oh damn does it feel good to be so close to him. So good.

I nestle my butt in his crotch, which earns me several hard, rapid smacks to my ass.

"Don't start," he growls.

"Can't help myself," I retaliate.

"Sleep, Rosa," he whispers. "Sleep. Tomorrow will be the day I punish you for disobeying."

"What? I don't know what you're talking about."

He shakes his head. "I stood on the other side of that door and listened to you."

"You heard me?" I manage to squeak out. "You were downstairs."

"I did. Told them I was checking on you, which was totally true. And it was the most beautiful thing I've ever heard. Also, it'll be the most painful punishment I've ever given you."

His cock twitches. He's turned on at the thought of punishing me, of course.

Uh oh.

I close my eyes and shake my head to myself.

I feel the weight of his arm on me.

"Are you sleeping here with me?" A little thrill of excitement washes through me. We've never shared a bed before, ever. We've held each other and kissed, but we've never snuggled in bed.

And God, but it feels nice to be held by him.

"Can't," he says with a sigh. "It's too risky. I don't want to be left in a position that could kill us."

I nod.

"But I'll hold you 'til you fall asleep, baby."

Ah, Santo. Don't let anyone ever tell you don't feel.

I keep myself awake as long as I can, so I can keep him here with me. It's like reaching for the edges of a dream when you wake, how the consciousness drives the safety of the memory away. I'm half asleep, forcing myself to stay awake so I can feel him next to me.

I love you, Santo, I think in my mind. And it's on that thought that I fall into a deep, deep sleep.

I wake the next morning to the sound of the other shower running.

In my sleepy mind, it's the nanny and I don't think much of it. God but she takes the longest shower.

Then my eyes fly open as I remember.

Santo.

He's here. In the flesh. Right on the other side of this room, in the shower.

I lay on my back and listen. I'd bet a lot of goddamn money he's taking care of business in there, if I know him. The guy's got the sex drive of a manwhore.

I won't think of that now.

I hear the shower crank off, then hear him turning the faucet on and off. I listen to the sounds of the bathroom door opening and his fumbling around for clothes.

"Santo?" I roll over in the bed, still naked. My damp towel's been put in the hamper. I smile to myself. He knows I like things tidy.

The door between our rooms opens, and he looks in at me. I look at him without bothering to hide it. At his abs and muscles, his inked arms and inked back, the heavy beard he's trimmed and groomed. Damn but it suits him.

"Ooh. The beard looks nice."

He gives me the glimmer of a smile. "Thank you. You sleep okay?"

"Like a baby. You?"

He grimaces. "Eh, not bad."

Footsteps outside the door. We both freeze, seconds before a knock sounds. He yells over his shoulder, "Be right there!" He slowly closes the door between our rooms without a word to me. I jump to my feet, grab a dress and bra from my closet, and run to the bathroom to get ready.

I do not want to look disheveled, like I just rolled out of bed. I don't want *anything* to look suspicious. I'm kinda known for being particular about getting ready, taking my sweet time about it, but a bitch can move when she needs to.

I hear voices at the door but don't bother to look to see who it is. I'm quickly applying my makeup and fixing my hair when there's a knock at the door between the rooms.

"Rosa, we need to head down for breakfast soon. You ready?"

"Be ready in a minute!" I yell, the same way I would respond to someone who was no more than a bodyguard to me.

But we both know better.

CHAPTER ELEVEN

Santo

I've always loved the thrill of a chase, the knowledge that something dangerous could happen at any minute. It's just a part of who I am. I don't like playing it safe, following the rules, which is probably why Narciso enjoyed training me as a hit man.

And I know something's probably broken in me, but it was the best job I ever had. The absolute *power* of it all, the need for perfect precision.

He broke me in easy, you could say.

"Asshole's been selling crack on the school playground."

Papa sat in his office, nursing a cigar. Mama didn't like him to smoke anywhere but in his office or the war room.

"Crack at the school?" I asked, my hands clenching into fists.

"Name's Frank Dudley. Slash his tire." Narciso's eyes met mine. "I want you to get there early, bring the right tools, don't get caught. You get caught, I'll order Romeo to beat the fuckin' shit out of you."

He'd done it before, and he'd do it again. Seeing the look of regret in Romeo's eyes every time he struck me was worse than the actual beating, and far worse than any punishment Narciso could ever inflict.

If he was a fucking schoolyard crack dealer, he deserved what I'd do to him.

"Just slash the tire?"

"Yeah, son," Narciso said. I felt a strange mix of pride and apprehension when he pulled out "son." "Just one. Driver's side front."

I researched the right tools, found out where his car was, and hiding under a black hoodie, discreetly slashed his tire until the air bled out of it. Stood, and walked back to the waiting armored SUV.

It wasn't until later that evening I heard the news story.

Frank Dudley, found dead, run over while changing a flat tire.

It was my first introduction to mob life, and wouldn't be the last by a long shot.

I loved drag racing with Mario, smoking weed with Marialena by the water, stealing cars before I could afford them. And I was damn good at it. I managed to escape juvi by the skin of my teeth, though Narciso's punishments when I was caught were probably worse than any juvenile detention hall would've been.

And now… Rosa. The forbidden jewel in the Rossi Family crown.

My Rosa.

Too broken to be loved by anyone less broken than she is.

Too ruthless to be understood by anyone "normal" or "sane."

Too beautiful to be touched by anyone who didn't worship the very air she breathed.

But even thinking of her's forbidden. Touching her should make me lose my goddamn fingers.

I've personally meted out punishment for lesser crimes than these.

The irony, or hypocrisy, however you want to phrase it, ain't lost on me.

I hear her frantically getting ready in the other room and stifle a smirk. Cute.

I open the door to Mario. His hair's still wet from a shower, and he's antsy, tapping his foot. "How's Rosa?" he asks, without a trace of accusation. The door to her room's shut tight. They know that we're in separate quarters here. They also know we're only a door away from each other, but we've been so careful to appear like nothing more than brother and sister. No one's ever let on they suspect a damn thing.

And honestly, until I came home this time… until I came back to America, to Rosa single and brooding… there was nothing to suspect.

I watched that woman take vows to a man who'd use and abuse his authority over her. Watched it as a made man, witnessing the lawful promises.

I drowned myself in pussy to quiet the demons that screamed in my head, and she knew it. I wanted her to know it. I wanted to make her jealous.

Never said our relationship was fucking healthy.

Mario looks over my shoulder before I answer. "Rosa's good. Didn't want to talk last night. I fired the nanny and went downstairs, barely spoke to her, but she's safe, brother."

What a douchebag move, to remind him of my vow to keep her safe. To distract him from the knowledge that she ain't safe from *me.*

"Good," he says, exhaling, then lowers his voice. "I'm afraid for the girls. It's the next move they'd make, I think."

"Agreed," I say, running my hand through my hair. "Agreed. Good damn thing we've got Montavio bulldogs on staff now, brother."

Mario grins. "Goddamn right."

The door to her bedroom opens, and Rosa comes out, looking as put together and refined as if she'd spent an hour getting ready. It's like her superpower.

"Morning, boys."

"Morning," we say in unison.

"Mama!" Natalia runs down the hall from Marialena's room, dressed in a pretty white dress and patent leather shoes. God help them all when this kid's a teen.

"Hey, baby," Rosa says.

"Uncle Santo, are you staying here?"

I nod. "Yeah, Natalia, I'm staying here for now, so I can watch over you and your Mama. We have to stay safe because we think there are people who could be threatening you all."

Natalia nods and grins. "Yayyyyyyy!" she squeals.

Mario laughs out loud, as we head downstairs for breakfast. "Hey, you don't get that excited when I come around."

"I do when you bring me rock candy from the store," Natalia says, ever pragmatic. In the past six months, Mario's taken to managing a car shop north of here, near Rockport, a quaint seaside town with little shops and a boardwalk. He buys Natalia sparkling pink rock candy on a stick that she goes crazy for.

"Rosa, you gotta talk to your daughter about her materialistic ways," Mario says with a wink.

"Nope," she says with a cool smile. "The sooner she learns that men should spoil her, the better."

Ah, right. I give her a discreet little pinch. She said that for my sake and doesn't really mean it. I lean over and whisper in her ear, "Ain't no one spoiled on my watch, woman. Don't think I forgot your punishment."

She flushes pink, probably more to do with fear that someone will overhear than anything, but Natalia and Mario are several steps ahead of us. Without a response, she pulls away and sniffs.

But she's wet, I know she is, and I'm going to tease her along as best I can.

People don't know Rosa like I do. They think she's materialistic and aloof, cold and even selfish. But she isn't. Her heart beats as strongly as anyone's, and she loves so deeply she's selective with where and how she shows it. While Marialena loves everyone and everything that moves, Rosa's more careful.

That makes it all the more special to me.

We have serious business to tend to today, all of us. Tavi's in full Boss mode, pulling out all the stops on who we investigate and who we interrogate. I've got a few leads but wanted to wait until the Montavios arrived to fill him in.

I don't care for anyone outside the Rossi family but the Montavios, probably because I know they're related to Mama. They're also just damn ruthless, and you gotta admire a family that's more ruthless than the Rossis.

The smell of bacon and coffee wafts through the air, and I push away the feeling that I'm on vacation. I'm not. The Family's in trouble, and it's up to me and all the made men of the family to ensure everyone stays safe during Romeo's absence.

But damn, it feels good to be back. To roam freely. To be with Rosa again. To be near all of them.

It isn't the same in Tuscany.

Romeo's exile was a sentence carried out because I kept silent. And a part of me hopes now that I'm about to tell them everything, the damn exile will be lifted. But I need to do it in such a way that Rosa isn't implicated. I don't want her to feel burdened by me.

Nonna comes flying around the corner with a rolling pin in hand, shouting in Italian at a girl in uniform, probably a new hire.

"Whoa, Nonna," Rosa says, quickly stepping ahead of me. She holds up a hand to stop Nonna's tirade, and asks her in Italian, "What's the matter?"

"She touched my bread dough!" Nonna replies in Italian, then curses her out.

Rosa turns to the girl. "Did you touch her bread dough?"

The girl can't be more than twenty. Her eyes fill with tears and she wrings her hands. "I didn't mean to. I thought it was Tosca's, and she asked me to punch it down and let it rise for a second time, so I did."

"No one touch my dough!" Nonna shouts, brandishing her weapon again.

Natalia, the little brat, giggles her little head off. Mario rolls his eyes.

"Nonna, it was a harmless mistake," he says in his suave way. I stand and watch them with my hands in my pockets. I don't fucking care about bread dough or new hires or damn near anything like this shit.

"Nonna, she didn't mean it," Rosa says. "Please, let it go this time."

"You no go my kitchen!" Nonna shouts, as Rosa turns her away and escorts her back to the kitchen. I take Natalia's hand, and Mario talks in a low voice to the new hire. I give him a side-eye. He is totally gonna use this to his advantage to get in the girl's panties.

"Nonna's funny when she's mad," Natalia says with a laugh.

"Nonna's funny pretty much any time she talks," I respond. She's got a ready wit and doesn't care to play games, so she cracks me up. I love Nonna and won't forget that she's the reason Narciso's tyranny came to an end. That woman may be a calzone-making machine, but she can wield a pistol as well as any of the Rossi women.

Natalia skips at my side, and my heart swells. She makes me feel alive, being around her like this. Sometimes I think others around her find her annoying, always asking questions, never staying out of trouble. But I like that she doesn't act *afraid,* like all of us did. Until we were old enough to defend ourselves from Narciso, anyway.

The Great Hall is empty, faint voices coming all the way from the dining room. We usually eat breakfast at The Castle in the Great Hall, but when we have guests or it's a special occasion, we feast in the dining hall.

But from here, the large windows show the measures we've taken for safety outside. Tavi still has the dogs chained by the front door, but he's brought every made man and man-in-training to secure The Castle. Armed men stand at every entrance, wearing comm devices, and a table in the dining room's set up with laptops and notebooks. Added surveillance.

We won't talk about business at breakfast, not with the littler ones and staff around, but after breakfast we'll adjourn with the Montavios to one of the private rooms.

"Santo." Sergio Montavio, younger brother to the late Nicolo, gives me a hug and slams his palm on my back. "How you been, brother?"

Sergio is another car aficionado, and in our youth, we spent many a summer under the hood of a car together. He winces. "Heard about the Maserati. Jesus, brother, I'll help you kick the ass of whoever's responsible."

"Thanks, man," I say, releasing him. "But I ain't sharin' that job."

He grins at me. "Atta boy." Then he sobers. "How's Tuscany?"

"Sucks balls," I say under my breath with a sigh, and he shakes his head.

"It's bullshit, eh?" he says in a low breath. While the Montavios aren't under Romeo's rule, they show respect at all times. We all do.

"Yeah, man."

"You comin' clean?" he asks.

I nod. "I'll tell everything I know today." There's no choice at this point. I'll have to be discreet, but it's time.

"Hey, motherfucker," Timeo, the middle brother, says. Montavios are good stock, good-looking guys, strong, respectable men who look like they just came over from Italy. Shorter and stockier than the Rossis, they're no less powerful and attractive. "Good to see you home."

Home.

It hits me harder than I expect.

"Thanks, man. Good to be home."

Staff mills about, filling coffee cups and bringing platters of pastry, but a large buffet sits up against one wall. One quick glance around the room and I find Rosa sitting beside Marialena, little Natalia on her lap. Vittoria sits beside them, and they're smiling and laughing.

Mama sits with her nephew, Ricco Montavio, as they catch up. Ricco's the only married Montavio and Boss to the Montavio family. When I look over, he's proudly showing Mama pictures on his phone of their new little baby.

Tavi sits at the head of the table next to Elise, Orlando and Angelina on the other side. Small tables surround the main tables with made men and guards, all dressed and fitted to the teeth with weapons. While everyone talks, socializes, and eats, I'm watching every exit and looking for anything out of place.

I greet each Montavio in turn. Last night we greeted them en masse but didn't take the time for personal discussions. Today we'll have a better time of it.

First, though, I have to check in with Tavi. I walk beside him, and he gestures to an empty seat next to his wife.

"Sit, Santo," he says. The ruthless brother-in-command looks tired. Weary, as if he hasn't had a wink of sleep in days.

I sit. I take a cup of coffee and decline cream or sugar.

"Takes it black," Tavi says, not looking at staff, but I look sharply at who it is. Everyone on staff knows how I take my coffee.

"New hire," Tavi says, reading my mind. "You know Romeo hired more staff after Leo's betrayal."

I nod. I do.

Leo's betrayal. The motherfucker double-crossed me. Betrayed us all.

So many things have changed in such a short time. I don't know how I feel about that.

"How many?" I ask.

"Four."

I nod, and sip my coffee.

"You hear from Romeo?"

Tavi nods. "One call. They have him in solitary."

I nod, approving. It's for his own damn safety. They'll know the most powerful Boss in New England's been taken into custody, so they'll keep him apart from the others, until we can get him out.

"And Flynt?"

"Working on getting him out."

I look around the room, talking to the Montavios, and I know today we get shit done. After breakfast, the inner sanctum and our Montavio guests will adjourn to the war room. Tavi will go over every detail of Romeo's imprisonment and the accusations made against him. And I'll tell them everything I know.

Everything.

But even though I've waited for this day, even though the danger to everything we know is imminent, knocking on our door like the Grim Reaper with his vicious scythe, all I can think about is Rosa.

Rosa.

The woman who to all others appears remote and aloof, the Italian ice princess.

But I know who she is. I know the intricate workings of her mind. I know what makes her heart beat faster. I know what she fears, what she hopes, and what she craves.

I excuse myself from the table and rise to fill my plate from the buffet table at the end of the room. I catch her eye and give her a barely perceptible chin lift. She smiles at Natalia, who's now sitting in her own chair, and rises. Stretches. Picks up her plate and follows me.

I take my time buttering a muffin. Pick up a large, slotted spoon and put fruit salad on my plate, one piece at a time, while she sidles up beside me.

"You get something to eat?" I ask nonchalantly.

"Of course," she says with a smile. I know her, though. She's probably eaten an egg and half a grapefruit.

I lower my voice. "Best keep your stamina up." She hides her face from the others and gives me a wicked, lopsided grin that makes me want to worship the damn ground she walks on. God, what that grin could do to a man. "Fortify yourself," I say, my voice low and raspy. "For later."

I watch as she slides a bagel on her plate, a hearty portion of fruit, and a few plump, sizzling sausages from a platter.

"Good girl."

"Jesus, this looks good."

I barely stop myself from jumping when Ricco's only inches away on my left.

Fuck. I'm losing my touch. Didn't even hear him get close. Did he hear me call Rosa my good girl?

Jesus. I'm not the kinda guy that slinks around. I hate this.

"Yeah, man, they pull out all the stops for the Montavios, eh?"

"Better than that slop they give you in the Big House," Ricco says, but his eyes are sharp and he's not laughing. Goddammit, I can't fuck around and risk everything.

"Got that right." Served time myself, and I wouldn't go back for anything. "Jesus, we gotta get Romeo outta there."

I hate the thought of my friend, my brother, my Don, alone and imprisoned. He needs to be here, in his rightful place of authority, even if that means I get sent back to Italy.

"We'll get him out," Ricco says with confidence. He blows out a breath. "That's why we're here."

Tavi rises and clears his throat. "I want all made men and guests to convene in the war room in twenty," he orders. I watch as he bends and kisses his wife's cheek, brushes his suit off, then turns to go to the war room himself.

Ricco and I sit with the others, but out of the corner of my eye I watch Rosa. My Rosa. She holds my gaze when she slathers cream cheese on her bagel and takes a big bite. No one else in this room knows why, but I do.

Good girl.

When we've eaten our fill, the made men of The Family and the Montavios head to the war room. At the far end of The Castle, the war room's tucked away in the very back, as private a place as you can get save the secret wine room in the cellar. Here, we've conducted business since before I can remember.

I remember the day Narciso brought me here and told me I wasn't to call him Narciso but Papa. That he'd be my father and take care of me the way a father should.

I wanted to believe that.

And in many ways, he did. What man hasn't borne the scars of his father's poor decisions at some point in his life? I guess that makes all of us, then, every brother I know.

The lingering scent of tobacco still hangs in the air, deeply embedded in the woodwork here. Whether it's Romeo's or Narciso's or any of the other guys', it doesn't really matter. It's a part of the rich history of The Family.

"This place should've been ours," Ricco says, sitting behind the desk in a swivel chair that Tavi normally takes. But he's grinning when he says this.

"Trade you The Castle for the villa," Tavi says with a twinkle in his eye.

Instead of The Castle, the Montavios inherited a whole villa in Italy just north of Tuscany and several vineyards.

Ricco taps his chin and looks at his brother. "What'd ya think, Timeo? Sergio?"

Sergio pretends to think things over as he nabs a chair and spins it around before he straddles it. "Maybe if they toss in that pretty redhead we met at the Christmas party."

Mario rolls his eyes. "Sassy's Marialena's friend. If you bang that chick—"

Ricco snorts. "This from the guy that looked up fuckin' ancestry to make sure he didn't bang his fuckin' cousin when he visited us last year. Stop thinking with your dick, bro."

"As if that'll ever happen," Tavi says with a snort.

"You laugh," Mario says, momentarily sober. "But shit was tight, dude. Girl was hittin' on me, found out she was like a third cousin twice removed." Sweat breaks out on his forehead. "Goddamn fuckin' landmine."

"Imagine, your biggest issue is making sure you don't fuck a blood relative," Orlando mutters, giving Mario a good-natured cuff upside the head.

Mario grins back. "I cover my ass, brother."

Tavi finally clears his throat to get down to business. Ricco quietly gets up from the chair behind the desk and gestures for Tavi to take it. He might give us shit, but he respects the hierarchy here, and we all know Tavi rules everything with Romeo behind bars. Tavi takes his seat and faces us.

"Flynt says Romeo's under arrest for involuntary manslaughter. Says the accusation's that Romeo drove under the influence and killed two officers in a hit and run."

Low whistles and curses fill the small room.

"Flynt also says they don't have any fuckin' evidence and he'll get the case tossed easily, but we should watch our backs in the meantime. We have time-stamped recordings of where Romeo was and when. We've installed new security cameras in the past few months, covering every vehicle and inch of this place."

Cold dread pools in my stomach and I drag in a discreet breath.

I didn't know they'd changed up security.

Has anything I've said or done to Rosa… has anyone seen…

"Let me scroll it, brother, will you?"

Tavi nods. "Mario already did but couldn't hurt to have a second set of eyes. Let's get it ready to give as evidence. We have a strong alibi for Romeo."

"Then what fuckin' grounds they using to arrest?" Ricco asks.

"The hit and run happened with his car."

"Jesus."

"Mario and I will look back through everything. Find out where that car was and why it happened, who framed him." My skin feels both icy and hot at the same time. I school my features with difficulty as I face them all. I clear my throat. "You guys know I've spent the last few months in Tuscany." Everyone looks at me with interest, likely interested in what I have to say. "And I decided when I returned to America that it was time to tell the truth."

I stand up straighter and hold Tavi's gaze above all. I can feel Orlando and Mario's eyes on me, but I watch Tavi. Tavi was the one I saved. He's the one that understands what happened that night. "I knew

Leo was a traitor, but I couldn't make an accusation against a made man of The Family without evidence. So I went to Tuscany to track him. To follow."

"How'd you know he was a traitor?" Tavi asks.

"Because I slept with his mistress's sister."

Tavi doesn't flinch. He knows there was a time when I slept with anything that walks. It did shit to exorcise my demons and only made Rosa angry.

Sometimes a guy gets it into his head that fucking anything with legs will eviscerate the memory of… *her*… from his mind. But it doesn't work. It's like turning on windshield wipers when your windshield's covered in mud.

All it does is smear things and fuck it all up.

"And the girl liked to talk in bed." I shrug. She was a pretty little Italian with big eyes and a wide mouth that liked to smile. She had no hard limits in the bedroom, and I used that to my advantage.

I regret it, though. I regret any woman I touched that wasn't my Rosa.

"So I played with her. Got her to tell me everything. And she told me Leo's mistress was making bank covering his ass and that he'd been in touch with the Regazza family through Anna Regazza."

Anna Regazza, Tavi's mother-in-law, planned to prevent Elise's marriage to our family so she'd inherit the money due her that went to Elise in the event of her marriage. Leo wanted a piece of that as well.

"Why didn't you tell us?" Tavi asks the most obvious question, and I have to be careful with how I answer. I did go behind their backs. I did choose instead to find out what I could on my own before I involved anyone.

What they don't know is that the truth implicates Rosa, and she doesn't even know it.

"Santo, you told me that everything would come to light. You told me it would all become evident. Were you talking about Leo?"

"Yeah, brother," I say, my voice husky. "I didn't tell you because I didn't know if you'd believe me."

Tavi shakes his head, disbelieving. "Since when did we treat you as anything less than a brother to us, Santo?"

Since I was exiled to Tuscany. Since I was cut out of their late grandfather's will. Since I was taken under Narciso's tutelage and taught vicious, barbaric methods the other boys were never taught.

Not that any of that is their fault.

I shake my head and lie. "Wanted to prove I could, Tavi."

It's… a half truth. I blow out a breath.

"Remember when your cousin Jenoah was killed? Leo knew about his death and helped make that happen, didn't he?"

Tavi nods slowly, mulling this over. I decide to attempt an evasive revelation instead of telling all.

"Jenoah wasn't the only one who was on the Regazza hit list. They knew one of your sisters overheard their plans as well."

"Which sister?"

I shake my head. "Don't know."

Lie.

"How do you know this?"

I frown. "I overheard a conversation between the heads of the Regazzas. I was in Tuscany when I heard that Leo was betraying us. And yeah, I was sleeping around. Wanted to save my own neck, so I didn't tell Romeo how I got the information."

Tavi frowns. "Romeo doesn't give a shit who you do or do not sleep with."

Only to an extent. We all know there's a "do not touch" list, and the only woman I have any interest in sits at the very top.

I shake my head. "He cares if I did it when I was supposed to be doing a job, and I felt like an asshole for failing at my job."

I'm not that guy. I'm not a wimp like that. But I need to take the hit.

They don't know that it was when Rosa spent time in Tuscany with Jenoah, her cousin, that she'd made friends with Elise. They didn't know she was at the springs in Tuscany with Jenoah and overheard the Regazzas' plans. I don't even know if she was aware of them, but the Regazzas were confident she was.

The plan to kill Jenoah was supposed to involve her as well.

ORLANDO WAS RELEASED *from prison and the boys and I had spent the night partying with him. He was married to Angelina, only then he believed she was someone else. Shortly after his marriage, he exiled one of the guards to Tuscany for trying to touch her. It was a harmless touch—helping her out of a vehicle—but Orlando's a possessive motherfucker.*

Rosa was in Tuscany, as she'd made friends there when she lived there during her time with her then-husband.

I knew she was in Tuscany. I knew she was no longer married. I fabricated an easy lie, asking Romeo to send me to Tuscany to oversee operations at the vineyard, but the truth was, I wanted to keep an eye on Rosa.

My Rosa.

I wanted to be near her, without the prying eyes of the brothers in The Family.

I told myself I wanted to keep her safe, but a part of me wondered if she had someone in Tuscany. If she'd fallen for someone while married to Mercadio. But I should've known better. Rosa never fell for anyone.

I watched her from afar, pretending to be busy with work, and if my presence affected her in any way, she never showed it. I could've been a newspaper delivery boy for all the attention she gave me.

It was just as well. I didn't need prying eyes on me, either.

It was in Tuscany I learned of Leo's betrayal and became a self-appointed watchdog for the Rossis.

It was there I heard everything.

Ricky Regazza, smoking a cigar on the balcony overlooking the Regazza family's estate. Smaller than the Rossis by a lot, the Regazzas still thought they were hot shit. Booze, weed, and women flowed freely, as if they could afford any of it, but at least when I got them drunk and high, they'd spill everything.

"Jenoah is a dead man walking, Santo, you know that," Ricky said, his glassy eyes watering as he looked at me. "Caught him overhearing our plans. And that girl—the Rossi girl."

My body tensed but I kept myself aloof, detached. "Marialena?"

"Nah, man. The older one. Cold bitch."

"Rosa?"

I'd cut his nuts off myself.

"Yeah. She was with him. Don't know what she heard, don't know what she didn't, but we won't take risks. He's dead." He took a swig of his flask. "Then her. You in?"

"I'm in."

Oh fuck was I in. I was in so I could personally kill the bastard.

BUT ROSA WENT HOME to America, never knowing about the plot to assassinate her that went unfulfilled. That never happened.

I pretended I was one of them. Fabricated political ties in the Middle East from when Narciso and I did business there and used it as a trading card to gain the trust of the Regazzas.

And fuck, it worked. They were greedy. They bought it hook, line, and sinker.

They believed me, only my trail was seen by the other Rossis, and Tavi came after me.

They thought me a traitor, which is exactly what I wanted them to think.

I should've told them the truth. I should've told them everything. But I knew telling the truth would implicate Rosa, then they'd blame her for everything.

And I couldn't do that to her. No, not my Rosa. I couldn't.

"Thank you," Tavi says. If he knows there's more to the story, he doesn't pry. "Thank you for telling us this."

I nod, and pretend I'm abashed. Ashamed.

I'm not. I'm fucking pissed, and ready to kick ass and take names.

"Now who do you suspect's behind the attacks here? Who do you think framed Romeo?"

I shake my head. "Whoever was siding with the Regazzas."

Tavi blows out a breath and shakes his head. "We'll need Elise."

I nod. "Yeah, brother."

CHAPTER TWELVE

Rosa

SANTO ONCE TOLD me he could feel me. When I entered a room. When I drew in breath. When I laid myself down to sleep.

When I came.

He felt the pulse of my body and the energy of my soul, as if we were irrevocably entwined with one another.

I thought he was being dramatic, which didn't make sense because Santo's the least dramatic person I know. But he's right. He *was* right.

I felt him before, and I feel him now. If I close my eyes, I could tell where he is right now, and it's not because I heard the men head to the war room. No.

It's something deeper than that. Some things defy logic.

I purse my lips and fold my arms on my chest. I suppose Marialena's taste for the supernatural runs in the family.

"Mama?" Natalia's on her bed, fluffing up her blankets.

"Yeah, baby?"

"Is Uncle Santo staying here with us?"

Uncle Santo. That's all he is to her. Her uncle, because he's a brother to me.

No.

No!

He never was, never could be.

I swallow hard. "For a little while, Nat. Just need him here so we're safe."

She frowns, as she arranges her stuffed bears on the bed. "He loves you, Mama."

My heart races. My hands go a little damp and sweaty. "Oh, honey, he loves all of us, doesn't he?"

But my voice sounds strange even to my own ears.

"Yeah," she says. "I mean, I guess. But he looks at you like you're special to him."

Oh, God. Out of the mouths of babes? If she sees that from him… who else sees? Would Mama or one of my brothers, or—

I sit beside her and pick up a fluffy pink dragon. I play with the iridescent tail and pretend it's flying. "And do you know he loves you, too?" I ask.

"Of course," she says with a nod. "He loves me and you. You and me. Uncle Santo will protect us."

My throat tightens. To Natalia, *love* and *protection* are synonymous. When I was a child, I knew no such thing. When I was her age, "protection" felt stifling and painful.

"Always," I tell her with a nod. And I believe that.

"Can't we go out?" Natalia asks. "I want to go *do* something."

Now that demand sounds familiar. When I was her age, I hated when we were forced to stay at home, and I'd beg my nannies or Mama to "take us out and *do* something." I didn't care if it was getting an ice cream cone or going shopping, I got restless and irritable when I was home too long, unlike Santo, who seemed to thrive in familiar places.

"I'm sorry, we can't, baby," I tell her. "Not until Uncle Tavi gives us permission."

Her lips turn downward in a little scowl. "And why's it up to *him*?"

Why indeed.

I exhale. She'll understand someday.

"Because Uncle Tavi wants to protect us too, honey. Now let's think about fun things we can do here without having to leave The Castle."

Her eyes light up like little lanterns. "Oooh. Can I go swimming?"

It's an unseasonably warm day here. Sometimes in the fall it's too cold to swim in the courtyard pool, but ever since Natalia's come, Mama's made sure the room's kept warm and the water's heated.

"I think we can arrange that," I say with a smile. I'd like a good swim myself. "And maybe Aunt Elise will make cookies with you later."

Elise seems to crave homemade cookies daily, and no one's more willing to sample her wares than Natalia.

But even with the little plans we make that involve coloring, making playdough in the kitchen, watching a Disney movie, and swimming after lunch, I feel my own heart unsettled.

Outside the window to The Castle, guards stand at attention, heavily armed. Either Natalia hasn't seen them, or she thinks nothing about men holding weapons outside our door.

I'm not sure how I feel about that.

Finally, we make it to the courtyard for a swim.

"Mama, I'm so excited you came, too," Natalia says. I know what she means. Normally, she'd go swimming with her nanny or I'd sit by the pool fully dressed and read or scroll through my phone. Today I've decided to join her, a rarity for me and something she loves.

"I'm glad I came, too," I say, squeezing her hand.

The courtyard's almost enchanted, with bright green shrubbery bordering the pool, and bright rays of sun streaming in. And I'm enjoying myself, but my mind isn't here.

"Mama, catch me!" Natalia giggles and screams, diving under the crystal water. I smile sadly to myself, paddle after her and dive in, and when I come up we're both laughing, water streaming down our faces.

I feel him.

I keep my face placid and my gaze on Natalia, but I feel his eyes on me with the force of a laser.

"Uncle Santo!" Natalia cries, splashing past me to get to him.

"Havin' fun, little fish?" he asks, leaning forward to put his elbows on his knees. His gaze flickers from Natalia to me, then down to my bikini top and back again. My cheeks flush pink.

Natalia goes to splash him, and he leaps back just in time.

"Don't you dare," he says with a wicked grin. I wouldn't put it past him to jump right in after her. She giggles and tries to splash him again, but he ducks the water, grabs a pool noodle from the side of the pool and slaps the water in front of her with it. She squeals with laughter as droplets rain down around us.

I walk up the stone steps to leave the pool. I feel his eyes burning into me. Scouring me. Scrutinizing.

I swallow hard and look away. I can still feel the tingle on my skin where he touched me. I can still remember the sound of his voice in my ear, the promise of what he'd do to me when we're alone later.

And I long to be alone with him *now.*

But he'll keep his stoic expression, and I'll keep mine.

It's the only way.

"You guys find anything out?" I ask, as I tip my head to the side and towel-dry my hair.

He gives a noncommittal shrug, still holding me in place with his gaze. "Got a few leads."

"Any word from Romeo?"

"Spoke with Vittoria this morning. How's she doing?"

I shrug. "She's okay, I guess."

He only nods, still scowling. God, I love that scowl, and I don't know why.

I hear voices outside the courtyard in the dining room. "You girls hungry for lunch?"

I shake my head. I had a protein shake after my workout and that huge breakfast, so I don't feel hungry. "I'm good, but I'll go with Natalia and you."

Natalia pouts at having to get out of the pool, but Santo leans in and whispers something to her that makes her grin and hop to.

"What'd you bribe her with?" I ask, as she slides into her flip flops and heads to her lounger to get dried off.

He only shrugs, and damn if that isn't sexy, the nonchalant slope of his shoulders, the sharp cut of his eyes.

God, I want him to touch me. I want him to take this towel out of my hands and rub it over me, drying me off. Santo would make it sexy. *Everything* he does is sexy, from brushing his teeth to tying his shoes. I guess it's the "make my day, asshole" attitude he wears, as if trying to prove he's impervious to threats or attacks.

But we can't touch here. He can't do anything that even hints at intimacy, because they'd pick him off so fast it isn't funny.

"I have to get dressed," I tell him as we enter the dining room.

Natalia's got a towel wrapped tightly around her hair, and she's pulled on a little terry cloth sundress cover-up.

"Marialena?" I signal to my sister, who nods with a grin. "I gotta get dressed. Keep an eye on Nat?"

She grins and takes Natalia by the hand. "Of course, no problem." I glance over at the table, where Nonna's set out a large platter of homemade macaroni and cheese and chicken tenders, a clear nod to a child's palette. Yeah, there's no worry about Natalia eating any of this.

I walk ahead of Santo. As if I'm not aware that he's walking close to me.

As if I'm not vividly aware that I'm wearing a wet bathing suit, that we're heading to my suite alone, and that no one can suspect a thing, because he's following orders issued by Tavi.

"You guys find out any more about Romeo?"

He blows out a breath and shakes his head. "He called Vittoria, and said he has the option of hiring an attorney or using one provided for him. Hasn't said much, but he's mentioned to Tavi he's working with Flynt."

It doesn't feel right.

I nod, still concerned, as the front door opens and Mario heads in.

"Thought we were on lockdown?" I ask Santo drily. "Now I don't believe for a minute that you guys are only having the women and children on lockdown."

Santo narrows his eyes on Mario. "Where were you?"

"Checking surveillance footage by the cars. And you?" Mario grins good-naturedly, daring Santo to give him shit.

"Just checked the footage in the war room. All looks clear. We'll check in later."

Mario's eyes come to me. "You swimming, Rosa?"

"Took Nat for a dip. She's bored out of her mind."

He winces. "I'll do something fun with her later. Show her how to drag race or something."

"Go for it," Santo says. "And I will happily kick your ass."

Mario leaves us, chuckling, and we hear him talking to Nonna in the other room.

My heart squeezes. I don't want to be here. I want to be alone with Santo. I don't want my *entire, bustling* Italian family eavesdropping and snooping.

God, sometimes it's *stifling.*

I trot up the stairs ahead of him. He's walking so close behind me it should be illegal, and would definitely draw suspicion if anyone was here right now.

I feel his eyes on my legs, and suddenly remember his promise to punish me later when we're alone.

I open the door to my room, then step aside as he does his usual sweep of the place.

"No scary boogeymen or robbers hiding in my shower?" I ask innocently. He only grunts in response.

"You sure you checked the heating vents?"

"Fuck," he curses. "Don't push it, woman. You're already in trouble."

I blink in surprise. Didn't actually expect him to take me seriously.

I walk to my room tentatively, shivering from the cool air that comes through the vents.

"Vents clear," he says.

It's broad daylight out, my entire family is here, and doing anything with him is so risky it's insane, and yet I can't help craving him. I remember what happened last night and want *so much more.*

We've never done much beyond kiss, and it isn't fair, it's not right that the only man I've ever actually cared about has always been off-limits to me.

Ah, but there was that one time…

No, there were a few times…

The door lock clicks behind me. My pulse races.

His voice is a low whisper no one would ever hear on the other side of the door.

"Swimsuit off, sweetheart, while I check Nat's room and the nanny's shower. When I come back here, I want you stripped and naked and laying over the bed." The rough sound of his voice makes shivers erupt on my skin. "It's time for your punishment."

My thighs clench, and I squirm with delicious apprehension. When I don't respond right away, he steps quickly toward me, grabs my hair and fists it in his thick palm. "What do you say, Rosa?"

"Ow," I whisper, making him grin wickedly. Those full lips, that crooked smile...

"Yes, sir," I whisper.

Something crashes in the nanny's room. I stifle a scream when he shoves me behind him and cocks his gun. "Get down," he snaps. I fall to the floor for cover. "Who's there?" he shouts.

"Please, Mr. Santo, please, it's just me—"

I blink in surprise to see a house cleaner, dust rag and spray bottle in hand, leaving the nanny's bathroom. She looks at me, still dressed in a damp bathing suit on my knees behind Santo, and Santo.

Fuck.

"We thought you were an intruder," I breathe. I gasp in air and let it out again.

Did she hear anything?

Did she see anything?

Our position here alone could be… compromising.

Santo hasn't dropped his weapon.

It's no surprise that he hasn't let his guard down yet until he sweeps the nanny's room, too.

"Stay down, Rosa," he orders in a low growl. This time, I don't question him. I do exactly what I'm told.

Is someone else here?

Did they put her up to this?

But when Santo goes into the bathroom, I hear nothing. I stay exactly where I am.

"Go," he says. "No more cleaning this room until we call you."

She leaves the room so fast she's a blur. The door slams shut.

I'm still on my knees. "Do you think—did she?"

"No," he says.

"What if she—"

"I don't fucking *care,*" he says in a heated whisper as he steps over to me. He grabs me by the hair and drags me to my feet. His eyes are wild, his temper out of control.

This is the Santo I know.

This is the Santo I love.

This is the Santo I crave.

"Bed," he whispers in my ear. "Naked." He licks my cheek, and a shiver skates down my spine. "*Now.*"

I stand up and he releases my hair but sends me to the bed with a searing parting smack to the ass. I hiss in a breath but don't miss my stride. When I reach the bed, I strip and lay belly down over the side of the bed as he told me to, as he continues his close inspection of the nearby rooms.

I close my eyes and melt into the bed. My upholstered bed frame makes it comfortable, with no metal edge pushing against my belly. In the darkness, I listen to Santo. He makes a phone call, his deep rumble of a voice warm and seductive. The no-nonsense edge to him makes me shiver in anticipation.

I swallow hard.

I remember…

I WALKED DOWNSTAIRS AFTER MIDNIGHT, *my stomach rumbling with hunger. I was on a hunger strike at dinner, angry at Papa's latest decree to move us to Tuscany for the summer. I didn't make a show of it, but had no appetite, so I'd pushed my chicken and peas under my pasta and feigned a headache to go upstairs.*

Hours later, the hunger woke me and I hoped the kitchen would be vacant.

I got my wish. My bare feet made no noise on the tiled floor as I walked quietly to the pantry and opened the door.

Something caught my gaze outside the window. A shadow passed the window with familiar slouched shoulders, head bowed.

Santo.

Early June by the ocean in New England was sometimes chilly. I grabbed a box of fruit snacks Mama bought for Marialena, pulled my sweater tighter, and headed out the back entrance to the pavilion. We were overdue for a midnight soirée in our favorite hiding spot.

I paused at the door. Even the dogs slept quietly. Far in the distance in the hallway between the Great Hall and coat closet, a grandfather clock chimed midnight.

The enchanted hour, when footmen turned back into mice and princesses became regular girls again. How I longed to go from a princess to rags.

Not many would understand that.

Santo would.

He thought me asleep, so I crept quietly out the back door and made sure to jimmy the latch so we could get back in.

I followed him. Down to The Castle wall, past the pavilion, past the garden. Clouds covered the moon, and I was sent into temporary darkness, but the next shiver of a wind sent the clouds sailing away again. I followed the moonlit path to where Santo sat, under the stars, his back to me.

"What's a girl got to do around here to get some attention?"

He didn't startle or even look my way but sat up straighter.

"Get your ass over here and sit."

At twenty-two years old, Santo was more bossy and commanding than most full-grown men I knew, and considering who my family was, that was saying something.

"Say please."

"Now."

"Oh fuck off.*"*

"You are *way overdue for a spanking, aren't you?" He clucked his tongue.*

I grinned and sat beside him. I went for broke and leaned my head on his shoulder. Wordlessly, he wove his fingers through mine and wrapped an arm around me.

"You cold, baby?"

I shook my head. I was never cold snuggled up against him.

I closed my eyes and breathed him in. I lived for these stolen moments.

I knew if my father ever found us out, there'd be hell to pay, but when we were alone it almost didn't matter. I could almost convince myself that all would be okay.

Santo was the only one I could be myself with. The only one who didn't expect me to play nice or act the part of the lady I never wanted to be.

"Brought snacks," I said, shoving the little box of fruit snacks between us.

He snorted. "Uh. Thanks."

His voice sounded gruffer than usual, so I sat up straighter and looked at him. I stifled a gasp.

"Jesus, Santo."

Gingerly, I reached a finger to his swollen cheek and puffy eye, my own eyes filling with tears. "Does it hurt?" I whispered.

He shrugged. "Nah."

"Who?"

He looked away. "You know who."

"He didn't make one of the boys do it, then?"

"Not this time. Did the honors himself."

I wondered sometimes if Santo's own brand of sex-laced discipline with me was a way for him to take back control, to re-write the narrative so to speak.

It worked for me. I craved his rough touch, losing all control to him. I knew why, at least in part.

He was the only one I trusted.

"I hate him," I hissed. "I hope he dies a terrible death."

Slowly, he removed my hand from his face and kissed each finger, one by one. "Men like him always do, baby."

Did he believe he was a man like him?

"Let me fix it."

"You already are."

I swallowed the lump in my throat, knelt before him and framed his beautiful face with my hands. The boy with the haunted eyes had become the man that stole my heart.

Only ours wasn't a romance story. We both knew our story could only end in tragedy.

Slowly, gently, I brushed my lips over his cheeks. I kissed each tender, bruised spot until his eyes closed. I relished the clasp of his hands around my back, how he held me. I felt so small and fragile in his grip.

I nestled myself on his lap as he tugged me forward, straddling him. He reached for me and brought me to his mouth, his fingers on the back of my head. My heart pounded along with his. We both knew that wicked punishment or even death awaited us if we were caught. Somehow, it made the moment that much more magical. A romance forged in prison.

My mouth parted as his did. I whimpered when he licked my tongue. I craved more, needed more, but tonight wasn't about me. His hard erection pressed into my ass, so I wriggled a bit until he groaned. Still kissing, tangled tongues and soft lips, I reached my hand to his belt buckle and unfastened it.

He didn't stop me.

I didn't breathe as I fumbled for the clasp and dove my fingers down inside. I closed my eyes as I touched his hot, throbbing cock. I'd never touched a man before. He'd felt me up and made me come over his lap, but I'd never touched Santo.

I had to make it better. I wanted to bring him one small moment of joy, something to take his mind off the daily misery he dwelt in.

Still kissing, I fingered the tip, felt the precum moisten my fingers and used it to glide up and down his shaft. I moved to the side to give myself more room. His hands slid up my sides and down, then cupped my breasts as I jerked his cock.

"Rosa," he groaned, still kissing me, words muffled between our connected mouths. "Baby."

I love you, I thought. I love you so much it hurts me inside. I love you so much... so much.

His head fell to the side, but he still gripped me. Intent on pleasing him, I followed his cues to move my hand up and down. He pulled my hand to his mouth and licked my palm. I glided my moist palm over his hardened cock and relished every second of his guttural groans.

"Fuck, baby. You're gonna make me come. Stop, Rosa," he whispered.

I shook my head. "Don't make me stop. I want to do this for you. Let me."

He didn't fight again. His hips jerked with every stroke of my palm. He gripped the back of my head, yanked me to him, and slammed his mouth on mine as his hips jerked and he came with a groan I'd remember forever.

I slowed my strokes until he slumped against me. He held me.

"Fuck, baby," he repeated, in a calmer tone now. Less tortured. I loved the sound of his voice.

I laid my head on his shoulder.

"Feel better?"

"You always make me feel better."

CHAPTER THIRTEEN

Santo

I PACE THE OUTER ROOM, while I imagine her laid out on the bed. I feel as if I've been given a gift, but my time is short. Like I hold a genie in a bottle. I only have three wishes. The sooner I make my wish, the sooner my riches and good fortune will evaporate. And where I'll be when the dust settles… I might be grateful to harvest fucking grapes again.

I silence my phone and place it on the table. After the meeting with Tavi and the others today, our jobs are straightforward. Read surveillance. Search for clues that will lead us to whoever's betrayed us. Use Elise for an inside job, if necessary.

Tavi will want to avoid that if possible, and I don't fucking blame him.

I hear Rosa's soft breathing in the other room and thank God that I have her with me.

For now.

Goddamn, what I wouldn't do to make that always.

I'm told I'm a solid strategist. If I am, why can't I unlock the key to the one mystery I've never known how to solve?

Make Rosa mine.

I hear her fidget on the bed and head to the doorway. My heart swells when I see her, naked and trusting, her fearless blue eyes meeting mine across the room. Slowly, I slide into the dominant headspace I reside in. My need to correct her. The craving I have to overpower her.

I finger the buckle of my belt. "Why do you need to be punished?" I ask, leaning my shoulder against the doorframe.

"Do you think she saw us?" she asks.

In two strides I cross the room and slam my palm across her ass. I want her here, focused and present. Measured pain, followed by pleasure, will do exactly that.

"Answer the question."

Arousal glistens on her thighs, and she gently parts her legs.

"I touched myself when you told me not to."

"Mmm." I nod, stroking my palm over the faintly raised skin in the shape of my palm on her gorgeous ass. "And you know you need a spanking, don't you?"

Slowly, she nods.

I knead the tender flesh and suck in a breath when her own breath hitches. I savor every inhale and exhale.

"To answer your question, of course she saw us. Will she tell anyone? I don't fucking care. What'd she see? You, next to me, on the bed? Whatever. She shouldn't have been in here."

I stroke my fingers between her legs.

"Good," she whispers. "I don't care either, then."

"Will you care when I whip your ass?"

She whimpers. I knead her flesh harder, firmly, and she hisses in another breath.

"Whip my ass?" she whispers.

I lean down and brush her hair off her neck with my free hand. "Yeah, baby. Whip your ass. Do you really think a little slap and tickle is all you deserve?"

"You never gave me a little slap and tickle," she reminds me.

I shrug. "It's all relative, isn't it?"

I bring the massage lower, to the tops of her thighs. I stroke between her legs. I feel her damp folds, the pulsing need between her legs.

"Touch yourself when I punish you," I whisper, just as I move my hand away. Obediently, she spreads her legs and fingers herself.

I stand back and reach for the clasp of my belt. Her hand freezes. Her shoulders rise, and her eyes widen.

"Santo…" she whispers.

"Keep. Touching."

With a quick snap and slither of leather on fabric, I slide my belt from my waist and make a loop. I snap the leather. She strokes and whimpers.

"When I tell you not to touch yourself, you'll obey me," I say, savoring the words of command and this brilliant woman's submission to me. It's the greatest gift anyone's ever given me.

She nods. "Yes. Yes, I will."

I slap the leather against the fullest part of her ass, hard. My dick throbs on impact, and my mouth waters at the beautiful pink stripe on her naked skin.

"If you disobey me, you'll be punished."

She nods, just before I give her another hard flick of leather, this time on the other side.

I lecture and spank her while she works her pussy. My own body thrums with need and want at the sight of her reddened ass, her legs spread wide, the way she comes up on her toes and sways in time to her lashes. We're too far from the main entrance to her chambers for anyone to hear, but at this point, neither one of us cares.

Maybe we should. Maybe we should be more discreet. All I know now is she's on the cusp of coming while I whip her, and I don't want to take that from her.

Over and over I lash her, over and over she strokes and whimpers.

"Will you obey me?" I ask, just before I give her the hardest smack I've given her yet.

"I—I will," she whimpers. Her hips jerk.

"Come, baby. You ready to let yourself go? Come."

I whip her again, a gentler strike, but she's thoroughly submerged in this. She takes every stroke of the belt. She absorbs the pain. So fucking gorgeous.

I drop the belt and crouch next to her, take her fingers off her pussy and place them beside her.

"Get up on the bed," I whisper. "On your back and spread your legs. Hands clasped behind your head."

She quickly obeys. I kneel in front of her, part her legs, and breathe in deeply. The scent of her arousal makes my dick pulse and my balls tighten. I want in her so badly, but first I want to taste her.

I spread her legs, inhale deeply, then stroke my tongue between her folds.

I groan at the sweet, heady taste of her. Her fingers stab into my hair, anchoring onto me. I lift her ass and squeeze, and when she whimpers, I lick her again. I fuck her core with my tongue, then suckle her clit. Her hips jerk and spasm and she's panting with desire.

With a strangled cry, she comes on my tongue. She comes so hard and so long, she's hoarse when she finally comes down onto the bed and softens beneath me. I give her pussy a gentle kiss, making her spasm in aftershock.

"I want you in me," she whispers. "Santo, please."

I shake my head. I've never fucked her before. If we do, we cross a line we can't ever uncross. "Rosa," I whisper. My voice trails off. I can't protest much, because I want it as much as she does.

"I'm on birth control. Use a condom. Do whatever the fuck you need to, Santo, please."

I remember the first day she touched me, how I came so hard I saw stars. Her touch was magical, and I'd wanted her so long I came alive when she touched me. Since then, we'd played around and I'd touched her, I'd made her come as well. But never… God, never.

"If not now, when?" she whispers, her eyes filling with tears. Her slender hand reaches for the top of my jeans and unsnaps the top snap. My hard cock springs free. She licks her lips when she strokes it, and once more I'm that boy craving a hand job from the most beautiful girl I'd ever seen.

"Please," she whispers.

I bend and kiss her cheek. She strokes again, and my cock throbs at her touch. Slowly, she slides me along her belly. "In me, Santo. Please. I've got condoms."

"Soon, baby," I whisper, and I mean it. "Soon. Not now."

She yanks my head to hers and kisses my cheek.

"When?"

"I want to take my time with you. I want to feel you."

I want to remember you.

With a small nod, she strokes my cock. My hips jerk. She slides to the floor in front of me, her sex-sated eyes on mine.

"Let me taste you."

I sit on the edge of the bed and spread my legs. I hold her gaze when I nod. She takes me fully between her lips.

"Fuck," I mutter. Outside in the hall, voices rise and footsteps fall, but it's only background noise. My total focus is here, with her, the feel of her tongue sliding up and down my shaft.

I relish every stroke of her tongue. I jab my fingers in her hair and pull, eliciting the sweetest moan from her. She's so eager to please me, I've never seen anything like it in my life. Her hands knead my thighs, then one hand cups my balls while she sucks my cock. I feel the rising need, but with every jerk of my hips and groan that escapes my mouth, she only sucks more eagerly.

"I'm gonna… fuck, baby," I groan.

She nods in approval, closes her eyes, and sucks when I come against the back of her throat. She swallows and eases me to completion, her own moans filling the room as if this is all she's ever wanted, right here with me.

I can't think beyond the blinding bliss, the feel of her hands, her tongue and lips and perfect submission to me.

She nestles her head in my lap when I'm sated. My breathing comes hard and fast, and hers like fluttering butterfly wings. I lift her onto the bed and hold her, but minutes later, her hand strokes my chest, she lifts off my shirt, and her bare cheek presses up against me. When her tongue flicks against my nipple, my dick's hard again. I reach for her breasts and fondle and suckle while she does the same, whimpering when I touch her between her legs.

"Sit on my face," I order with a slap to her ass. She scrambles up, limber and eager, her knees spread over my ears while I suckle her needy pussy and she takes my cock again.

I make her come on my mouth and she sucks my dick over.

And over.

And over again.

"Fuckin' two-person orgy," I mumble, drunk with sex, my beard and nostrils filled with the sweet, seductive scent of her pussy. Her cheeks are flushed and her eyes half-lidded.

"Fucking perfect," she groans.

"I have to be downstairs in an hour," I tell her. We sat out lunchtime, but many did. I have to clean up and get ready to do my work, she's got to check on Natalia and check in with the girls. I hear approaching footsteps and freeze with her still on my chest. The room's heavy with the scent of sex.

But the footsteps only retreat. "Come shower with me. Don't wash your hair. Get dressed and head downstairs while I work on surveillance."

She stays snuggled up against my chest before she nods and sighs. "I will. I wish we didn't have to hide.

I wish we could share this room together forever, and that you could fuck me for real."

I kiss her cheek. "I know, baby. I want the same."

"And I want more than this," she says, her voice shaky. "Santo, I know eventually I'll be sent to someone else. And I know Romeo will do his best to make sure…" her voice trails off like she can't even talk about it. "I don't want anyone else," she finally says.

I don't respond at first. I'm not sure what to say. She knows I share this sentiment, but we both know I can't declare my love for her and fuck everything our brotherhood stands for.

"How do you know?" she says, tracing her finger over my collarbone. "How do we know that if we told Romeo how we really feel…"

I sigh. I've asked myself this over and over again.

She doesn't know the vow I took that supersedes all others. She doesn't know Romeo's already promised her to someone.

"Maybe this time…" her voice trails off.

"Babe, I'm on probation. They sent me to Italy to exile me, you know this."

She sighs.

"I do. But Romeo isn't the one in charge now, is he?" Rosa asks, a wicked gleam in her eye.

He is, but at a distance, and we both know this.

I roll her over on top of me and hold her to my chest. Her heart beats along with mine.

"What if?" I ask her.

"What if what?"

"What if you were mine." My voice is choked as I hold her to me. I run my hand along her back, the soft skin melding to my touch. "How would that change things?"

"We wouldn't have to hide, for starters." She laces her fingers with mine. "We could be openly… well, just with each other." She kisses the palm of my hand. "We wouldn't need protection. I could have your babies, Santo."

Fuck.

Fuck.

"I'll have to prove myself to the brotherhood, Rosa. I have to start there."

She looks up at me, her eyes wide and a little surprised. "Do you think that would work?"

Not if she's fucking engaged to another man.

I hold her gaze and don't betray what I know. I can't do that to her, nor to Romeo or Tavi. I know beyond a shadow of a doubt, betraying that confidence would end with swift and merciless punishment.

"I don't know."

She winces and looks away.

"What?"

"I just remembered that time one of Elise's bodyguards..."

I look away. It's a time none of us wishes to remember.

"She thought she was in love with him, didn't she?" she says softly. "But she was just a kid."

"Just a kid? She was eighteen years old. Old enough to know better."

Old enough to be sent off in marriage to someone else.

"Who was it?" she asks softly. I know what she means.

Which one of us was the one who pulled the trigger? Who ended his life?

"You know who I am, Rosa."

She nods.

"Then you know who it was."

We sit for long minutes while the sun sets. This is borrowed time. Soon, they'll be looking for me, if they aren't already. Soon...

"I have to go," I tell her. "We'll have to be careful. We've spent a lot of time with each other today."

Suddenly, she sits up, her eyes wild. "And what if I don't care?"

Her voice is louder than before, careless. She scowls at the door as if defying someone to overhear us.

"Don't talk like that, Rosa."

"Like what?" she says, even louder.

"Rosa." My voice holds a warning edge. She bites her lip and shakes her head.

"No. No, I know." She sighs. "Let's get through this, Santo. Do what you think you have to. Let's get Romeo out of jail. Then… then let's see what we can do."

CHAPTER FOURTEEN

Rosa

THE DAYS PASS SLOWLY, but I don't mind it. Normally, I'd be out of my mind with boredom, dying to get back into town with Elise for the fall collection reveal. I love this time of year, but it isn't the same when we're all stuck within the walls of The Castle.

Don't get me wrong, there are far worse places for one to be confined in. We have the full staff here preparing our meals, and with the exception of the basement levels and outside grounds, we have the run of the place.

We haven't hired a new nanny for Natalia, but there are so many here to occupy her for now, I barely see my little girl except for the few nights she spends in her own bed. When Tavi lifts our lockdown, that will change.

Santo's still here. And Santo is very, very much present.

Always.

He keeps himself distant and brotherly when we're around anyone else, or in the near vicinity of a security camera. He panicked once when Tavi first told him they'd revamped the security system, but after a thorough sweep with Mario, he discovered there was no evidence of the two of us that's suspect.

And the maid hasn't said a word.

Still… a part of me feels as if we're waiting for the other shoe to drop. Like the deep, dark secret of our love for one another will be brought to light, and that we'll regret the consequences of what we've done.

I don't, though. I don't. How could I?

Santo is the only one for whom my heart beats. The only one that truly loves me, the way a lover should.

"I'm bored," Marialena announces over lunch one day. We've gone swimming, made playdough with Natalia, made knotted fleece blankets to donate to charity, done family yoga which was wildly amusing, learned how to make Russian teacakes, and brewed new iced tea recipes. It's nice having the cousins here, though. They're funny and easy to get along with, even if I know they're ruthless and stern like my brothers, when they feel the situation warrants it.

And Jesus can those boys eat, too. Mama's getting groceries delivered damn near every day, like we're a bonafide restaurant. Orlando's using his vendor account to order restaurant-sized everything, and Tavi's having his staff in the North End keep us readily supplied with their decadent homemade pastries.

Elise has cooked us lamb shanks and steak, whatever her pregnant heart craves, Nonna's plied us with every delicacy Italy has to offer, and Mama's made her homemade bread so often, the house smells like a permanent bakery.

Last night, Elise showed me how to make *Zuppa Toscana,* a savory soup made with sausage, potatoes, and a broth laced with cream and wilted spinach. When he ate it, Santo asked me in a whispered breath if I'd marry him.

No one's attacked us. And yet, the threat lingers in the air like the smell of gun smoke after battle. No one questions Tavi's lockdown.

"You can help me pick the new inventory for the upcoming winter collection," Elise says. "I'll need it done early before the baby comes."

I know she's been talking at length with Tavi and Santo about her family, but no one's offered any information, and I know better than to ask. But something tells me she'd welcome a change of topic right about now.

"I'm game," I say with a shrug.

"What'll that take, like, ten minutes?" Marialena says, rolling her eyes.

"God, I wish," Elise replies.

Then Marialena's eyes go wide. "Oooh. Oh, I have an *idea*. You guys, I have the *best* idea." She jumps up. "I just have to talk to Mario…"

She runs from the room with her eyes alight.

"What's she up to now?" Santo mutters, refilling his espresso cup. I've barely seen him since yesterday. I practically have to sit on my hand to keep me from reaching over and squeezing his. Between his absence and Elise's, I suspect something's going on, I know it.

"I have no idea," I tell him honestly. "Says she's bored."

Santo smirks. God, I love his smirk. It makes me want to jump him. "When we were little, remember what Mama would do if we told her we were bored?"

"Oh God," I say with a laugh. "We'd have to clean this house from top to bottom, until Papa put an end to *that*," I say with a grimace. Papa hated his children doing "menial labor." Said it was undignified.

We're finishing up dinner, but Santo's just come in from outside. I'm not gonna lie, I'm super jealous he gets to go outside when the rest of us are stuck indoors. We all are.

"Eh, let her have her fun," I say with a shrug.

"All of you out!" Marialena says, entering the room and clapping her hands. "Well, everyone but Natalia. Everyone else, scoot!"

Santo gives her a withering look. Tavi eyes her suspiciously. "What the hell are you doing?"

"It's a surprise," she says in a singsong voice.

"Marialena, you can't goof off now," Tavi says sternly. "We're still on soft lockdown, and if you do anything that jeopardizes our safety—"

"Tavi, *relax,*" she says. "Take the stick outta your—" Then she clamps her mouth shut and shakes her head. "Promised myself I'd be as respectful to you as I was to Romeo, so I will not complete that sentence."

"Thanks," Tavi says, giving her a sidelong look.

"Trust me. Don't you trust your baby sister?"

"Ah, no way," Orlando says from across the room.

She rolls her eyes. "You'll see."

I'm working with Elise in the reception room on the emergent winter collection, a new batch of imported leather bags, lightweight woolen scarves, and a cashmere collection that makes me want to sigh in bliss, when we hear Marialena from the Great Hall.

"Come one, come all! The next movie showing is at seven p.m. sharp."

Elise and I exchange a glance.

"Did she say movie showing?" Elise asks.

"Ah ha."

I see Santo's shadow pass the doorway as a group text comes in on my phone.

Movie night, just like when we were kids. Great Hall in ten! Wear your jammies and bring your pillow!

"Is she outta her fuckin' mind," Tavi mumbles as he walks in the reception room and comes straight to Elise.

"Oh, I don't know, I think it's a fantastic idea." Elise grins. "I thought I smelled popcorn…"

"Oh, you smell popcorn alright," Mario says. He enters the room with a large paper sack of popcorn. "She had me bring in the machine we used to use for the St. Anthony's festivals back in the day, you remember?"

"Jesus, dude, you're sprayin' popcorn all over the damn place," Tavi says.

Mario rolls his eyes. "One little piece." He picks it up and pops it into his mouth.

I roll my own eyes.

"Well, I don't know about you guys, but if I have the option of spending the rest of the night staring at my phone or reading a book or *whatever,* I would rather watch a movie and eat popcorn that's gonna clog my arteries than anything." Plus, I don't like to disappoint Marialena. It's like kicking a puppy.

I head upstairs to grab my jammies. Natalia's obviously already raided her drawer, and I would hazard a guess that she's wearing the mermaid jammies with the iridescent tail. I fold the clothes that are strewn over her bed and pile them into her drawer, when I hear the door creak open.

Santo shadows the doorway, eyeing me thoughtfully. "Should bring down that big blanket," he says. "You know, that huge one Natalia likes to snuggle under."

I give him a wary look. If he thinks he's gonna get frisky right there under the noses of the entire family...

"What?" he asks innocently. "Cut me some slack, Rosa."

"Oh, right, like that'll happen." I give him another wary look. "You have that look in your eyes."

"What look?"

The door shuts behind him, and a second later I hear footsteps.

Dammit. We're getting too familiar, too lax. We have to remember what's at stake.

"That look that's nothing short of *predatory,*" I hiss.

He stalks over to me. "Do you blame me?" When he reaches me, he threads his hands around my waist. "I've got the most gorgeous woman in the world here." God, I love the heavy weight of his hands on my body, the warmth of his touch seeping straight through my clothes. I love the sturdy bulk of him, the surety and size. I love knowing that when he's with me, I'm safe.

The past few days have felt… almost normal. If anyone suspects anything, they haven't said a word.

I doubt that they have.

Or maybe I'm just fooling myself.

He leans over and nibbles my earlobe. "Wear the pajamas you have with the little hearts on them."

I wear bulky, oversized pajamas to bed when I'm here. I have no reason to wear anything else.

"Those are huge. I practically have to hike them up over my ass."

His grin widens. "Exactly."

I groan. "And if I don't? Jesus, I swear you men think with nothing but your dicks."

"If you don't, I'll do this," he says. He sits down heavily and jerks me across his knee, raises his palm—

"Hey! Santo!" I hiss, wriggling out of his grip before he can whack my ass for all to hear.

"Rosa," he whispers back. "Thirty seconds."

I roll my eyes, and he shakes his head with a waving motion toward the air. I quickly change into the pjs and join him in the other room. I halt when I see a black bag sitting on the edge of the bed.

"What's that?"

"Your toy."

My… toy.

I knew I'd only seen the barest hint of Santo's kinky side.

"What toy?"

He pats his leg in response but doesn't say a thing.

I glance at the little clock on the bedside table to note the time. "Marialena's expecting us in a few minutes…"

"I don't need more than a few minutes."

Oh, boy.

He slides me onto his lap, then gently pushes me over one knee. I brace for a spanking even though there's no warning, but none comes. I squirm, waiting for him, when I feel him fumbling in the bag. He takes something out, squeezes it onto his hand, then slowly lowers my pj bottoms.

My breath is coming in ragged gasps, and I squirm waiting for what he's doing. I know he likes control.

I like giving it.

I know he likes to command.

I like to be commanded.

I know he likes to dominate.

I love to submit.

Only to Santo. My Santo.

I close my eyes when he caresses my bare ass and kneads one cheek, then the other. I squirm as he parts my legs and warm liquid pools between my ass cheeks. I try to look over my shoulder but can't see anything. I whimper when his fingers slide through the liquid, easing my cheeks apart. It feels so wrong, yet arousal pulses through me like wildfire at the taboo touch of his fingers. Parting me. Squeezing me.

"Breathe, baby," he whispers in my ear. I draw in a breath, and as I let it out, his finger slides past the ring of muscle.

Oh, *fuck.* I'm deliciously aroused and can hardly breathe, but when he pinches my ass with another reminder to breathe again, I draw in a ragged breath. Even though he's fingering my ass, my pussy throbs, slick arousal coating me just from the way he touches me.

"You'll wear these jammies and this plug," he says. For one crazy minute I think he's talking about his fingers, but then cold metal grazes my ass and replaces his fingers. I feel so full, I gasp. My breath is frozen in my throat.

"What. Is. That?" I whisper.

"Pretty little jeweled plug, to remind you who this ass belongs to."

"I don't remember you claiming it," I toss back at him. Pushing him. Maybe even goading him a little. I lose my mind at the thought of him fucking me like this, in the most vulnerable way possible.

His hand claps down so hard my back arches. It feels...different when he's plugged me.

"Thought I made it clear you were mine," he whispers.

"You hinted at it," I tease.

"Ahh. Noted. Tonight, let's have a talk about making all that clearer."

I swallow hard, consumed with the vibration of his voice, the fullness in my vulnerable body, my throbbing clit. "I'm game."

"Thought so. Now stand and let me see my handiwork."

I stand, feeling a little foolish with my pajamas pooled around my ankles and my butt on display.

But when he frames my ass with his hands on either side and clucks his tongue approvingly, I feel… I feel like a goddess. Like he's worshipping me.

"Yeah, *fuck yeah,*" he whispers. "Better than I imagined."

"You've imagined sliding a butt plug in my ass?"

"For fuckin' years."

Oooo. Well then.

"Pull 'em up and turn around. Lift your top."

Hoo boy.

Slowly, I obey. The oversized pajamas pull easily up over my butt, even though it feels like nothing should fit comfortably right now. I lift my top, and watch as his eyes gleam appreciatively. "Mmm. Jesus, you're a masterpiece, woman."

I smile in thanks when he takes a small plastic sleeve out of his pocket. He crooks his finger at me to come to him.

I walk slowly, curious what he's got planned next.

He wets his lip and swallows, before he slides his finger under the sealed zippered edge of the bag and opens it. Wordlessly, he removes two little things that look like suction cups.

I stare, unbelieving, as he laves one with his tongue and slides it on my breast. "What is *that*?" I ask. His wicked glare is answer enough. With a twist and wiggle, he eases the suction cup over my nipple. Sharp, delicious waves of arousal course through me, as if he's licking and suckling my nipples.

A strangled cry comes from me when he eases the second cup over my other nipple.

"Santo," I whisper. "Oh, *fuck*."

He falls to his knees and tugs my pajama bottoms back down. Parts my legs and bends his mouth to my aching, sopping pussy.

I anchor myself onto his shoulders as his tongue meets my throbbing point of need. My head falls back. Every pressure point in my body seems centered between my legs. I'm vaguely aware of the plug in my ass, the suction cups on my nipples, and *blissfully* aware of his mouth on my pussy.

One stroke. Two. Three strokes and my knees go weak as I soar into climax. If he didn't hold me, I'd collapse, right here against him. I writhe and come, spasms of pleasure wracking my body. It feels like I've got a harem of men working my body to climax with every little tool of torture he's used.

Finally, when I slump against him, he gives me a wicked grin and wipes his hand across his mouth.

"Go, baby," he says with a nod. "Keep 'em on until I tell you otherwise. Let's go watch a movie."

CHAPTER FIFTEEN

Santo

THE GREAT HALL'S been transformed. The shades have been drawn, the lights dimmed. Large screens have been pulled down over the walls and comfortable chairs arranged for sitting. The popcorn maker of our youth sits against one wall, and a table set up with movie theater boxes of candy beside it.

Rosa walks in, holding a large fluffy blanket. She yawns as if she's tired, but I know she's tired because she just came on my mouth, and the plug and cups I have on her are working her to her next orgasm. That one will wait, though. I might be a kinky bastard, but even I won't make her come in the Great Hall with her family nearby.

Could take her to a coat closet, though.

"Ooh, are those Raisinets?" she says when she sees the candy.

"You've always loved those," I say with a smile.

I used to buy them at the school snack cart, back when they let you buy junk food and soda. I'd slide the boxes into my bag and surprise her when I got home. Those, and Junior Mints were her favorites.

"Hands off the Raisinets," Mario says. "I want those."

Rosa frowns and grabs the last box. "Nope. I saw them first."

"Rosa," he says warningly. It's rare the girls get in on a Rossi family food fight, but it happens sometimes.

"These," she says, tearing the box for emphasis and shaking some into her mouth, "are mine!" And to my surprise and probably everyone else's there, she pops a few in her hand and whips them at Mario.

They bounce off his forehead while he stares at her, his mouth agape.

"Did you just throw candy at my head."

"Duh. Not only did I throw candy at your head, my aim was spot-on, wasn't it?"

"Oh, you wanna play that game?" he says, nabbing a box of nonpareils. "It is *on.*"

"Not the chocolate!" Elise protests. "C'mon guys, at least use the gummy stuff."

"Not my Sour Patch Kids!" Marialena protests.

But it's too late. Nonpareils and Sour Patch Kids, Swedish Fish and Starburst fly around the room like a downpour from heaven. Natalia comes in the room with Mama and squeals with delight. "It's raining cannndddyyy!"

Mama takes one look, puts her fingers to her mouth, and whistles so loudly, we all freeze. Been a while since I've heard that, but we all know she means business.

"What is going *on* here?"

"Oh, Mama, we're just watching a movie," Marialena says innocently.

"My God," Mama shakes her head. "After the movie, y'all are gonna sweep that floor and make this place tidy, you understand me?"

Everyone mumbles and agrees, while Marialena flickers the lights and tells us all to get to our seats. Natalia beckons me and Rosa over to snuggle on a huge bedroll she's made on the floor, right up front. Rosa sits cross-legged beside her, winces, and gives me a reproachful look. I discreetly hold my fingers at my eyes and swivel them back to her, to remind her I'm watching her.

She'll be ready to combust by the end of this movie. I watch as she slowly sticks her tongue out at me, almost like she's mocking me, but then she moves her tongue around the edge of her lips to tease me.

Under the dark shadows of the Great Hall, while everyone else is watching the movie, no one sees the little seductive flirt.

At first, I think it's just a regular movie, some Disney cartoon I'm barely paying attention to. Beauty and the Beast? The girls seem riveted and Natalia sings along in her sweet, high-pitched voice, but most of the guys seem bored. We entertain ourselves with popcorn and candy, and Mario makes subtle wisecracks Mama and Natalia don't hear about the Beast nailing Belle.

"Is his *dick* beastly?" Mario mutters, shaking his head. "No wonder the girl's crazy about him. Who wouldn't wanna be nailed with a nine-inch dick?"

Tavi elbows him but Orlando and I snort with laughter. Sergio joins in about those claws of his and Belle's pretty yellow dress being torn to shreds, and Timeo makes a wisecrack about little beast-like bambinos. But when the credits come on, the screen flickers.

"Movie ain't over," Marialena says in a singsong voice. "You guys are gonna like this one."

The screen goes black, and the room quiets. I reach under the blanket for Rosa's hand as a picture that's gotta be thirty years old pops up on the screen.

"Oh my God," Mama whispers when the camera flickers to the church. She's holding a baby swaddled in a white blanket by the front door, looking suave and put together as always. God, Papa still has black hair, and his eyes aren't as haunted as they were when I knew him. It was before he'd taken the throne as Boss, before his father died of a stroke. Before his older brother committed suicide.

"Marialena, where'd you get these?"

"Papa's desk," she says quietly. "Thought they'd make a fun movie night."

The old video camera from the Eighties didn't hold a candle to the current equipment we have. The video footage is jerky and grainy, but we're all there... all of us.

A hush falls over the room as we watch clip after clip.

"My God, your hair," Tavi says to Mama. Her perm was a sight to behold, and even Rosa, when she was school-age, had wild and crazy hair she didn't tame until her early twenties.

"This was before you came to us," Rosa says, holding my hand under the blanket. To others, it will look like we're just sitting together, watching a movie. Natalia snuggles up to Rosa's side and giggles at everyone's pictures.

"If this is the one I think it is," Mama says thoughtfully, her voice trailing off.

And then there I am, a gangly youth with a perpetual scowl. In one short video, Marialena's first Communion at church, Romeo puts an arm around me and takes a picture. My chest swells and

I grin at the camera, so proud to be one of the Rossi men.

"There you are," Mama says proudly, halfway across the room.

Rosa's hand stills in mine. I stroke my thumb along the top of her hand and wonder what she's thinking. I know what I was thinking that day.

It was the first day Romeo ever taught me how to shoot a gun. We'd been attacked by a local rival, and I had no weapon. I used what I had, though. A nearby branch I used as a club, my two fists that were unrelenting when the shit hit the fan. And I knocked them down and restrained them until Romeo came and brought Papa to take over. Back then, the older made men of The Family were the inner sanctum until one by one, the Rossi men of the brotherhood grew of age and were inducted.

Papa was so damn proud of me. *I* was so damn proud. Mama cried, and Rosa wouldn't even look at me for days. I think it was the bruising and stitches I needed around my hands after delivering a near-death beating.

When I made my first million, I celebrated with wine and alcohol and women from all over the damn state. My brothers said a night of liquor and the best sex of your life were just what the doctor ordered.

We sit for another hour, reminiscing. I'm back in the headspace of a child. I never wanted to be there. But now that I am... I wonder.

Is this what I wanted?

"It's so funny to see you all when you were little," Natalia says. "Mama, you were so pretty even then."

I almost agree with her out loud but catch myself just in time. She was. She really was.

"I'm glad the dogs didn't bark through the whole movie again," Natalia says. "Remember when we were trying to watch and they wouldn't stop barking?" she says to Marialena.

Mario and I look at each other across the room. Tavi's already got his gun pulled.

"I haven't heard them at all, have you guys?" Mario asks the room.

Tavi's on his feet. "Everyone to their rooms," he orders in that voice no one dares to disobey. "Mario, Sergio." He jerks his head to the door.

"On it," Sergio says.

Mama's pacing by the door. "Why haven't we heard the dogs, Santo? Why?"

"I don't know, Mama," I tell her, as I pace the room and head to the windows. It's unusual so many of us are gathered in one place for that length of time. Even meals are much shorter.

If any bastard tried to get to us when we were right here, if they hurt our dogs…

"On second thought," Tavi says before he leaves. "You all stay here. Better to keep everyone safe in this one room before we leave."

"How long?" Mama asks. We don't respond, because we know she isn't talking about how long we'll be here. She's asking how long until the threat against the family is lifted, when we can all go about as usual again.

"I don't know, Mama," I tell her, shaking my head. "I don't know."

I keep everyone behind me in the Great Hall and pace by the courtyard. I see nothing by the windows. I pull up surveillance on my phone and am taking a look when it rings.

"Dogs have been knocked out, Santo," Tavi says. "They're unharmed, but dead asleep. Sweep the footage from where you are. See what you can find."

I go back to the security footage. Two hours ago, nothing, the faint barking of the dogs from one angle of the camera.

One hour ago.

A pedestrian on foot, wearing a hooded jacket. Kneels by the fence and gestures for the dogs. The dogs can't reach anyone by the fence, because we set it up that way. They're too dangerous to allow any pedestrian to reach them. They take something out of their pocket and push it through the fence.

"What's that?" Rosa asks. She's standing over my shoulder, her eyes glazed. I've been caught up watching surveillance, but she's been turned on while she watches everything right from where she is.

I shake my head. "Not sure. I don't know..." my voice trails off. "Can't see who it is."

"They fed something to the dogs, didn't they?"

I zoom in closer and see small dog biscuits pushed through the fence, far enough to tantalize the dogs.

The hooded figure rises and walks away, but before they put their hands in their pockets, I see something. Looks like a shadow across the back of their hand.

"You see that?"

Rosa nods. "Hand tattoo, isn't it?"

"Hand tattoo?" Timeo's behind me, scrolling the same footage on his phone. "Hand tat like that's Castellano, brother, no?"

I shake my head. We're one step closer to finding who's threatening us. "I don't think so. Castellanos have no beef with us."

Tavi and Sergio come back inside. "All clear outside. Vet's on their way and I'll fill everyone in as soon as I have more information."

I show them the screenshot I got of the security footage. Tavi scrubs a hand across his chin. "Castellano, Timeo says."

"Nah, man," Dario says. He's pacing near Orlando. Cracks his neck, spreads his shoulders wide and bounces on his feet like he's going into the ring. "You remember hand tats like that, bro?"

Orlando nods. "That's Campanelle, isn't it?"

What if they're working together?

We've got some work to do.

"Everyone upstairs," Tavi says. "We're safe for now."

"Tavi, how much longer?" Marialena asks. Elise stares at Tavi, curious as well. I bet she's dying to get back to her shop before the baby comes.

"Not yet," Tavi says with a sigh. "We stay right here."

And yet my gut instinct says something's off, that something isn't right.

I don't like to think I'm a pessimist, but I've seen shit go down. I've learned to trust my instincts, and I know something's very wrong. The time of peace and hiding like this can't last for long, and I feel that's exactly what we're doing wrong.

"How much longer's right, Tavi," I say in a low voice. Still, it seems all eyes in the room swing our way. I told Rosa I'd prove myself to the brotherhood, and the smart thing to do would probably be to keep my head down and do exactly what the boss tells me. But I can't help the question now. How much longer do we sit here waiting? How much longer to be holed up like sitting ducks waiting for the next blow?

"What else would you have me do, Santo?" Tavi asks.

"Aggressively seek out who did this to us." I look around the room. Mama and Nonna and Natalia watch me from the doorway to the courtyard. "This is a conversation for a much more private audience, brother."

"Santo's right, Tavi," Rosa says. "This isn't how Romeo would want us to handle things, is it? We haven't gleaned the respect of everyone in the North like this."

Tavi nods. The measure of a good leader isn't just his fearlessness, but his willingness to listen to those he leads. His humility.

"This is a conversation for a more private audience. Santo's right about that, too. Tomorrow, we move. Tomorrow, we talk details. I don't wanna lay around and wait any longer than you do. If anyone is going to threaten our family, I'd rather come out with fists. Tonight, I want everyone to be scrupulously careful, you get me?"

We all nod and head to our assigned stations. Rosa gets Natalia in bed, then heads to her own bed. I know she's waiting for me. I primed her to be waiting for me.

I scroll through footage after footage, looking for more clues. Anything that will tell us who's doing this and why. I think of Leo and the Regazzas. Tomorrow I'll ask Tavi what questions Elise has asked, how far she's gotten.

But tonight might be all that we have. Tonight might be the only time I'm with Rosa again. Tomorrow, we could be ripped apart and sent in different directions.

Tonight might be all we have.

Tonight, I'll make Rosa mine.

CHAPTER SIXTEEN

Rosa

I'M LYING on the bed on my back, thinking over the night's events. The hot-as-fuck session I had with him right before we went downstairs, the way he lit my nerves on fire, set me off like fireworks, then put me on a low simmer for hours. A low simmer, left unattended, will grow to a boil.

Yeah, that's about where I am right now.

I figure he's preoccupied, but it still doesn't feel right taking the tools he's used on me off without asking him first. It feels deeply intimate, and there's something about them that makes me incapable of defying him, as if he holds the key to my submission in the palm of his hand. And maybe he does.

I feel like there's something in the air, as if something terrible's about to happen. I can see it in Santo's eyes, too. He knows as well as I do that threats like this culminate in violence or the like, but if we don't know where the threat is coming from or why, it's hard to know how to defend ourselves.

I hear him pacing in the other room and gingerly bring my fingers to my breasts. The little suction cups have held tight, my breasts tingling. I trace the edge of one. Just the edge.

"Did I give you permission to touch yourself?" Santo's low rumble of a voice comes from the doorway. I look over at him and don't stop circling my breast. I watch him with my head tipped to the side. He's kept his voice low so he doesn't wake Natalia, but her door's shut tight and I know she won't hear.

I can tell he needs to control me tonight. I can tell he needs to dominate.

Like a vampire feasting on blood, Santo craves my submission to fuel him. It feels like a sort of honor to serve that need for him. For Santo, I'd bare my neck.

I swallow and squirm, still focusing on him.

"Kinda dying over here, baby," I whisper, parting my legs. My butt tingles, my breasts tingle, my belly swirls with need. I came on his tongue before the movie but that seems like a long, long time ago.

"Can't have that," he says in a whisper. He crosses the room and comes to me, sits on the edge of the bed and eyes me. "Let's get these pajamas out of the way." With a tug and whoosh, he quickly divests me of my clothes. They fall into a tumbled heap on the floor.

Yep, that's why he wanted the baggy ones.

There's something in his eyes that worries me. He looks… sad. As if he knows that tonight will be our last night together. As if he knows something I don't. I watch as he eyes my body.

"I want to make love to you, Rosa," he whispers. "My beautiful Rosa. A woman like you deserves a name so pretty." Slowly, he drags his finger over my navel, where my bellybutton dips, then traces the swell of my hips. Unlike the times of before when he made me climax, I feel… different now.

Whereas before, I felt as if he lit my nerves on fire and I craved the release and intensity of orgasm, now… now I want something more. Deeper. I crave the intimacy of being with him.

We've been emotionally connected with each other for as long as I can remember, so it feels like the natural progression of things. And what if we have no more time with each other? What if this is it?

He bends and kisses the swell of my breast before he slowly releases the suction cup. I draw in a breath at the quick spike of pain before it melts into something warm and delicious. I sigh.

Next, he removes the second suction cup. I'm already aroused, already on edge, craving the mind-numbing release and connection with Santo. Our brief time here together, under the pretense of my protection, secured here in the room where no one can stop us, we can finally seek the intimacy we both crave.

"On your knees," he whispers, gently pushing me onto my belly, then hiking up my knees so I offer myself to him. He presses my breasts to the bed, making my ass rise higher. "Jesus," he mutters, and I half wonder if he's praying. "*Beautiful.*"

With gentle hands and a firm touch, he touches the plug. I tighten, but his hand comes to my lower back to steady me. "Easy, baby," he whispers. "Let go. Relax."

I relax my muscles, and as he divests me of everything, I feel bared, my nerves electrified. I swallow hard and close my eyes, and relish the feel of his large, rough hands on my body.

"Good girl," he whispers hoarsely. "You're so fucking beautiful."

He kisses my lower back and I shiver, before he gently rolls me over.

"Let me undress you," I ask gently, when he grasps my wrists and holds them down, those deep blue eyes capturing my attention and my heart. "Let me?"

His lips quirk up. "Go for it."

My hands shake a little when he releases me, whether it's nerves or tension, or the eagerness of a woman in love, I don't know. Maybe all of the above. He kisses my cheek and brushes a finger across my lips. I kiss his fingers, and they linger.

Slowly, as if I'm unveiling a masterpiece, I remove his shirt. My hands move gently but purposefully over his body. Exploring. Wandering. Roving. An exploratory touch with love and purpose. He shifts his shoulders, his muscles bunching, when I lift his shirt over his head. Then he descends back to the bed, bracing himself on his palms before he traces a finger over mine.

I lick my lips when I reach for his belt and unfasten the sturdy metal buckle. I've watched him unfasten his belt a hundred times, and I never lose interest in the intimate movements of his hips and hands.

I tug his belt off, curl it into a loop, and lay it to the far end of the bed next to his shirt. I take a minute to admire him, the strength and vital force that's all Santo—his curved biceps and toned abs, decorated in ink that makes my heart beat faster. Every tat has a story, every story part of what makes him who he is.

I lift his wrist and bring the rose tattoo to my eyes. No one else but me knows that along the edge of the rose in fine script lies my name.

Curl of an "r," a loopy "o," the swirl of an "s" and the hint of an "a." I thought it risky when he got it, but no one knows it's there. No one but me and Santo. As it should be.

I kiss the palm of his hand, the tendrils of letters on his rose tat, and remember the day he got it.

"I'M GETTING *the rose tattoo today," he said as he pushed his hair out of his eyes. We sat along the edge of The Castle wall, discreetly hand in hand.*

"You're being inducted, then."

"Rosa, I've already taken vows to your brothers and your father."

I nodded and gently leaned my head on his shoulder.

"There's no going back then, is there?"

"Why would I?"

"Why would you what?"

"Ever go back?"

I shook my head. "It's just so... irrevocable. So permanent. It's like once you make the vows to the brotherhood, you're... you're never the same."

"It's not like that, Rosa. That's exactly *what it is."*

Later that night, we met in the war room. My father was in Italy and my mother had gone to bed, my brothers gone there themselves after celebrating Santo's new ink in town. Romeo wasn't around much, building real estate investments in Boston, and back then, when my father was out of town, we all eased up a bit.

Not Santo, though. Never Santo. Being an inducted brother at such a young age meant constant vigilance and never taking anything for granted.

So we met in the war room because I wanted to see his new ink.

"I've got a surprise for you," he said. Still bandaged at first, when he removed them to show me, his new tats looked like fresh slaps across bare skin, red and angry to the touch.

"It's your name, Rosa," he said softly, pointing a finger to the swirl of text along the edge. "It's discreet so no one will ever think it anything but a rose stem. But I'll know what it is. I'll know what it says."

"Oh, Santo," I said. I cried that night. It seemed most of my memories with Santo involved my tears. "It's... beautiful."

"WHERE ARE YOU?"

Santo kneels over me, half naked, his stern eyes probing and curious.

"I was remembering the night you got that ink. Remembering how it made me cry."

A soft smile ghosts his lips before he sobers. "It did."

"Santo," I say softly, my fingers edging into his jeans. I grip him tight so he doesn't move.

"Yeah, baby?"

"You said that night that you took vows to my brothers *and* to my father. Why say it that way?"

A look I can't identify flickers across his face before he shrugs. "Not sure why you remember it that way."

"I just do. Was there meaning in that?"

"There's meaning in everything, Rosa."

He bends and kisses me, silencing my mouth and quieting my mind. "Finish undressing me, baby," he whispers. "Tonight will be special, and I want to savor this."

I give a quick nod before I unbutton his jeans. My hands tremble when I push them over his hips, and he helps me get him out of them by pushing them down, his hands atop mine.

I take them off and pile them beside his other clothes until he kneels before me wearing nothing but boxer briefs stretched tight across his muscled hips and firm ass.

"I remember when you used to play baseball."

"One season, twenty years ago."

"Perhaps, but the sight of your ass in those tight pants… mmm, a girl doesn't forget a thing like that."

I grip his ass and squeeze. His cock, already stiff, throbs in his boxers and stiffens even more, the hard length obvious and arousing. I want to feel him inside me. I've never had Santo inside me, and I can't think beyond the need to feel him.

With the firm touch of a man who knows what he wants, he captures my arms in his strong fingers and places them by my sides. Slowly, he lowers his weight on me in a way that isn't stifling but reassuring, his mouth caressing mine in an almost-kiss that hints at things to come.

"I want you," he whispers in my ear. "I want you so bad I can taste you."

Between the foreplay earlier and his control over me, and the slow revealing of his naked skin next to me, I shiver in need and want. I swallow hard and my eyelids flutter closed. He kisses one, then the other, as if blessing my dreams, but when his mouth meets mine, this time he's more insistent than ever.

Tonight's the night. Tonight, Santo will make me his in every possible way. Tonight, we become one.

My eyes stay closed as he kisses me, his tongue licks mine and I release a guttural groan which he swallows with the next kiss. I graze my teeth along his lip, and a low, deep moan, all male and all Santo, permeates my pores. I inhale the deep, masculine scent of pine and strength, clean and vivid and mesmerizing. I lose myself to the firm exploration of his fingers, the possessive grip that only affirms what I already know: Santo loves me, and I love him. Only a lover could hold a woman like that.

My heart races when he nips my lip. Tongues and teeth and hurried breaths, whispers and promises and prayers. His fingers stab into my hair and mine grip his muscled shoulders. My hips rise to meet his, and he glides his legs over mine. I feel his hardened length through the fabric of his boxers, and my own barely clad body meets his in wanton abandon.

"Rosa," he groans in my ear, thrusting his still-clad cock against my body. "Fuck, woman."

"I want you, Santo."

"And I'll have you."

I nod, so eager to feel him in me, I make short work of pushing down his boxers. I savor the feel of him on top of me, his large hands roving over my bare skin as if memorizing every curve and plane. His lips along my neck make my skin erupt in fire, his fingers soothing the burn only to deepen the heady feel of need.

He moves his hips in time with mine, and the wait is agonizing bliss, a yearning need that says *all of you, now* while savoring every breath and touch. I can't breathe. I can't think. I can feel and touch, ignited by his every breath and movement.

With rough, perfect hands at my knees, he parts my legs.

"Take 'em off," he growls in my ear. I grip the elastic band at his waist and yank them down, eager to see his cock at full mast, a deep shade of red with his own pumping blood and need. We take one glorious moment to stroke our naked legs against one another, mine smooth and his rough, mine small and slender and his like massive tree trunks.

I hitch up my knees and wrap my legs around his, my bare pussy beckoning him to come closer. My arms around his chest tighten, and for one agonizing second, I can't breathe from the anticipation.

His lips join mine as he glides into me. I sigh with relief as jolts of pleasure ripple through me. The first thrust makes me cry. By the second, tears flow freely down my face. He kisses the trail of tears with kisses that anoint me, and trembles before he thrusts again.

"Fucking perfect," he says in a hoarse whisper. "Christ, woman, I'll never forget this until the day I die. I'll remember this. Fuck, I'll remember..."

My legs tremble with need when he thrusts again, spasms of electric perfection tingling my limbs and arms and pelvis. His thick cock fills me to beyond capacity, but when he rocks his hips, the too-full feeling dissipates to a cloud of utter bliss that covers every inch of me.

"Santo," I say on a whimper, when he thrusts again. He throbs inside me, as if holding himself back.

I feel as if we've waited this long, I can't wait another minute.

My need to climax rises with my rapid breathing. I scrape my nails along his back and he grips me harder with every firm thrust. The rhythm of his movements sends blissful awareness through my body, every nerve ending electric and pulsing.

"Come with me, baby. My sweet Rosa."

There's something about a man like Santo melting to gentleness that makes me yearn for him. My heart beats along in time to the tempo of his thrusts, until my head falls back and the Earth shatters into a million brilliant shards around me. Bliss floods my limbs in perfect time with his own hoarse breathing and hips melting into me. I come so hard I can't breathe, stars blinding my vision.

He curses in English and Italian, his words incomprehensible, prayers or curses or a mixture of both, until we lower back to Earth, panting and grasping each other as if we hold each other here with our frantic embraces.

"I love you, Rosa Rossi," he whispers in my ear, and I swear I hear pain in his voice when he whispers again, "and I'll love you until the day I draw my last breath on Earth."

His damp forehead meets mine. I barely trust my voice in this magical realm somewhere between heaven and Earth. I pant my own confession in the quiet stillness. "I love you, Santo. I love you. I always have, and always will."

We lay there in the darkness until our breathing slows and our damp skin cools. I shiver, but he still lays atop me, still in me, our bodies joined. He finally slumps onto an elbow but still keeps my fingers entwined in his.

As if releasing me will make the moment vanish forever. We stay like that until I'm half asleep, my eyes too heavy to hold open. We stay like that as if it's our last night on Earth, and tomorrow, we'll be torn apart forever.

"I love you," he says as he cleans me up and tucks me in, as if now that he's said it, he can't stop saying it.

"I love you," I whisper as my eyes flutter closed under the weight of sleep and he holds me to his chest.

"I love you," he says when he wakes in the middle of the night and holds me again, his movements frantic and hurried until his hands find mine in the dark. I breathe it in my dreams and when I wake, when the light finally peeks along the edge of the window, Santo's gone.

CHAPTER SEVENTEEN

Santo

FUCKING KILLED me to leave her.

Killed me.

But we both have reached the point from where there is no return.

Either we go our separate ways and hold the knowledge of who we are forever, and I uphold the vows that I took and make the ultimate sacrifice.

Or I break the vows I've taken and choose Rosa instead.

The choices are dismal and my options few. Either choice means turning my back on someone I love.

I told her I'd prove myself to the brotherhood, that I'd make them realize who I am. But with Romeo in jail and the knowledge of her betrothal imminent, I don't trust the outcome of any choice right now.

So at the first break of morning light, I extract myself from her with difficulty. When she stirs, I kiss her cheek and brush her hair back off her damp forehead. Her hair's a gleaming masterpiece, and I bend close so I can breathe her in. The simple scent of her's like an elixir I crave more and more.

I rest my hand on the top of her head, tracing the memory of her so no matter what happens, I hold her with me.

My eyes fall on the rose tat on my arm. A vivid reminder of the vows I've taken that mean everything.

I leave her sleeping deeply, and check on Natalia next. She's asleep as well, tucked up against her stuffed animals, a fluffy pink blanket tucked under her chin. I've always envied the way a child can sleep so undisturbed, without the worries of the world wearing them down. I kiss the curly top of her head, and tuck the blanket back around her shoulders.

I change into clean clothes in the guest room and check my messages.

TAVI: *Romeo gets out today. Flynt worked his magic. Meeting downstairs ASAP, all made men report to me ASAP*

. . .

FUCK.

On the one hand, we want Rome out. But the truth is, if Romeo's out that means whoever's been threatening our safety could act at any moment. They could feel as if their time is up. If I know Romeo, and I like to think I do, he'll come up with his fists swinging. Not that I fucking blame him at all.

And Romeo will want to move forward. Solidify his plan to wed Rosa to a Campanelle, because joining forces through marriage makes us nearly impenetrable.

I love Romeo like a brother and want him out of jail, but the small window of time we had is at an end.

With one final glance at Rosa and Natalia's closed doors, I know I have to let them be. I check in with the guard at the door, close it quietly, and head downstairs to check in with Tavi.

We meet in the war room with cups of espresso. Staff's brought platters of croissants and muffins, but none of us touch them. Tempers are taut. Everyone's on edge.

"Fill us in, Tav," Mario says. Mario's the only one who reaches for the platter of pastry and takes three large croissants onto a plate. He takes a big bite, flakes falling from his mouth like rain. "What's up?"

"Flynt called me early this morning, found a loophole in Romeo's arrest. Pulled some strings, will have him home this afternoon. It's all kept quiet, so no one knows yet, but as soon as word gets out..."

"We're fucked," Orlando finishes. Tavi nods.

"Bring it," Mario says. "I'm sick of fuckin' lying here waiting for the next goddamn attack."

"Agreed," Sergio says. He sips his espresso, black, before he continues, his dark brown eyes zoned in on Tavi. "You've done an impressive job keeping everyone safe here, Ottavio. None could fault you. But we aren't bred to be sitting ducks waiting for an attack. We always work better when we take the lead."

"Agreed," Timeo says, nodding. He cracks his knuckles, the picture of menace to anyone who isn't family.

Tavi nods, leans back in his chair, and puts his fingertips together. "We keep everyone on soft lockdown. We bring Romeo home today. We anticipate another move but scour everything we can until we find a lead, then we follow that lead like goddamn bloodhounds."

Ricco grins. "Now you're talkin', brother."

I stand, pacing, running my hands through my hair. We're on the verge of a battle, and my need to move makes it impossible to sit still.

"We secure every entrance but double the manpower, yeah?"

Tavi nods. "Yeah."

"How will you double manpower?" I ask.

"Got the Montavio men coming in," Sergio says.

"Tavi, you ain't gonna wanna hear this, but we need a thorough questioning of every fuckin' Regazza. You know I told you the truth, man. You know that."

"I do, brother."

"I'll question the Campanelles with Santo," Mario says.

Tavi looks at him sharply. "You know something I don't?"

"I know Santo's the most ruthless motherfucker we've got," he says with a grin. "And we'll drive a sweet ride to do the job."

"Perfect. Go."

When we leave a few minutes later, I'm satisfied that the Castle's safe. Montavio men, like bulldogs, man every entrance in conjunction with our own. Anyone who'd try to attack us now would have to be one stupid son of a bitch.

Tavi's gone with Orlando to pick up Romeo. Mario and I've gone to investigate the Campanelles in my Ferrari. Imported straight from Italy, it's my second favorite car, a sweet ride I'll enjoy taking into the heart of Boston.

But I have my suspicions, and as soon as we're free and clear on the highway, I kick up the speed and ask Mario a question.

"Another reason you wanted to investigate with me, brother?"

He gives me a shit-eating grin. "You know me too well, don't you?"

I nod and scrub a hand over my brow. "Let's have it."

"I scoured the footage we had with you the other day, and did it again when we were zooming in on whoever came onto our property the other day."

I nod, switch lanes, and accelerate. It's a cold fall day, so I don't roll the windows down. Leaves have begun to fall, heralding the approach of another cold New England winter. Still, I'd rather be here freezing my ass off than in warmer Tuscany.

"Saw some footage I think you'd better explain," he says.

I give Mario a sidelong glance. I'm not usually one to take a threat idly.

"I'd better?" I ask, even as I know it's probably better to take it from here myself, not rock the boat.

"Yeah, Santo. I ain't blackmailin' you, you know that. I'm not that fuckin' low."

"I know you aren't, but I also want you to come out and fuckin' say what you have to."

"I saw footage of you and Rosa."

A muscle ticks in my jaw. "What kind of footage?"

He blows out a breath. "You need me to get into detail, man?"

"I really do."

Nodding, he taps his fingers on his knees. "We installed another camera down by The Castle wall. I didn't see anything incriminating, Santo, but you and I both know she's betrothed to a fucking Campanelle."

I turn away and don't respond.

Fuck.

"And we further know that if what I saw on camera was right, you didn't touch her the way a goddamn brother does."

I don't reply. He isn't saying exactly what he saw, but I go over what we've done by The Castle wall. There were enough times I touched her, or said something in her ear, that it isn't worth getting fucked in my head over what he says.

There is no footage of her bedroom. No one knows I've gone way, way beyond anything that's been recorded.

"Why are you telling me this?" I ask him. My voice is a little hoarse. If Mario tells the others…

"Because you covered my ass so many fuckin' times, bro," he says. "And I know if you have any feelings for my sister, she'll never be safer." He blows out a breath. "And I *also* know that if Romeo, Tavi, or Orlando found out, your ass is fucked."

I don't respond at first, but when he doesn't continue, I urge him. "Go on."

"You got anything to say?"

I think about it.

"Rosa is promised to a Campanelle," I tell him. "I know this."

"Yeah, brother. But if you touch her, Santo— I mean, I know you guys have always been close, but if you cross that line…"

Already fucking crossed that line.

Over, and over, and over again.

I sigh. "I know."

"It ain't worth it, bro," he says softly. "I scrubbed those files so no one will ever see what you did. But you can't fuck this up. Romeo would kill you. I know he would. You remember…"

"I remember."

I know I can't fuck it up. I took a vow none of them even know about that prohibits me from touching her. I blow out a breath and nod.

"Break whatever the fuck it is off, Santo. You have to. I won't tell anyone. But if you don't..."

His voice trails off. He doesn't need to finish it.

"I hear you." I want him to know I'm listening, that I won't fuck this up. "Mario, The Family's everything to me," I say, even as my heart breaks at the thought of turning away from Rosa. "You know I'm loyal to the fucking core."

"I know that now, but there was a time I wondered, Santo," he says. It's rare Mario sobers, but when he does, we pay attention.

"I know. I won't hurt her, Mario, and I know she's promised to someone else."

IT'S rare Mario looks threatening. But it's a look on his face now. I know this is the concern not only of a made man of the Rossi family, but Rosa's brother. Mario is one of the gentler sort, he hates conflict, even though he is the best man to have at your back in a fight. So the stern look on his face gives me pause, and his assumption that Romeo would end my life confirms my own suspicions and fears.

"I would never hurt her, Mario."

"But you being with Rosa would hurt the family," Mario says, pointing out something that I feared from the very beginning. "Which is why I will not do anything with her. Which is why I will see Rosa married to someone else and not protest."

Mario gives one curt odd. "After we end this, our conversation never happened."

I've been given one extra life, like a cat's nine lives. I'm probably on my goddamn eighth.

"Then all I'm telling you is, be careful."

I nod soberly. I will be. I have to.

We pull up the long drive that takes us to our rivals' home.

"Jesus," Mario mutters under his breath. "Shit like this gives Italians a bad name."

Thick columns line the driveway topped with lions' paws carved in stone. Gold accents glitter at the lions' manes, and I wonder if it's real gold. Some people, like Romeo and the rest, are wealthy without flaunting it, although The Castle is barely a subtle home. Still, they like to travel, they like good possessions, they invest in their future and the future of their family.

But then some people? They flaunt it.

The Campanelles are definitely in the latter group.

A circular drive shows cars of every kind, custom deals. Teslas and Jaguars, BMWs and Ferraris, Aston

Martins and Porsches. Sports cars and luxury cars, vehicles of every type one could imagine. The home has a fountain out front, a garden fit for a king, and staff milling about doing yard work.

I roll up to an iron gate.

"May I help you, sir?" A uniformed guard speaks on a loudspeaker across from me.

"Here to see Carmine, please."

A pause, then, "And who are you, sir? Do you have an appointment?"

"Please tell him the Rossis need to speak to him, and we come in peace."

Muffled voices and a series of clicks. "He'll let us in," Mario says. "He never misses a chance to show the fuck off."

He's right. Half a minute later, we hear the squawk of the loudspeaker, followed by, "Come in, sir. Please leave your car with an attendant."

"Just do it," Mario breathes. "They'll sweep it for bombs and bugs."

"How do I know they don't put their own fuckin' shit in here?"

"You don't," he says with another grin, as if welcoming the Campanelles to bug us. "I'll handle it."

"So you're the brains behind this, and I'm—"

"The brawn, you sexy motherfucker."

"I am so gonna kick your ass when this is over."

"Aw, Santo, still hittin' on me? Touché."

Uniformed men walk to our car and bow when we exit. I hand the keys over with reluctance. "This car is like one of my own flesh and blood," I warn the guy. "You treat it that way."

"Yes, sir, of course, sir," he says with a nod.

We walk inside and Mario chuckles at me under his breath. "Come to Daddy, shiny car."

I grunt under my breath. I fuckin' mean it.

We're greeted by another rash of uniformed personnel welcoming us into the house. This shit's ostentatious as *fuck*. Gleaming marble floors, life-size paintings of every one of the Campanelles, a chandelier that hangs under a spotlight, casting diamond-like reflections on the floor below. The faint scent of expensive perfume hangs in the air. A minute later, I see why.

"My, my, Mama didn't tell me we have visitors," a pretty, feminine voice says from above us. We look up at the landing to see a stunning blonde in high heels, her skirt halfway up to her ass, walking down the stairs.

"Mamma mia," Mario mutters to himself. "Gonna have to go to confession after this shit."

"Behave yourself," I warn him.

"Fuckin' flirting with me again, eh?" he quips.

"And who do I have the pleasure of meeting today?" blondie asks with her head tipped curiously to the side. She extends a hand to me, her wrists covered in bangles, her nails pointy and red.

"Mario Rossi," Mario says warmly, turning on the charm. I swear she melts under the heat of that flirtatious look.

"Mario Rossi," she says to herself. "Now *where* have I heard that name before?" She thoughtfully taps her chin. "Ooh, you're not the one that drag races, are you?"

He gives her a boyish grin, and she wags her finger at him. "Bad boy, Mario, now I know you."

Turning to me, she gives me the full dazzle of her brilliant smile, but she doesn't even ping my radar. She's as fake as a three-dollar bill, and as cheap as a cardboard cutout. "And you?"

"Santo," I say, reaching my hand to her.

"So pleased to meet you, Santo," she says. I believe I see challenge in her eyes when I don't return her warmth or cordiality, like I'm a harder man to conquer which makes me that much more appealing to her.

Heavy footsteps sound down the hall. This place is much more modern than The Castle, but smaller. Hell, every house is smaller than The Castle.

"Well, well, well, if it ain't my future brother-in-law." A hefty guy in a suit lumbers toward us, large and intimidating, with beady black eyes that look oddly out of place, like beetles pinned to a card. He's dressed richly, and wears so much gold I'm fucking blinded. "And you are?" he asks.

"Name's Santo. Came to ask some questions."

"Ah, Santo." He strokes his chin. "Rumor has it you fell in with the Regazzas and betrayed your family. Surely that can't be true if Romeo's sent you to do his busywork?"

"Romeo's not with us," I tell him, probing to see if he knows. No flicker of surprise.

"Oh, right. Jail, was it?" He strokes his chin again. "Come, let's sit in my office and discuss why you're here."

It doesn't take long for us to get to his office, and when I arrive, I'm not surprised to see it's as opulent as the rest of the house. His men stand on each side of his door holding fucking machine guns like this is a military operation.

Goddammit. Maybe it is.

"Drinks, boys?"

"I'm good," I say. We both decline.

He folds his meaty, damp hands and gives me an oily smile.

"Now cut to the chase," he says. "You came here uninvited. Your Don is in jail. I've been asked to marry one of the Rossi women, and I've agreed to wipe your debt clean once she's mine."

I clench my hands under the edge of the desk, where no one can see them.

"We've been under attack, and we came to ask questions."

"Questions?" He tips his head to the side with a fake look of benign curiosity. "What sort of questions?"

"We found footage of one of your men drugging our guard dogs," Mario says in a cold, angry voice. "We know it was one of yours because of the hand tat."

"Not us," Carmine says with fake innocence. "We've been traveling abroad and just returned last week."

"So someone with Campanelle ink feigned allegiance to you and came to my house?" Mario asks. "You sure about that?"

"I'm sure," he says tightly. "Anything else I can help you with?"

Something isn't adding up. He's acting too innocent. He knows shit.

"Mario, Rosa's your sister, isn't she?" he says. "She's so pretty, she looks like a little Catholic schoolgirl." His grin turns sour. "Tell me, does she suck cock?" He grins when Mario's face goes red.

He knows exactly who we are, and he sent someone to our house.

"Don't fucking talk about my sister like that, bro," Mario warns. "Don't do it. We came here to have a casual conversation, real friendly-like, right? Shut up about my sister."

Carmine Campanelle… I remember his ruddy, puffy face. I remember what the Regazzas told me about him, too.

When Carmine sees Mario's reaction, he gets a snake-like look on his face. His eyes narrow. "She's no good to me if she ain't good in bed, Rossi. And I've waited a long, long time for this. I can't wait to spread her legs. I can't wait to take her back to my house and treat her like an Italian princess. I'm gonna truss that girl up—"

I'm over the desk before he finishes his sentence. I break his nose with the first swing of my fist. Mario hits the door and barricades it while I beat the shit out of Carmine.

I slam my fist against the side of his face, feeling bone break. He reaches for a button on the desk but with the blunt flat of my hand, I break his fingers.

"You came to our house, Campanelle. If it wasn't you, it was one of your fuckin' minions. We came here for answers, and you're giving them to us. Tell me why you sent someone there."

He shakes his head and tries to push me off, but I've got him in a death-like grip. "We're gonna scour your files and see what we find. Mario." I jerk my head at Carmine's phone. Mario grins and heads over.

"Don't you fucking—"

I slam my hand across his face so hard, his head snaps back and he whimpers. If this were Romeo, and someone attacked him in his office, they wouldn't have made it this far. Romeo's got better protection, and Romeo would wipe the floor with an attacker. This guy, though, has gone soft. Given too often to rich food and laziness in his premium imported leather chairs, getting those goddamn blow jobs he says he wants from Rosa, his body is soft and plush and easy to manipulate.

"Read it, Mario."

Mario scrolls down, scowling.

"Guy named Franco reported back last night. Says…" he scrolls down further. *"Motherfucker.* Sent a scout to get a layout of Rosa's room."

I lift Carmine up, slam my knee into his ribcage, and when his head comes down with a strangled cry, I slam his head on the desk, push it under my palm to hold him in place and call Rosa.

"Hello?"

"Baby, you okay?"

"Yes, Santo, I'm fine. Why?"

"No reason. I'll explain later. Stay close to your guards."

I hang up the phone before she says *I love you.* I can't have Mario hear that, even if it makes me crave her even more.

"We'll get Romeo on the phone with you. You see, Carmine, he's home today, Romeo."

Carmine's eyes go wide. It's news to him. "Couldn't hold him in as long as you'd planned, could you? Now this is what you're gonna do, boss. I'm gonna let you go. You're gonna wash your face and keep your fuckin' mouth clean. And you'll tell your family why you ain't marrying Rosa Rossi."

He shakes his head. I kick him again, grab him by the front of his shirt, and shake him hard. "You got our boss sent to jail. You trespassed on our property. You talked disrespectfully about Rosa Rossi." I curse under my breath. "You dirty motherfucker will keep out of our family or we go to war. And last I checked, Carmine," I say with a warning thread in my voice he'd better heed, "we've got three times the manpower you do, we own more property, and *you're* the motherfucker tappin' underage girls. That'd look real nice if you get yourself in jail, wouldn't it?" He wouldn't last a day, made man or not. I mentally thank the traitor Regazza for giving me a bargaining chip.

Mario straightens and heads for the door. "Thanks, man," he says. "Got the name we need and no need for a douchebag brother-in-law. Excellent."

The door slams behind us. We just threw a fucking grenade at the Campanelles.

CHAPTER EIGHTEEN

Rosa

BRIGHT SUNLIGHT POURED *into the large bay window where I dressed. The angels themselves couldn't have fashioned a more beautiful day. Birds tweet outside the windows, and Mama's set up the garden to look like a fairy wonderland.*

I stare at myself in the mirror and suppose from the outside I look pretty enough.

"Beautiful."

Santo's deep voice comes from the doorway but it's a mocking tone with a cold edge. I turn to him, dressed in bridal white.

"Didn't know you'd be here," I whisper.

"Why not?" he asks with a scowl. "Not see the Mafia Princess married to her Prince Charming?"

I turned away from him. It was too painful to listen to his taunts, and I knew it would make me cry.

"Go away. My makeup's been done, and I'll have to ask them to fix it if you make me cry."

I tried to sound aloof and detached, but my voice would *wobble at the end.*

"Go ahead. Cry. It won't do you any good now," he says. I look to see him take another long sip from his flask.

It was a morning wedding. He probably never even went to bed the night before. Still, he looked handsome as sin in his tux, a trail of ink showing at his neck.

"Go away, Santo, you're drunk."

Don't go. Stay here. Don't let this happen.

But those were the words that couldn't be said aloud.

He only took another sip and looked at me, bleary-eyed and unfocused. It broke my heart.

"He's a good man," I lied.

He shut the door behind me with a bang *that made me jump. Stalked to me. Placed his hands on my hips. The two of us stared ahead into the full-length mirror and captured each other's eyes. It was strange, staring into his eyes as he stood behind me.*

"He's a bastard."

I don't argue with him.

"You're beautiful, Rosa," he whispered. "So damn beautiful. You're an angel straight from heaven."

The tenderness in his voice almost broke me.

If we were caught now, the consequences would bring my whole family to ruin. Anthony Mercadio would rant and rave and demand repayment in some terrible form from Romeo. And Papa... I couldn't even bear to think what Papa would do.

To me.

To Santo.

I'd be beaten and locked up.

Santo would be killed.

"Santo..."

My voice was choked when he gently brought his lips to my neck and kissed me. My eyelids fluttered closed, and I stifled a cry.

"No, Santo. No," I said, but it was a weak plea for him to stop.

But stop he did.

He pulled away from me at the sound of high heels clicking in the hallway. Louder. Coming closer.

"Go ahead," he whispered in my ear. "Take the son of a bitch's name. Wear his ring. Say those vows." He released me and stood apart as the heels clicked louder.

I braced myself for scathing parting words, for him to call me a liar, for anything but what he did.

"If he hurts you, I'll kill him," he said softly. "Painfully and slowly." He took another swig of whiskey and his eyes shone with tears when he said, "He doesn't deserve a woman like you. Fuck it, no one does."

The door between rooms clicked shut as he left, as the door to my dressing room opened for Mama.

"Aw, sweetheart," Mama said gently. "It's normal to cry on your wedding day."

SANTO CAME to me before he left.

He gestured for me to go into the room, pushed me in, and kissed me.

It was a kiss that knocked me off my feet and told me he loved me. I felt that kiss travel from my lips to every fiber of my being, warming me from the inside out.

But it was a kiss with a flavor of farewell. And I don't… like to think I'm a superstitious person, but my mind travels back to the horoscope Marialena read on her birthday. The sense of foreboding I felt even then.

Santo kissed me because he knew something was going to happen, like a solider about to take his position on the front line of battle.

I doubt he felt he was going into dangerous territory so much as he felt something threaten the stability of… of *us.*

I've spent the day doing the usual things. I played with Natalia, and we bought a few more dresses online. Sometimes retail therapy helps, sometimes it doesn't.

It didn't help me today, but it cheered Natalia up.

I went over the incoming inventory lists with Elise and picked out some sweet little baby gifts to buy for Elise and Tavi.

I played with Angelina and the baby, and helped Mama cook the hugest batch of marinara I've ever seen, then convinced Nonna to make not one but *two* batches of her biscotti so we'd avoid Rossi Family World War III.

I gave myself a manicure and read a few chapters of a book, but my focus was elsewhere. From the courtyard window, I looked out to where Santo's car was supposed to be. He took the Ferrari. I wonder why.

I texted him on the private phones we have that aren't regulated with security measures, then, when I noticed Vittoria pacing nervously around the house, poured the girl a cup of spiced coffee and binge-watched HGTV. We managed to conclude that updating the mansion would be a full season of updates all on its own.

I waited.

And I waited.

And I waited.

"Where's Natalia?" I asked Mama after lunch.

"She went to Marialena's room," Mama said absently, checking on her marinara. She tastes it, frowns, and adds more salt.

I feel tired. Bone tired.

When I hear the crunch of tires on gravel, I stop myself from running to the door to greet them.

But it isn't Santo and Mario. It's Romeo, with Orlando and Tavi.

Don't get me wrong, I'm not *unhappy* to see Romeo. Mama and Nonna burst into tears and hug him, dampening his charcoal gray suit. He comes to me and gives me a bear-hug when he finally escapes their grip.

"How've you been, sister?" he asks.

Oh, Romeo. My eyes water with tears. I want to tell him everything. I want to plead with him on Santo's behalf. But even though Romeo loves us, I've seen how his loyalty to the family trounces all.

And I won't do that to him. I can't.

I also know that I couldn't do that to Santo without talking to him first.

So I do what I've done for decades when it comes to my true feelings.

I lie.

I smile through tears and swipe at them impatiently. "Just so happy to have you home, Romeo."

He kisses my cheek and holds me to him. I give myself one minute, just one minute to *breathe.* To exhale and be held by my brother. I may be the older sibling, but he's been the head of this house so long, it almost feels as if he's the older one sometimes.

It feels good to be held for that one moment in time.

Then I release him and give him to his wife.

"Your wife has been the very picture of grace and dignity during your absence, I'll have you know."

Vittoria laughs. "If you call eating cookie dough straight out of the freezer graceful and dignified, then I guess I'll take that as a compliment."

"Oh, that's so forgivable it's barely sinful," I say with a smile. "Romeo, do we know who's behind it?"

"I think so," he says with a frown. "But not now, Rosa." He looks around and sees the Montavio cousins for the first time. "My God, now this is a welcome party," he says.

Sergio claps him on the back, Ricco gives him a bear-hug, and Timeo fist-bumps him. "Tavi called us in, Rome," he says. "And you'll have us with you for as long as you need us."

Romeo thanks him, greets the others, and welcomes Dario, as I hear Santo's car pull up to the top of the drive. The door slams hard. His feet hit the ground and they're running.

"Shit," Tavi says, as the door opens and Santo and Mario come in.

"Romeo," Santo says, ignoring everyone else in the room. "We have to fucking talk, and now."

Romeo nods. "You two safe?"

"For now," Mario says.

"Good," Romeo says.

Frowning, he looks around the room. "Where's Marialena?"

Mama's on her feet. Mario whips out his phone.

"Who saw her last?" Tavi asks. He tries to hide the panic in his voice, but we can all tell he's concerned.

"She was with me this morning," Vittoria says, paling. "Isn't she just upstairs?"

But after some phone calls and a thorough search, she's nowhere to be found.

I look to Santo. He sees the panic in my eyes and he's at my side in two steps.

"We'll find her."

"Santo," I whisper, my voice choked. I open my mouth to speak, but I'm too frozen in fear to make the words come. The gentlest touch on my lower back and I open my mouth.

"Natalia was with her."

Vittoria shakes her head. "Oh my God. I'm so sorry. What if she… is she okay?"

My skin prickles and my body goes cold. I reach for my phone, and try to still my trembling hand. With shaking fingers, I text Marialena.

Hey. Where are you?

Nothing.

I call her, but it only goes to voice mail.

"Jesus," Tavi mutters under his breath. "Mario, call her guard." He spins and looks to Orlando. "Check security footage, see if you find anything." He curses under his breath.

Dario is the one who takes the lead. He pulls out his gun and checks the ammunition. "Anyone check surveillance?"

"I will," Mario says, but before he leaves, he makes a call. He shakes his head. Then makes another. And another.

No.

No.

Not my baby sister. Not my *baby,* not Natalia, my little one who is everything to me. And Marialena's the light of our lives, the North Star in a world of dark. I might be sometimes cold and even cruel as a method of self-protection, but I love them. I pace the room. I can't think about them being hurt.

I can't think about it.

"Can't get her fucking guard," Mario mutters. "Jesus."

Santo's jaw tightens. I know he wants to go out to search for her. He doesn't like sitting around waiting, making phone calls. He likes to see things for himself, to control the outcome.

I text her again.

And again.

And again.

"Take me with you," I whisper to Santo. "Take me with you to find them."

He turns furious, cold eyes to mine. "Are you out of your fucking mind?"

"I know Marialena," I tell him. "I know how to find her. I know where she'd hide."

My phone buzzes. I lift it up to see one text from Marialena. My heart thunders.

"She texted me!" I scream, my voice shaky but loud enough to catch everyone's attention.

I hit the text.

Marialena: Rosa. Help.

I fall to the chair, my knees giving way.

Me: Where are you? Are you okay? Marialena, where are you?

No response.

"No answer. She isn't answering," I say, as a panicked well of fear presses on my throat. I can't breathe. "She won't answer."

"Track her phone," Tavi shouts. And this is why the man's Underboss. He keeps his head when the shit hits the fan. "If she texted, she's got it. She's got her phone. Someone check her goddamn phone."

Santo's already got it pulled up on his.

"Tracking's off." He swivels to Vittoria. "You said she was outside?"

Gun at the ready, Santo yanks the front door open and races out.

I follow, determined, and the others come with me.

"We'll scour the grounds," Santo says. "No one could've taken her without our knowledge. They're here, somewhere on the grounds. Fuckers must've kept someone hidden where we didn't see. Came out when we left."

His phone rings. Mario.

"Yeah? *Fuck.*"

My brothers and cousins pour out of the house.

"What is it?" Tavi asks Santo.

Santo shakes his head. "Mario says the surveillance cameras were off."

"Fuck," Tavi says. "How the fuck did that happen?"

By the grim look on Santo's face, I suspect he knows more than he's letting on right now.

I text Marialena again for the hell of it, when it suddenly dawns on me that I don't hear the dogs. Goddamn it.

"Santo, the dogs. Where are the dogs?"

He doesn't answer but paces past the fence. I lean against the cold metal of the chain-link and listen. The dogs are always here, but if they're not here…

Romeo steps in front of me. His deep barrel of a voice resonates over the grounds as he calls the dogs.

Everyone goes quiet. Far in the distance we hear the rough rasp of a dog's growl.

"By the wall," I whisper. "By the wall?"

I run faster than anyone else. My daughter. My sister… my sister and daughter are in danger. My heart beats so fast I'm nauseous. My shoe, my *stupid* designer shoe, catches on a rock, and I start to go sprawling. But I don't fall. Santo runs beside me, and he catches me before I crash.

"You okay?" he asks gruffly.

I nod, shaking, and for half a second I wish he'd swing me up in those big arms of his and take me with him. But I'm not a wilting wallflower. I'm not now and never have been.

I kick off my shoes, begin to slide, then lean into the steep descent of the hill to get to our favorite spot. My spot and Santo's.

Marialena's protecting Natalia with her body, pressing her up against the wall in front of them. A man I don't recognize holds a leash with the dogs only inches from the girls. They're salivating, chomping, and Natalia screams.

I don't think. I grab my heel and whip it as hard as I can at the dogs. I miss by a yard, but Santo's faster than I am. With a roar that makes my hair stand on edge, he orders the dogs to stand down and launches himself at the man.

A solid slam of Santo's fist connects to his jaw. It snaps back and he howls as Santo sweeps his leg and sends him hurtling forward. I knew Santo was ruthless, but I've never seen him fight like this.

There's a *blast* of a gun and screams. Someone tackles me to the ground and pins me. I claw at him, but he doesn't move. "Stay down," he orders. Dirt blurs my vision. "Get him!" yells the man above me.

I shove him off. "Stay fucking there!" Dario growls at me. He reaches for my arm, but I pull away. Santo.

No.

No.

Santo lies slumped over. The dogs lick his pale, lifeless face as my brothers and cousins swarm like a pack of rabid beasts.

CHAPTER NINETEEN

Rosa

TIME MOVES SLOWER when you're pacing at death's door.

Breath grows shallow when you're breathing your last.

Hope begins to flicker as the evening vigil wanes.

Romeo let me and Mama go with them to the hospital. Several others—namely the Montavio cousins and our newest recruit, Dario—stay behind to secure our hostage and check on Marialena.

I take Natalia with me to the hospital. I can't bear to be apart from her. Marialena stays home under a doctor's watchful eye.

“Mama,” Natalia says, her little voice shaky in the cold waiting room. “Will Uncle Santo die?”

I close my eyes. I can’t bear to think of it, but I know it could happen. I shake my head and don’t respond at first. I can’t.

I don’t know the answer this time, and it feels so wrong to lie about it.

“Pray, honey,” I whisper to her, because I don’t know what else to say. My family may be invested in terrible things, and I may have done grave things for which there is no forgiveness. But the childhood memory of kneeling in church resurfaces with a vengeance when I’m staring at the brink of the death of the man I love.

The only man I ever have, and we never even got to love freely. I never got to give him the full measure of my love for him. It isn’t fair. It isn’t *right.*

I’m not surprised to see Nonna, dressed in her signature black and grasping her faded rosary beads, sitting on a folding chair in a corner of the room. Her eyes are closed but she isn’t asleep. I can tell by the way her lips move in recitation of prayer.

Finally, *finally,* the doctor comes out. He sees all of us sprawled like someone’s let loose a passel of overgrown teens from a late-night party. My high heels, long since kicked off, dangle helplessly from my fingers by their straps. Romeo’s collar’s undone, Tavi’s face is drawn, and Mario paces in front of the vending machines, buying Natalia candy that sits untouched on a table in front of us.

"Who... do I speak to?" he says gravely. The doctor's a serious sort of man with a bushy gray moustache and a neatly trimmed beard, his scrubs wrinkled from a long night's work.

Romeo stands and extends his hand while I slip my shoes back on. "Romeo Rossi."

The doctor bows his head and speaks in a hushed tone to Romeo. "I'm sorry to tell you this," he whispers, his eyes furtively moving around the room. "Mr. Rossi. We did everything we could..."

I stand, wobbling. I feel as if a cold chill was just sent down my spine. Santo... my Santo... I feel as if I could handle literally anything but... but *that.*

It can't be. I won't believe it, I can't. Not my Santo.

Romeo sinks to the floor and covers his face with his hands. I go to him and put my hands on his shoulders. One broad hand covers mine as Romeo weeps.

"Doctor Follet. Doctor!" A frantic nurse rushes into the room, her cheeks flushed. "He's awake, Doctor. Come quick!"

Romeo and I stare, open-mouthed, as the doctor turns on his heel and runs.

I can hardly handle the abruptness of it all, feeling as if I've been doused in a bath of ice water then set to tumble dry on high. I blink and stare before I remember who I am.

I am Rosa Rossi. I am the eldest of this family. I've buried one husband and am raising a child. I've guided and cared for every one of my siblings and been the best daughter, mother, and lover I know how to be.

And I belong to Santo, my fearless Santo.

I square my shoulders and leave the others behind. I don't care what anyone thinks. I follow Romeo down the hall.

Wordlessly, he takes my hand and gives me a little squeeze. "Stay strong," Rome says. "We have to stay strong, sister."

I nod.

"Never buried a brother before," he begins.

"And we won't start now," I finish.

Romeo gives me a sad smile.

But when we reach the room, they won't let us in. Two male nurses block our entrance and shake their heads. "No, sir. No one can come in now. You must—"

Apparently Romeo doesn't much care that he was just released from prison. In one swift, fluid movement, he draws his gun. "Let me in there. I won't cause any harm, unless you keep us out."

The first nurse holds his hands up in the air, stepping back, and the second nurse talks to him in a whispered voice. I catch *Rossi family, mob, stand back.*

"That was a bit over-the-top, Romeo," I chide, but he ignores me, pushes the door open, and gestures politely for me to enter, as if he's taking me to dinner. The gun is nowhere to be seen now.

We enter the room but stand out of the way as doctors and nurses do their work. Lights flash and machines beep. Santo has so many tubes and wires I can hardly see him, but I focus on his chest. It heaves in and out, up and down.

He lives.

I turn my head to Romeo and bury my face in his shoulder, stifling the sob that comes hard and fast.

"He's alive," I whisper to Romeo.

"Thank fuck," Romeo says in a hoarse whisper.

After a lengthy wait, while my heart beats fast and my palms grow sweaty, I utter silent prayers.

Just let him be okay.

I will let him go.

I won't ask for anything else, if you just let him live.

I will walk away and never look back. I will live the rest of my life alone, if only Santo will live, if only he can get another chance at life. He deserves this. If anyone deserves another chance, it's Santo.

"Mr. Rossi." The doctor walks to Romeo, shaking his head, and finally gestures for us to come closer.

We walk tentatively, as if we walk too fast we'll harm Santo. Santo's eyes are closed and his breathing's shallow, but he lives.

"He rallied, sir. I've never seen anything like it," the doctor begins, but I'm not there, I'm not listening. I made a promise that if he lived, I'd walk away.

I'd give him back.

He was never mine to begin with. He should be free.

Free from the demons that plague him, free from stifling expectations and ungodly demands, free from the tortured conflict of hiding his feelings for me from the others.

I love Santo, and true love means letting him go.

So there in the hospital room, while words I barely comprehend float in the space between death and life, words like *coma, near-death,* and *very low expectations of recovery,* I give Santo back. I love him enough to detach myself from any selfish motive.

I sit by his bed and hold his hand.

CHAPTER TWENTY

Rosa

SANTO LIES in a coma for three days.

But he breathes.

They are the hardest, most painful days of my entire life. Every second that passes seems like it lasts an eternity. My mind's a chasm of silence, and I can barely put two thoughts together.

It hurts to breathe. It hurts to blink. I can't eat or sleep.

For three days, I steel myself against whatever will happen next. If I'm married off or he is, if he survives and wants me for his own… I'll tell him no. I have to.

I've made a promise and I'll keep that promise.

I keep my vigil like a sister would, holding his hand and talking to him through it all. Natalia visits and thanks him for saving her. She tells Santo she's sad Uncle Romeo got rid of the dogs, but she understands why.

I watch his chest rise and fall. I watch the beeping monitors and see the quiet nurses walk in and out between armed guards in the hallway. Police prowl the hall, but at a word from Romeo, they quietly disappear. Sometimes I forget how much power my brother wields. He holds the lives of so many in his hands.

The entire time Santo's under, unaware of who's with him or what's going on around him, I detach myself from his heart. I tell myself it's in his best interest, that I can't and won't allow myself to be selfish. Selfish me wants Santo to myself. But I know the devastation that would bring to our family. Selfish me wants to confront Romeo and tell him the truth, but I know it's the last thing The Family needs right now.

The last thing *I* need.

I almost lost him. I won't do it again, and definitely not by my hand.

Mama visits and talks to him through the stillness. Nonna visits and prays over him. Father Richard visits, as does every man of the brotherhood. Marialena wrings her hands and whispers prayers and tells me he'll be okay.

It's hard not to break down. It's hard not to cry and hold him, to grieve what could've been and reveal how I truly feel. I have to stay strong. For him. For the family. For all of us.

On the fourth day, he opens his eyes. At first, he doesn't see me, staring ahead in the darkened room. I reach for his hand and give him a gentle squeeze, but the lump in my throat makes it difficult to talk.

"Hey," I finally say.

And when he swings his gaze to mine, he finally looks… alive. Thankful we're alone, I bury my face beside him and weep.

For the loss of everything that could've been.

For the near loss of the only man I've ever loved.

For the way I've been detached and misleading, for anything I've ever done that's hurt this good, loyal, fearless man.

For the road of recovery he has ahead of him and the knowledge that I'll only be with him as a sister.

I weep for who we were and who we'll have to be next.

He rests his hand on the nape of my neck reassuringly. "Baby," he says softly, his voice hoarse and almost painful to hear. "Rosa. Shh, baby. It's all gonna be alright."

I only cry harder because I wish I could believe it to be true.

CHAPTER TWENTY-ONE

Santo

I STARE out the window at the churning sea and sit up. I stifle a groan.

Jesus, I forgot how much it hurts to recover from a gunshot wound. Bullet tore through my chest and caused damage to my lungs but missed my heart. Could've been fatal.

"Dodged a bullet," Mario quips when I finally get back home to The Castle for our in-house doc to tend to me.

"When I get outta this bed I'm gonna kick your ass for that," I tell him.

"I look forward to it," he says with a grin.

They did an X-ray and an ultrasound to assess the damage and proclaimed me "lucky." Blood test showed no infection and proper kidney function, and an endoscopy showed no further internal damage.

The bronchoscopy was a bitch of a test, but thankfully no damage to the lungs that's irreparable. I'm told they almost lost me that first night. I don't remember much of anything.

They did surgery the first night and again the second. I have a vague memory of Rosa and Romeo, but they felt distanced and worried. I couldn't open my eyes, but I heard their voices. And I felt Rosa with me.

It was the fourth day when I could finally open my eyes, and the eighth day they reluctantly sent me home.

Romeo can be persuasive.

And our doctor at The Castle knows his shit.

"You're lucky, Santo," the doctor says to me when I wake after being transported home. "You're damn lucky."

My entire body's on fire with pain, and breathing hurts. I can whisper to talk but not much else. I don't feel that lucky, but I can draw breath. That's what fucking matters right now.

"They gave you a tetanus shot, and you got a blood transfusion," he explains. "Almost needed an endotracheal tube but you're stubborn. You breathed on your own and didn't need help from a respirator."

I don't want help from anyone. I'll do whatever shit I can on my own to get better.

"They did surgery to repair damage, to clean the wound, and retrieve the bullet," the doctor explains. "But found it was a clean entry and you're remarkably unharmed."

I wonder what *harmed* would feel like. *Unharmed* feels like fucking shit.

Still, I'm thankful.

I nod and don't reply. It hurts to talk.

"You'll have to follow my instructions for recovery," he continues.

"No sex for a month and you can't smoke or drink," Mario says from across the room.

"Can I kick his ass?" I ask the doc.

"Four more weeks before you do any ass kicking."

"Better watch your back, motherfucker. Long time to plan strategy," I tell Mario. My voice sounds like it's been dragged through hell and back.

"You'll do the breathing exercises illustrated here," he says, waving a white sheet of paper at me and placing it on the bedside table. "Once you're able to get up and about, you'll walk two or three times a day. This will prevent clotting and help you heal, but it'll be painful."

Pain can be fucked. I'll do it.

"No lifting anything heavy and Mario's right about one thing, do nothing that will cause physical stress for the first three weeks. Do what you can to sleep comfortably. No lying on your belly while the injury heals. Sleep with your head propped up to aid with better breathing. My assistant will be in here three times a day for dressing changes and wound care, and you'll take sponge baths during that time."

"Sounds fantastic," I lie. "Thanks."

He pats my hand. "You came out of this alive, Santo. We're all thankful. Now we gotta keep you alive."

I nod. "Yeah. Sounds like a good idea."

He gives me a heavy dose of painkillers, then leaves me to my brothers, who surround me like worried little hens.

"You guys are practically fuckin' clucking," I mutter, and close my eyes. They feel so heavy.

Romeo chuckles. "Worth it," he says.

My eyes fly open. "Jesus, I forgot you were out. God, what have I missed?"

"A lot," Romeo says with a sad smile. He shares a look with Orlando and Tavi. "But you gotta rest for now. It's best for you."

I nod and don't move. I want to know where Rosa is, if I can see her, but I won't risk revealing anything. Not now, when I need to make sure she's secure.

"Natalia?" I ask. "She okay?"

"Marialena and Natalia are fine, thanks to you," Romeo says. He sits at the side of my bed and leans forward, his elbows on his knees and fingertips pressed together. "You took a gunshot from the Campanelle camper," he says. "I'll explain it all later. Campanelles made a deal with the Regazzas, but the Regazzas ratted them out."

Tavi speaks up. "Elise had a word with a cousin, who came to her. Won't tell us his name, but says he knows what they're planning and it's an inside job for them. They never forgave you for killing one of their own, Santo, but Romeo's making them an offer they can't refuse."

I don't ask what the offer is. I don't wanna know.

"The dogs?" I ask next.

Romeo sighs. "We surrendered them to our family in Tuscany. They're thriving there. No children, only made men there, so it's better for them to be there."

"Sorry, Romeo," I mutter. It hurts to talk.

"No worries, brother," he replies. "They were like pets, but I don't trust them after they've been tampered with and bribed. It ain't right."

I nod. It hurts to even do that. "I get it."

"We made it brutally clear to the Campanelles that we won't suffer another attack," Mario says. "They swear they had nothing to do with it, but we know the man who shot you was associated with them on the periphery. We ain't fucking around with this."

I barely listen. I know Romeo's right, if anyone's a threat to us we have to end that and *soon.* But it seems we've maybe ousted the threat to us thus far.

"Seems you paid a visit to Carmine?" Romeo asks.

I open one eye and nod. "Yeah, we did."

"Good work," he says with a curt nod. "I'm confident we'd get a further attack from them if you hadn't put the fear of God in him."

"Put the fear of something in them," I mutter. "Not sure if it was God."

Romeo's eyes glint at me with the hint of a smile.

It isn't until the sun begins to set that the door to my room opens, and I see her eyes cast in darkness.

"Rosa," I say, my voice a hoarse croak.

She rushes to me, sits by the side of the bed, and gingerly puts her head next to mine on the pillow.

"I don't want to hurt you," she whispers. "I can't, Santo."

I reach my hand to her hair and stroke her gently. "I'm getting better. I'll get over this bullshit."

"I thought we lost you," she says, shaking her head. "We thought you were gone."

I gently stroke her hair and don't speak for long minutes.

Romeo is home and the threat against us has been silenced for now. Laughter comes from down the hall, and I look at her curiously. "What's that all about?"

"We've had a lot of visitors recently," she explains. "Sassy's here with Marialena, Nonna's sister came from Italy, and Mama has been cooking all day long."

My stomach growls. "Damn, I'm hungry."

"I'll get you food," Rosa says, rising, but I tug her back down.

"I want you here more than I want food."

"Santo…" She bites her lip, and her voice trails off.

Something's wrong.

"What is it?" I ask.

When she doesn't answer, I tighten my grip. "Rosa," I warn.

"Romeo says I was engaged to a Campanelle. He's called off the wedding, for obvious reasons, but… Santo, you know we have to… end this." A lone tear trails down her cheek. "I gave you back in the hospital. I made a promise to God that if you lived

I'd never ask for another thing, that I wouldn't pursue anything. That I'd… I'd let you be free."

Being apart from her isn't freedom.

I don't respond.

I have to talk to Romeo.

"I'm moving to Tuscany," she says finally. "Romeo says he's strengthening the family now that we have the Montavios and Dario with us. I asked if I could go back to Tuscany and he said yes. He has… he has someone in Tuscany he wants me to marry."

Again, I don't respond. I hear her pleas, I hear her cries, and they echo my own fears. I've thought for years there's no future for me and Rosa. How could there be?

"When do you leave?" I ask.

She grimaces and looks away. "That's it? When do I leave? That's all you want to know?"

I squeeze her fingers and she looks back to me.

"Tell me."

"Day after tomorrow," she whispers. "It's for the best."

People use that line so often it almost ceases to have meaning.

It's for the best.

Voices sound outside along with heavy footsteps. She stands and moves to the side so we're not touching. The footsteps fade.

"See? I'm tired of waiting," she says with a cry. "I'm tired of hiding. You don't deserve it any more than I do. You lived, Santo, and I promised if you did, I'd let you go."

Still, I don't reply. She's afraid, and she doesn't know what I do. She will soon.

"Come here," I order. My voice is hoarse, and my body weakened, but she hears the command in my voice. When she reaches the bed, I take her hand. "I didn't live so we could go our separate ways. Trust me, Rosa. Can you trust me?"

Her voice is soft and hollow when she nods and whispers, "Of course. I always have and always will."

"Then go, Rosa. Do what you have to. Let me do what I have to." I squeeze her hand. "But don't lose hope, baby. Don't."

She gives me a look that says she wishes she could believe me. I know that look. I know that feeling. When you've been beaten down and hurt so many times, you fear trusting again. You fear the next blow to your heart will shatter it irreparably.

But I have a plan, and I'll show her what I have in mind.

I have no other choice at this point. The only other choice is to give her up, and that's not something I'm willing to do. I fought death and lived to tell about it and might face it again, but I'm beyond the point of caring. I love this woman with everything I have. *Everything.*

And if they fault me for that, they aren't who I think they are.

I lift my cell phone and make a call. Romeo answers on the second ring.

"Jesus, brother," he says. "Like getting a call from death's door."

I can't help but snort. "Death's door says we need to talk. Tomorrow morning, war room."

"Got it."

Rosa's brows rise in surprise. "Did you just tell Romeo what to do?"

I shrug, then wince. Damn, forgot how much that hurt. "What if I did?"

"Getting bold, Santo," she says with a sad smile.

"I almost died, babe," I say softly. "I don't fucking care anymore. Now help a guy outta bed, will you?"

"You supposed to get out of bed?" she asks warily.

"If I'm gonna do what I have to, it's the only way."

She still looks nervous, but takes my hand none-theless. I brace myself on her shoulders and push myself to standing. Pain radiates from damn near *everywhere,* but I push through it. I grit my teeth and breathe more rapidly, rising above the pain. Welcoming it. I imagine I'm being hammered in fire, refined and perfected through the pain of it all.

I wasn't raised to be a fucking wimp, and I won't start now.

"Go," I tell Rosa. "I'm gonna shower. Get myself out of bed. Don't give anyone a reason to suspect why you're here so much, and join us in the Great Hall tomorrow morning, got it?"

"Santo…" her voice trails off and she shakes her head. "Santo, I…"

"Rosa." I pull her to me and grip her waist for support. It takes all the energy I have. "I've never needed you to trust me so much in my life. It's crucial."

"But Santo, you heard what I said—"

"I heard what you said, and I did what I had to, yeah. I'll do what I have to, yet. But for now, I need you to go, and I need you to do what I said."

She squirms uncomfortably, as if nervous to let me go. I fix her with a stern glare.

"And if you don't, when I'm better enough to swing my arm, your ass feels my palm, woman."

She bites her lip and heeds the warning. "Alright, alright," she says. "Going." But before she leaves, she lifts her head to mine and kisses my cheek. "God, a girl doesn't know how bad she misses bossy until he's back."

"And a girl doesn't know how bad she needs to be dominated until she's splayed out beneath her man, ass bright red and welted, under his total command."

"Oooh," she breathes with wide eyes. "If you need me, call me."

"I will."

I give her a chaste kiss on the lips and send her on her way. I'm not gonna call her, not tonight. I have to do what I've planned.

The next morning is a bright, sunny morning that gives me hope. I don't believe in omens, and I don't believe in good luck. I believe people either work their asses off to get what they want, or they don't. And I also believe I have the choice to be the person that does.

The calls I make are painful. It's a matter of signing away a part of who I am to become the person I'm meant to be. Rosa will cry when she learns the truth, but I have to do it.

I have to.

The deals go faster than I expect, thanks to the Montavios and a few other connections I have.

When the clock strikes eight, I rise and ignore the flare of pain along my side and belly. I toss a few more painkillers back and swig them down. Marialena hooked me up with the good stuff, the little brat.

I'm thankful.

I head downstairs and hear stifled gasps of surprise from the local guards.

I ain't supposed to be out of bed yet, but I've got shit to do.

Everyone's in the Great Hall, and I mean *everyone.* Sergio and Ricco and Timeo, chatting with Mama and Nonna. Romeo and Vittoria, Orlando and Angelina, Marialena and Mario with Natalia and Rosa. I feel her eyes come to me, but I don't look back. I need her to stay strong.

Nonna hugs me and Mama plies me with food, fresh-squeezed orange juice, and coffee, but I don't eat much of anything. My nerves are on fire, adrenaline coursing through me.

"We're going shopping today," Sassy tells me with a grin.

"The hell you are," Dario says, fixing her with a look that tells me he means business. "You talk to Romeo about that first?"

"Jesus," Marialena mutters. "Read my cards last night and read something about a beast of a man thinking he can boss me around, but I burned those cards." She gets in his face.

Well, then. I haven't seen her this fired up in a while. Sergio eyes them thoughtfully and pours cream into a little cup then splashes hot espresso in it.

"Marialena reminds me of my sister," he says to Dario. "Feisty as fuck and into all that Tarot shit."

"Uh, *hello!*" Marialena says. "I'm standing right here?"

Dario shakes his head. "Romeo's put me in charge of security for you two, and there ain't no way you're sashaying your asses into town to do something as stupid and pointless as shopping." He takes another cup of coffee from the staff.

"He didn't," Marialena says with her hands fisted. "If you're lying to me—"

"What're you gonna do?" Dario asks, a teasing smile on his face. He gives a fake shiver. "I'm so scared."

Her jaw drops open in wide-eyed shock. "You —you—"

Sassy rolls her eyes. "Whatever, sis," she says. "We'll talk to Romeo. I made him cookies, and he's always liked me."

Dario smirks and drinks his coffee.

"Tell me about that sister of yours," Dario says to Sergio.

I shake my head. Tempers flare and feelings abound in the Great Hall. It's good to be fucking back.

Mario eyes me from a table at the far end of the room, nursing a cup of coffee. He crooks a finger at me. I walk to him, though it hurts to do it.

"Yeah, brother, what is it?"

"You got that look in your eye," he says. "Like the one you get before a hit, or before you buy a car, or whatever the fuck hair-brained bullshit you're planning next. You gonna rock a fuckin' boat, aren't you?"

I shrug but don't respond.

"Jesus," Mario mutters. "Give a guy one damn chance at life again and he loses his goddamn sense."

"You oughta talk."

At least I'll have one brother who's got my back. I hope, anyway.

When Romeo stands, the inner sanctum stands alongside him. Tavi and Orlando, me and Mario. Romeo gestures for all made men to follow him, talks low in Vittoria's ear.

At the last minute, I change my mind.

No. I don't want to do this in front of the inner sanctum. I want to do this in front of everyone.

I shake my head at Romeo. "Let's chat here, where everyone can be present."

Rosa eyes me and her fingers travel to her neck. She fingers a thin band of gold. I do a double-take and look closer. Goddamn, I didn't know she still had that necklace. I gave it to her when I turned eighteen. Worked all summer to buy it, told her to take it back to college with her. She wore it until she married, and I assumed she'd lost it.

Solid gold, entwined around the most vulnerable part of her body where her lifeblood pulses. I feel the meaning in my core.

I draw in a breath and release it slowly. Stand and clear my throat. Soon, the room begins to quiet and finally all eyes are on me.

But I look at Romeo when I'm talking. He sits beside Vittoria. Pretty unlikely he'll pull a gun on me while his wife is watching, though he could drag my ass to the dungeon, and it wouldn't take long.

"I've got something to say."

"No shit," Mario mutters, but Tavi's stern look silences him. I flip him the bird sideways so the ladies don't see and he grins back at me.

Romeo's eyes are like lasers on me. I meet his gaze head-on.

"Rosa told me the plans you have for her. To send her to Tuscany and marry her off. And I want everyone here to know, I object."

The room is as silent as it could be. Even the staff's frozen in place, as if waiting for the other shoe to drop.

Romeo says nothing.

I clear my throat and look to Rosa. This might be the last thing I ever say but goddamn, I'll die happy knowing I said it.

"I love your sister. I've loved Rosa since before I knew what love even was. Rosa isn't marrying anyone in Tuscany, Romeo. And if that means my life is forfeit for defying your decision, then I stand before you all now, and I'm here to tell you, I'll lay down my life before that happens."

A muscle jerks in Romeo's jaw. Orlando's on his feet. Tavi stares with wide eyes. Mario pulls out a flask and tips it into his cup. Sergio's eyes dance at me, and Rosa's quietly crying.

"Go on," Romeo says, as he takes another sip of espresso. "This was worth jail time to hear."

Mama stands and her voice wavers. "Romeo—"

"No, Mama. Let him finish, please."

She clamps her mouth shuts with a stifled cry and sits.

"Santo, you know what this means," Romeo says.

I swallow and nod. "I do. And fuck it, Rome, if you're gonna order me killed, don't make one of them do it. I'll do it myself before I put that on the souls of any of my brothers."

Romeo stands and anchors his hands on his hips.

"You got something else to say?"

I nod.

"I took a vow to your father, years ago. I vowed to him that I would never marry. I vowed that I would let every one of you ascend in rank before me, because I wasn't a blood relative." I clear my throat. "But I won't let a vow to a dead man hold me back from what's right any longer."

Romeo nods slowly. Processing. Absorbing. His face is a mask.

I go on.

"I sold my cars, every last one of them. I've sold my real estate. I sold everything I own and I'm offering you every penny as a reverse dowry. If she's with me, she doesn't solidify our family, and our coffers don't profit, I know that. But I'm offering ten mil of my own money and a lifetime of service to you."

Rome shrugs. "But in Tuscany—"

"Fuck Tuscany. Your sister deserves to be married to someone who loves her, and that man is *me*."

Romeo raises his hands. I hold my breath, waiting for him to command me to be taken away, or for him to draw a weapon of his own.

Slowly, he begins to clap. *Clap.*

His lips quirk up at the edges. "It's about fucking *time,*" he says, shaking his head. Then he sobers, and his voice goes hard. "You think I'd marry any one of my sisters to someone who didn't worship the damn ground she *walked on*?"

I listen in silence, my body tense, vibrating in pain, but I stand my ground.

"Do you think I would give my sister to anyone who wasn't prepared to lay down his goddamn life for her?"

He stalks over to me and gently rests his hand on my shoulder. "You knew the stakes tonight. You knew it all, and you were willing to risk everything for her. Then you, my friend, are the only one who deserves to marry Rosa."

Rosa lifts her hands to her face and sinks into a chair. Mama wraps her arm around her and holds her, rocking gently back and forth. I don't trust my own voice. I swallow and open my mouth to speak, but no words come out.

"Go, Santo," he whispers. "Go to her. We'll begin preparations tomorrow."

"I don't know if I should kiss you or deck you," I tell him.

He grins. "Probably smart to choose none of the above."

"Oh my God," Marialena says out loud, then she jumps to her feet with a wild *whoop* that makes everyone chuckle. "Oh my God, you two will make the most beautiful babies I've ever seen in my *life!*"

"Jesus," Mario mutters, as if he can't quite wrap his brain around this yet.

The girls are crying and hugging Rosa, but I make my way to her and hold her from behind. My heart beats so fast and hard, I can't think beyond the pounding of blood in my ears.

Sergio turns to Dario. "Looks like it might be smart to introduce you to my sister sooner than later." He shrugs. "She's young, though, you'll have to wait a while."

Dario only chuckles.

Vittoria pushes herself to standing and clinks her coffee cup with a spoon. "I—I have an announcement to make."

We all look toward her. "First, I have to say, Romeo, I love you. You're a scary guy but you're my scary guy, and I love how loyal and faithful you are to this family." Her eyes grow soft. "Everyone here wants to solidify the family. Including me. And we all know that children are one way to make the Rossi name stronger."

Romeo's eyes go wide, and his mouth drops open.

"Before Romeo was arrested, I found out some news. I hadn't even had a chance to tell him yet, but

I will now, in front of all of you." She grins at Romeo. "We're having a babbbbyyyy!"

"Could've told him that *before* I put my life on the line, Vittoria," I mutter. "Softened him up a little, eh?"

She grins, and everyone laughs. "I'll make sure to keep him softened up so he doesn't change his mind, Santo." She raises her glass of orange juice. "A toast!"

There's clinking of glasses and Nonna whispers words in Italian, Orlando holds Angelina close, and Tavi rests his hand on Elise's back.

"To the Rossi family," Vittoria says. "To family bonds and fearless loyalty."

Voices erupt all around us and we tap our glasses together to cheer. "To the Rossi family!" everyone echoes.

Rosa stands, turns to face me, and buries herself in my chest. I hold her to me and she tucks her head against my shoulder. "Santo. I… that was so brave of you. I love you. I love you so much."

"And I love you," I tell her, right there in front of everyone. I say it again, loud and clear, for everyone to hear. "I love you, Rosa Rossi. Will you marry me?"

She grins at me and swipes impatiently at her eyes. "Stop making me cry and the answer is *yes!*"

We cheer and clink glasses again. I hold her to me.

"I lost you once," I whisper to her. She fits in my arms like she was meant to be here. "I lost you once, and I won't lose you again."

"You are going to be an insufferable husband," she says with affection. I love the way she bites her full lip.

"Baby," I whisper in her ear. "You have *No. Idea.*"

A glass shatters on the floor, and silence quickly descends in the room. All eyes go to Elise, who stands in a puddle of water. She grimaces and clutches her belly. "Guess what," she pants, her eyes wide. "I—I think all this drama broke my water."

Tavi gasps. "Santo, can I take your—goddamn it, you sold *all* of them?"

"Tavi, honey, we probably have lots of time," Elise says patiently. Then she turns to me. "Did you really sell all of them?"

"I ain't takin' his money," Romeo says, "so he can buy whatever his pretty little heart desires."

"Doesn't help us get to the hospital," Tavi mutters.

I grin at Romeo. "Good to have you home, brother," I mutter.

Romeo grins. "Will be even better to make you part of this crazy clan in more ways than one."

"Ooooh," Marialena says, wiping at her eyes. "It's all so beautiful," she sniffs.

Nonna bustles around, plying us with food and pleas to, *"Mangia, mangia!"*

"Santo," Rosa says softly. "I… I feel bad about what I said yesterday. Everything about… about letting you go."

"Shh," I tell her softly. "I understand."

"I just… wanted to protect you in whatever way I could," she says, shaking her head.

"I know. That's behind us, baby."

I think of the road ahead of us. It might be rocky, and there will be twists and turns like any other. But it will be our story that we'll write, our story that we'll tell. And after everything we've been through, I can only see, for the first time in my entire life, a happy ending ahead of us.

EPILOGUE

SANTO

Six months later

Rosa

I DON'T WANT a big wedding at The Castle. I don't want to be married with every member of my ridiculously large family looking on.

I want to wear Santo's ring and bear his children. I want to wake up every day beside him and go to bed every night curled up to his side. I want to laugh with him, fight with him, make sweet love to him, and be dominated, spanked, and taken hard.

I want to *live* with him. Breathe with him. Love with him.

Because I love him, and when I'm with Santo, my world no longer tilts on its axis. My world is right again. Santo was always mine, and I was always his.

We just had to fight to get there.

But fight we did, and we won't stop now.

Cousin Sergio's wildly amused by our decision to marry in Tuscany.

"What," he says on a shit-eating grin. "Don't want any more gossip, Rosa?" The cousins and aunts and uncles have been talking about Santo since he got here, and it's no secret that he wasn't included in my grandfather's will.

I roll my eyes at him. "I don't give a shit about gossip," I tell him truthfully. When you're raised in the mob like me, you learn to drown out the buzz of chatter over everything you say and do. "I don't want *anything.* No pomp and circumstance. No big to-do. No flowers or bridesmaids or *anything.*"

"We'll save it up for me," Marialena says, sucking on a lollipop the size of my fist. "I want *all* the pomp and circumstance on steroids with glitter and satin bows."

"Did you win that at a carnival?" I ask her.

She shrugs. "I have a stash."

"Your lips are blue," Sergio says grinning. She sticks out her blue tongue at him.

So Tuscany it is for the wedding. We stay at one of our villas, the rolling green hills in full bloom behind us. Only Mama, Marialena, Romeo, and Natalia come with us. That's all we want. Marialena and Romeo are our witnesses, and I couldn't deny my only sister a place by my side when I marry Santo.

Everyone else doesn't give us as much grief as we expected they would for not attending our wedding, but they're pretty occupied with Elise and Tavi's new baby girl, sweet Gia, a chubby little baby with pale blue eyes and round cheeks, who's got every made man in the family wrapped around her chubby little fingers.

Natalia, of course, is on cloud nine. "I have a new cousin *and* Uncle Santo!" she says over and over, before she frowns. "Can I still call him Uncle Santo? Anything else is weird for me."

I grin at her and tweak one of the pretty curls pinned to the top of her head. She is, of coursed, dressed in layers of pink tulle and satin and fairly floating with pure glee.

"Of course," I tell her. I bend and kiss her cheek. "I think he'd like that."

And soon, if all goes as planned, we'll have a baby of our own to call him daddy. I smile, my chest warming with the utter joy in the knowledge that Santo and I no longer have to hide our feelings for each other. That we can live the way we've longed to, as lovers with the blessing of our family. As one.

A gentle knock sounds on the door.

"Come in!" I call, expecting Mama. It isn't Mama, but Romeo, dressed in a formal suit, his hair still damp from a shower. His blue eyes warm at me, and he smiles gently. He looks a little older than he did when I first came home from Tuscany, but then again… I suppose we all do.

"Look at you two princesses," he says, giving each of us a kiss on the cheek. "Vittoria made me promise to take all the pictures I could." He grins and whips out his phone. "Smile!"

I toss an arm around Natalia's shoulders and grin at the camera as Romeo snaps pictures after picture.

"Beautiful," he says, satisfied, before he leaves. "For now. I'll have to take another few hundred at the ceremony and dinner."

I never dreamed Romeo would give us his blessing. After Santo's confession, Romeo refused any of Santo's money and gave it back to him, telling him to invest and save it to provide for his family.

"Have you seen that woman's taste in clothes and shoes?" he said. But he was only teasing. My entire shoe collection barely scratches the surface on the cost of one of his damn cars.

Romeo's been as supportive as I could wish for. I'm grateful. *So* grateful.

I want Santo to buy back his cars, but he doesn't want to. He says it's more important to him now that we get married and settle into life together.

"I'll buy another one or six after we've settled. They were important to me when I was married to *them,*" he quips. "Now that I'll be married to you, they don't matter as much."

But I know that's only partially true. He isn't himself unless he's getting his hands dirty under the hoods of a sweet ride.

There's a lightness to his steps and a glint in his eye I've never seen before. He smiles more easily. He sleeps all night without tossing and turning.

Santo looks…happy.

We have a small, intimate table laid for dinner, but after dinner, Santo and I are flying away on a honeymoon. I wanted to go away, and I didn't care where. I left the details up to him, and he's been grinning to himself for weeks planning it out.

"How far?"

"Far enough," he said.

"How long?"

"Long enough."

I don't really care, I just like teasing him. Finally, he tugged me onto his lap, kissed my neck, and my mind went blissfully blank.

"Do you trust me, baby?" he asked quietly. I closed my eyes against the rush of emotion that nearly choked me.

Trust.

Such a simple world with such a complicated meaning.

"Of course I trust you," I told him in his ear. "Why else would I let you blindfold and take that wicked riding crop to me?" Oh he does like to play, and I am his favorite toy.

That makes both of us.

"Do you *really* trust me?" he asked.

I turned and buried my head on his shoulder, wrapped my arms around him, and nodded. "I've never trusted anyone more in my life."

So, we're honeymooning anywhere out there in the world, and it could be Taiwan or Hawaii or Alaska, and I don't care. All that matters to me is that we're together.

After all we've been through, we need this.

Eventually, we'll find our way in the family again. Maybe he'll work in Tuscany, or maybe we'll buy a home near The Castle. Possibly something in The North End. We'll frequent The Castle, but I've lived there long enough. It's a place I'd like to visit, not a place I'll call home any longer.

Another knock at the door, and Natalia takes my hand.

"Ready, Mama?" she asks with a grin.

Santo dedicated his whole life to my family. He took oaths that nearly broke him. And now? Now I'll take oaths of my own, to the man who means everything to me.

"I'm ready," I tell Natalia, smiling. I am *more* than ready to take this step. This *leap,* even. To gracefully enter the next season of my life.

Santo

ROSA'S GRINNING, blindfolded.

"Why Santo," she says teasingly. "Didn't know you'd get frisky on the ride there. Hmm. Now, where could we be that we can't fly directly to, but can get there in five hours?" She pouts a bit, sucking in her lip. "Gosh, that could be a *lot* of places."

I drag the edge of my thumb underneath her collarbone and watch her shiver. "I'll get frisky anywhere, anytime I want to," I tell her.

"I love when you talk dirty to me," she breathes.

But this time, the blindfold isn't a prelude to a night of sex-filled sensory deprivation and earth-shattering orgasms. This time, I don't want her to guess where we are until we get there.

No direct flight from Florence to the Amalfi Coast, and since we have hired drivers, we thoroughly enjoyed our road trip. The Amalfi Coast honeymoon's one of the top-rated spots in the world, and I know she'll love it.

I won't have to look over any grapevines. Answer any phone calls. Flex any muscle.

"Hint," I tell her, tickling her underarm.

She giggles and squirms.

"They're known for the best limoncello."

She worries her lip. "Hmm. Oooh, it's on the top of my head. No…can't be that, we didn't cross any water… no, not that, we couldn't fly there, no direct flights you said… hmm. Oh! Oh, Santo, did you take me to the Amalfi Coast?"

Grinning, I flick off her blindfold and let her look. "Oooh, you *did!*"

She claps her hands with glee.

Natalia's gone back to America with Tosca and Marialena, giddy with a full week away from us where she'll get spoiled and pampered. I'll miss her —we both will, but I'm damn near giddy with the knowledge that we're a small but tight family now— me, Rosa, and Natalia. The family that was meant to be.

The Montavios took the news well, and Sergio's already hinting at marrying a non-blood relative of the family to someone in his bloodline, to give us a "solid front like no other." Dario's up for nomination, then.

Mario's pacing, the only brother among us now unmarried, and though he swears he'll never settle down, I can't deny he looks a bit wistful sometimes. And as a made man of the Rossi family, in the end he won't have a choice.

Our driver opens the door and another gets our bags as we step into the warm breeze off the ocean. I booked a private hotel right on the water with a private cabana and full coast to ourselves.

"Oh, Santo," she says, her eyes alight as she looks at our sun-kissed surroundings. "It's *beautiful.*"

I went looking for something romantic, and not too far from Tuscany where we'll stay for a long while before we decide on a permanent residence. The food in Ravello and the little island of Capri is reason enough to come to the Coast, but I knew Rosa would adore the charming little villa and fresh seafood and wine. Me? I just want to be with her.

"I've always wanted to come here," she says softly, her eyes feasting on the turquoise Tyrrhenian Sea. "I can't believe I never have." She hasn't even seen the resort I've picked.

It isn't as crowded in the spring, though it's warm and sunny. The real flux of tourists won't come until a few months yet. So the best part? *No one knows us here.*

"*Ooh,* will we visit Capri? I've always wanted to see the Marina Grande."

"Your wish, milady," I saw, kissing the back of her hand.

For some reason, the gesture makes her close her eyes and lean her head on my shoulder. "Oh, Santo," she whispers.

Oh, Santo.

Two words I'll never tire of hearing.

"Yeah, baby?"

"I love to see you happy."

I hold her tightly and breathe her in. "Happy's an understatement, Rosa. I've never felt anything like this before. It feels… damn, woman, I don't even know how to describe it?"

"Right?" she whispers.

I kiss her forehead and hold her to me again. "That's a good start," I whisper. "This is right. Me, you. Us. We've been part of a family together, and that's something that will always be a part of who we are. But there comes a time… when the family doesn't define you. No matter how loyal or dedicated you are, you have to find your way, you know?"

"I do know," she says. "I don't even know if my brothers have realized it themselves, but they all have as they began their own families, all but Mario, but he'll get there. And I think the two of us finding our independence apart from the rest may have been hard-won, but it in the end, it had to happen."

We ride in silence to our villa.

"The view's breathtaking," Rosa says, sighing as she looks at the sunset on the water as brilliant as blue diamonds.

I'm staring at her, though, with her delicate features and grace, she's stunningly beautiful.

"It is," I whisper. "Breathtaking."

She turns and catches my eye, and for the first time in so long, laughs out loud without reserve. Turning to me, she tangles her fingers in mine and presses her head to my chest.

"I love you. I love everything about you. And I need to thank you, Santo."

I kiss her fiercely, gripping her face between my hands.

"Thank me for what?" I stare in her eyes.

"For everything," she whispers, her hands atop mine. "For your loyalty to my family but your sacrifice for *me.* Your willingness to give up… everything that mattered to you."

"Rosa," I tell her, shaking my head. "None of it mattered when it came to you. *You're* what matters in the end."

We sit in silence, watching the landscape pass us.

"It feels almost surreal, doesn't it?" she whispers. "That we're finally together. That we don't have to hide. That the family's at peace with no one attacking us…"

I decide now's *probably* not the time to tell her of the latest whispers of the Feds on our tails. It ain't the first time and it won't be the last time. We've got this. We always do.

"One moment of peace," I say to her.

"And a lifetime of promise," she finishes.

I silence her with a kiss, as we bask in our happy ending.

PREVIEW

Oath of Seduction

Chapter One

Emma

I SHIVER when a brisk wind kicks up my skirt, the crimson fabric fluttering around my knees like the wings of a cardinal.

My mother hated red. She said it was the color whores wore.

She would know.

But I like it. Red's full of energy and life, the color that symbolizes many things throughout various cultures and times—life and courage, anger and love. *Passion.*

I wrap my arms around myself to warm up, trying to be impervious to the biting wind.

"Happy now?" I ask her, my voice tinged with bitterness. "You got your way. I'm alone now. Just like you always wanted. Only now you're not here to mock me anymore."

Bitterness coats my tongue, even through the salt of tears. I swipe at them angrily. I vowed when I was fifteen years old I'd never shed another tear for her, but sometimes tears come when I don't want them to.

I lift up my chin, defying the cold waterfront breeze to chill me. We've left winter behind, but the cool spring air hasn't yet warmed, still holding on to the last vestiges of winter on the coast. A chilly wind whips over the water, pebbling my skin.

But I like the cold. I like the taste of the salty air, even as it turns my lips blue and I shiver. I like the raw boldness of it, the gusty bellow of a silent power that knows no bounds.

I step out further, the pointed, shiny tips of my shoes—death-defying heels I wore in honor of the occasion— edging toward the precipice.

Jump, a little voice in my mind tells me.

No one will miss you.

You won't have to fight anymore.

Jump, and let the water wash it all away.

I stare at the blue-green waves laced in white, churning like a monster's rage, boiling and simmering below as if defying the cold March air.

I laugh at the voice in my head.

Give up so soon? I taunt. *Never.*

I have a mission. A job to do. I've worked all my adult life to get here and won't let one low moment push me into doing something stupid and reckless.

That's not who I am.

I want wild, though. I want to do something that doesn't follow the rules, that doesn't make sense. Something... *bold.*

I don't know how long I stand there, but the sun sinks from eye level to barely noticeable, nothing more than a splash of fading orange on the horizon. And with the setting sun, a deeper cold sets in.

My stomach churns with hunger. I don't remember the last time I ate. I didn't skip food because of grief. No, grief was the bitter herb I tasted a full decade ago. I'm beyond caring at this point. The tears aren't tears of regret but of anger, though why I'm angry, I couldn't say.

I've got a ways to walk, but I chose it this way. I wanted to be alone. I *craved* being alone. Sometimes, walking alone's the one thing that clears my mind.

My mother made it easy. Hardly anyone came to her funeral anyway, save a harried-looking woman wearing a too-tight dress and scuffed flats. She didn't look at me. She didn't talk to me. She dropped a wilting rose on my mother's dead body, then left with her head hung low.

And I didn't care. I still don't.

Ah, that's right. I ate two mints from the little glass bowl in the waiting room. A meal for an ant, not someone like me. Fuck it, I'm starving.

Another brisk wind makes me shiver again. My legs wobble on the edge of the cliff. I'm in danger, and I know it, but I crave the bolt of adrenaline that courses through me when I look over the cliff's edge. It helps make the little voice in my mind that coaxes me to jump to fade a little.

I listen to the waves. I close my eyes, my arms spread out wide to stay balanced. They say it's harder to remain still with your eyes closed. My lips tip up in a grin.

I didn't get to where I am by being reckless and dangerous, but damn if it doesn't exhilarate me.

I focus on the details around me. It centers me somehow.

I've never really known how it works with me… I'm not like other people. When I was younger, I didn't know enough to pretend I was ordinary, but learning to feign mediocrity's a skill one learns with age.

When I was little, I pretended I had superpowers. I almost fooled some of my friends. The power of observation when others are blind to details does seem almost supernatural.

Not everyone could tell you that the sun sets today at precisely 5:38 p.m., that tonight we have a full moon, that there are three cars parked in the nearly barren parking lot below the cliff, that there used to be an ice cream shack there, and maybe it returns when the weather warms up.

I could tell you the woman who came to my mother's funeral today was a hooker, but that was an easy one. She was the only friend my mother had, and yet she didn't know who I was. It didn't surprise me that she didn't know my mother had a daughter.

I could tell you in kindergarten everything about my teacher's wardrobe, clothing size, a full catalog. I could tell you what she drove, what she ate for lunch, and that she had two crooked front teeth and dyed her hair every other month. Not because I spied, but because I simply couldn't shut my brain off. When I saw something, my mind automatically catalogued it. At one point, my mother and her then-boyfriend thought it smart to have me see a shrink.

"I don't know what's wrong with her," my mother hissed at the desk when asked why she'd brought me in during my freshman year of high school. Long after my father died. "The girl's a freak. She's way smarter than she should be at her age."

Her boyfriend only cringed. Assholes don't like when the woman they're screwing has a smart kid. They sniff out bullshit.

I tuned it all out. Tuned her out. I got used to it.

"Ma'am, you can't bring her to see anyone on the grounds of her being... unusual," the desk girl said as patiently as she could. Meanwhile, my cheeks burned with embarrassment. This was before I realized I could've just walked out.

The day you learn you can just walk is the first day of the rest of your life.

I come to with the sound of an approaching car. It gets louder as it draws nearer. I stand up straighter. I'm a little shaken I didn't hear it sooner, but the sound of the waves is louder than I expected and the wind howls in my ears like a mourning lover.

My eyes pop open. Those wheels are *moving* at an alarming rate, so much so I'm not sure they could stop now if they wanted to, not without careening off the edge of this cliff. I stare out at the fading sun, and listen to the sound of the wheels to see if they're approaching or leaving.

Definitely approaching, and at a good clip.

Someone's coming up here, and fast.

I'm a few feet away from the road that leads up here. I know, because I walked every damn step by foot.

I clutch my small purse to my side and swivel to see what's coming.

Who's coming.

A stunning red convertible, as bold and vibrant as the dress that clings to my legs when the wind kicks up, approaches from the east side of the cliff. The top's down. I can't see who's driving it, but whoever it is has a death wish, since they're going at least a hundred miles an hour.

God, to be that *bold*. That daring. To feel the wind in my hair and not give a shit if I lived or died. To feel the power of that engine with a tap of your foot.

I draw in a breath and hold it as they come nearer and nearer. I can see the driver now, and my heart thumps a little faster. I can't make out details, but I know from here it's a guy, he's big, and... yeah, he's *hot*. Dark brown hair that falls across his brow, a T-shirt that clings to his frame... Faint strains of classic rock echo in the wind.

He slows as he nears me. My heart beats madly, and I clutch my bag as if it could save my life.

With the grace of a stallion coming to rest, the car purrs gently as it slows, then stops only feet away from me. He's wearing sunglasses, his eyes hidden from me. Full lips tug upward in a smile, revealing perfectly straight white teeth, teeth that are too perfect, like the wolf's before he ate Little Red Riding Hood.

Wow. He could grace the cover of a men's fashion magazine. I'm rarely stunned by beauty, but this man… with his classic good looks and smooth, tan skin, I half expect him to speak to me in Italian.

"Hey, baby," the stranger says, his voice smooth and seductive. "I'm sorry to keep you waiting."

A shiver courses through me.

I blink in surprise. It's a classic pickup line, I know it, but that doesn't mean my heart doesn't beat a little faster at the heat that flares between the two of us.

My stomach rumbles, reminding me that humans need to be fed once in a while.

Fuck it.

My mother's dead.

Today begins the rest of my life.

I get one night of freedom before I recommit myself to my mission, my *purpose.*

I'm cold, I'm alone, and I could think of worse ways to spend my time than with an anonymous stranger in a sexy car. A woman like me trusts no one, but today, I'm feeling bold and reckless, and the guy, as hot as he is, honestly looks like he'd help little old ladies cross the street.

I swallow hard.

I wanted something different. Daring. Dangerous.

"I'll let it go this time," I tell him. My voice sounds a little raspy from disuse.

Who am I? I don't flirt. I'm not witty. Yet the words fly off my tongue as if a stranger says them. "Guess you'll have to make it up to me."

I step toward the car, but before I can open my door, Mr. Tall and Handsome puts it in park, launches his tall, muscular frame out of the body of the car, and quickly reaches for my door handle. He moves with the grace of a dancer, seductive vibes rolling off him like a lover, and right then, I'd empty my wallet in the back of his car just for a kiss from him.

"Now, you know better than to open your own door, doll," he chides in a way that makes heat rise in my chest. I'd do wicked things if he asked me to in that voice. "My mother would kick my ass for not behaving like a gentleman."

Doll. Gentleman.

Oh, I like that. All of it. For one brief moment, we've stepped back in time.

He has a mother that cares about him. I think I like that. Is that just part of the pickup line, though?

He opens the door and gestures for me to take a seat.

The interior of the car's wrapped in luxury leather. It's buttery smooth and soft to the touch, lending a decadent, pleasant scent to the air around us.

What am I doing?

Mmm. I take in a shuddering breath as he trots back to his side and folds his long, tall frame into the seat beside me.

I don't know where we're going. I don't know where he's from. And for the first time in my life, I like that.

I watch as he kicks the car into gear, and we take off.

I observe everything I can. It's my job.

Now that we're this close, I can tell he's definitely Italian, but his accent's faintly tinged with Boston, so likely born here. Dark brown hair, ruggedly styled, definitely mussed by the wind but it looks intentional… *sexy.* Tanned olive skin, and since it's March in New England, either he's gone to a tanning salon, or he's spent some time in a warmer climate recently. He seems way too masculine for tanning, so my bet's on option two. It's getting dark, but I can tell his eyes are so blue they nearly shine in the darkness. Most of the Italian men I've met have darker eyes, but blue's not out of the ordinary. Blue eyes likely mean he's from Northern Italy, then. Genoa, Milan, Tuscany.

I want to look deeper into those eyes.

The rugged cut of his jaw, shadowed with casually masculine stubble, is offset by an almost boyish pair of lips that look like he's perpetually smiling. Something tells me he can pull off a scowl that would make me melt. *Jesus,* those lips… A faint rose color paints his cheeks. His perfectly symmetrical face, the way he holds himself, makes him look like Mustang hired him for a two-page spread in a racing magazine.

The cut of his clothes suggests wealth. Paired with the car, that's a no-brainer. A quick glance tells me the Mustang is a custom job.

His phone's mounted on his dash, but even though it's off, it's plugged in and on. So either he's someone that doesn't like to be disconnected, or he's someone who's expected to be on call. Interesting. The screen's clean, free of smudges, but it's a smallish phone.

The car's impeccably clean, not a fleck of dust or crumpled paper or empty Subway package in sight, yet from where I'm sitting I can see flecks of mud on the hood.

He was driving fast, then. Maybe even racing fast. A car like this was built for speed.

I glance casually behind us and note a black leather jacket folded over the seat, but there's nothing else to note in the car.

Wrong.

My heart gives a quick thud when I glance again at the jacket. It's hidden, and it's discreet, but he's hiding a handgun.

This boy—no, *man*—is trouble with a capital T.

"How long have you been waiting?" he asks. Fuck it, that voice is sin personified. Sex on the rocks.

"Oh," I shrug quietly. My voice is a little shaky now that I've seen the gun. Weapons don't scare me. Half a second with that beauty in the palm of my hand and I could make it purr for me. But for a brief moment in time, I'd wanted to believe he was a good man.

Maybe he is.

But could a good man handle a girl like me?

And does that matter?

"I mean… a while."

Normal people would either ask for a name or offer theirs at this point, but I have no interest in doing either. And thankfully, he doesn't seem interested either.

"So," he says, reaching a large, heavy, masculine hand to my leg. I note it's the only thing about him that isn't model material, and I'm not complaining. His palm's rough and calloused, his fingers strong, the nail tips blunt. There's a silvery scar along the top of his hand, a gentle smattering of dark hair. When he moves his hand, I see a trace of ink on his forearm, but it's covered by his long-sleeved shirt.

The warm feel of his confident hand on my naked skin feels incredible. I sigh and move closer to him and make the decision right then, right there, that whatever he wants to do to me, I'll let him. I've never had casual sex, but tonight's the first time I've ever wanted it. Maybe even needed it, the freedom not to think, to not have to plot my every move and every step so they're perfectly aligned. To give myself permission for one night, just *one night,* to forgo perfectionism and live a little.

He traces his fingers so lightly on my thigh, I shiver. His touch is so electric, the wild part of my mind that doesn't dwell on reality imagines sparks fly from his fingers. His voice, a low rumble that somehow both commands and seduces, slides into my veins like a potion. "How do I make it up to you?"

I smile to myself, and it feels a bit wicked. Not only am I dressed in crimson, I'm wearing bright red lipstick (also not my mother's favorite.) I feel a bit like a sorceress.

I decide to go for broke. I'm diving in, head first.

"Sexual favors would work," I quip, allowing the faintest hint of an accent to tinge my words before I can stop myself. It's part of the appeal, I tell myself. Seductive and mysterious. I was born and raised right here in Boston, but he doesn't need to know that. I want to distance myself from who I really am.

Tomorrow, I'll leave. That's the beauty of a casual one-night stand. He has no expectations I'll stay, so I have no fear of hurting... him *or* me.

Wait. *Sexual favors,* I said. Does that sound slutty? Of course it sounds slutty. I wanted to sound flirtatious, but the line between slutty and flirtatious can sometimes blur.

I want to slam my fist in my mouth to shut myself up. Too late.

"Sexual favors?"

"Mmm, if you want to get back in my good graces."

Who am I?

But the next moment, his resounding chuckle tells me I answered correctly.

READ MORE

USA Today bestselling author Jane Henry pens stern but loving alpha heroes, feisty heroines, and emotion-driven happily-ever-afters. She writes what she loves to read: kink with a tender touch. Jane is a hopeless romantic who lives on the East Coast with a houseful of children and her very own Prince Charming.

You can find Jane here:

Jane Henry's Newsletter

Jane Henry's Facebook Reader Group

Jane's Website

BB bookbub.com/profile/jane-henry
facebook.com/janehenryromance
instagram.com/janehenryauthor
amazon.com/Jane-Henry/e/B01BYAQYYK
tiktok.com/@janehenryauthor

Made in the USA
Monee, IL
20 November 2022

18184541R00203